MMXV

THE WHITE REVIEW

EDITORS   BENJAMIN EASTHAM & JACQUES TESTARD
DESIGN, ART DIRECTION   RAY O'MEARA
POETRY EDITOR   J. S. TENNANT
US EDITOR   TYLER CURTIS
ASSOCIATE EDITOR   FRANCESCA WADE
ASSISTANT EDITOR   HARRY THORNE
EDITORIAL ASSISTANT   CASSIE DAVIES
DESIGN ASSISTANT   GABRIELLA VOYIAS
READERS   CARLA MANFREDINO, SCOTT WILSON

CONTRIBUTING EDITORS   JACOB BROMBERG, LAUREN ELKIN, EMMELINE FRANCIS,
                           PATRICK LANGLEY, BELLA MARRIN, DANIEL MEDIN,
                           SAM SOLNICK, EMILY STOKES, KISHANI WIDYARATNA

ADVERTISING   LOUISA DUNNIGAN, LUCIE ELVEN

HONORARY TRUSTEES   MICHAEL AMHERST, DEREK ARMSTRONG, HUGUES DE DIVONNE,
                           SIMON FAN, NIALL HOBHOUSE, CATARINA LEIGH-PEMBERTON,
                           MICHAEL LEUE, TOM MORRISON-BELL, AMY POLLNER,
                           CÉCILE DE ROCHEQUAIRIE, EMMANUEL ROMAN, HUBERT TESTARD,
                           MICHEL TESTARD, GORDON VENEKLASEN,
                           DANIELA & RON WILLSON, CAROLINE YOUNGER

THE WHITE REVIEW IS A REGISTERED CHARITY (NUMBER 1148690)

COVER ART BY SUE WILLIAMS
PRINTED BY PUSH, LONDON
PAPER BY ANTALIS MCNAUGHTON (OLIN CREAM 100GSM, OLIN WHITE SMOOTH 120GSM)
BESPOKE PAPER MARBLE BY PAYHEMBURY MARBLE PAPERS
TYPESET IN JOYOUS (BLANCHE)

PUBLISHED BY THE WHITE REVIEW, JULY 2015
EDITION OF 1,800
ISBN No. 978-0-9927562-5-3

COPYRIGHT © THE WHITE REVIEW AND INDIVIDUAL CONTRIBUTORS, 2015.
ALL RIGHTS RESERVED. NO REPRODUCTION, COPY OR TRANSMISSION,
IN WHOLE OR IN PART, MAY BE MADE WITHOUT WRITTEN PERMISSION.

THE WHITE REVIEW, 243 KNIGHTSBRIDGE, LONDON SW7 1DN
WWW.THEWHITEREVIEW.ORG

EDITORIAL

HAVING SEVERAL issues ago announced that we would no longer be writing our own editorials, the editors' (ultimately inevitable) failure to organise a replacement, combined with a marked lack of enthusiasm on the part of those people we invited to write on our behalf, has hastened our return to these pages. It might have dawned on those we approached, as it long ago dawned on us, that writing editorials is dull and difficult.

So, to what purpose should we put this page which remains, roughly nine hours before we go to press, accusingly blank? To proselytise here would be to preach – one hopes – to the converted. Should we instead use the opportunity shamelessly to ask you for money? It would after all be opportune – in September we launch a crowdfunding campaign offering such incentives to donate as a night-time peregrination in the sole company of Will Self (expensive), limited edition, specially-commissioned art works by previous contributors to the magazine (quite expensive), a drink with Ned Beauman (competitively priced), a set of artists' postcards (pocket money) and even the opportunity to meet the editors at a party (please form an orderly queue).

But no, it would be unbecoming of us. We, the unpaid directors of a registered charity in the United Kingdom (number: 1148690) 'specialising in artistically or educationally meritorious works by new or emerging artists and writers', would never so shamelessly prey upon the kindness of our readers. However loyal, big-hearted, munificent, tasteful and – may we say – well-dressed our readers might be. Readers who are committed to supporting literature and the arts beyond the penalties of what we are now obliged to call 'austerity', readers who believe that a vibrant, progressive, polyvocal cultural milieu is essential to the wellbeing of a society, readers who understand the importance of paying writers for their work. Readers who certainly don't need to be told that taking out a subscription to a magazine supports its long-term survival by providing it with a reliable cash flow during a time in which news-stand sales are falling and the margins are increasingly tight, nor indeed that such subscriptions can be purchased for friends and family via our website, thewhitereview.org. No, this is not the place.

Nor would it be seemly here to hype a publication already described as 'one of the best magazines in Europe' by the director of a prestigious London gallery not long ago named as the most influential person in the art world by ART REVIEW but who shall here remain anonymous, because we wouldn't drop names. A magazine 'growing in stature' (the NEW YORK TIMES), 'nothing less than a cultural revolution' (Deborah Levy) and – proving that it is possible (following the title of a series by Camille Henrot featured in THE WHITE REVIEW NO. 5) 'to be a revolutionary and still to love flowers' – hailed by VOGUE as a 'thing of beauty'.

Having dismissed those low impulses we will, instead, take the opportunity sincerely to thank those people who make THE WHITE REVIEW possible. Everyone with whom we've had the fortune to work, each of whom has had a hand in shaping the magazine; the many great artists and writers (included those featured within) who have allowed us to publish their work; others too numerous to mention without whose intelligence, support and friendship we would long ago have given up; and, last but not least, you, dear reader.

THE EDITORS

MADRID

BY

KEVIN BREATHNACH

> As a rule Don Jamie is not thinking of his misfortune; in fact, he usually thinks of nothing at all. He looks at the mirror fixedly and asks himself: Now who invented the mirror?
>
> Camilo José Cela, LA COLMENA (1951)

IT WAS THE MIDDLE OF WINTER when I moved to Madrid, but I had not banked on the cold. In the beginning I lived alone in Lavapiés, a neighbourhood just south of the Puerta del Sol, where the night I arrived the air smelled more or less of marijuana. My new landlord introduced himself as Iñigo. He said he lived nearby, that he was part of an improv theatre company. Since this seemed to be more information than a tenant needed to know, I took it to be an offer of friendship. When I expressed a less than entirely sincere interest in seeing his company perform, Iñigo's demeanour changed to one of nervous excitement. He directed my attention to a series of framed photographs depicting performances held in the Teatro Lope de Vega so long ago that he could not possibly have had anything to do with them. Here, he said, is Aurora Bautista in 1962. I see, I said, though I did not. The photographs were printed on what looked like black crèpe paper. They were dark and matted, and Iñigo seemed to have as much trouble as I did making out the figure of Aurora Bautista in 1962. Here, he said, moving on, is Maria Asquerino, also in 1962. I mean: Here. It occurred to me that the photographs were not worth framing. Perhaps it occurred to him too. Anyway, he seemed to remember his purpose. He said he'd call next time there was going to be a performance. He demonstrated how to fix the heating should it stop working and he showed me how to lock the door. Then he said goodbye. He did not call for almost a month. When finally he did, it was to let me know that the apartment would undergo a routine fumigation later in the week.

Only six months had passed since the first time I'd visited Madrid, shortly after my brother and his girlfriend moved into a place just off Gran Via. I stayed with them that weekend – we bought imitation sunglasses, spoke about the weather and the price of cans. After lunch each day, I wandered off on my own for a few hours, sweating up and down the same few central streets – Calle de Alcalá, Calle de la Cruz, Carrera de San Jerónimo – from which I developed the lasting, and probably inaccurate, impression of Madrid as a stranger, cheaper, pre-Hausmannish kind of Paris. Everything looked basically familiar to me, only more frequently curved, obscurely flourished, somehow more spacious too. I told myself that if I left Dublin again, Madrid was where I'd go. I could not remember another city in which I'd made the decision to walk up a steep stretch of road with no intention other than to look back down it.

One such stretch was Calle del Amparo, a crooked little side-street on a hill, my hill now, where I sat alone in Iñigo's apartment, somewhere near the end of the street, at a loss for things to do. Quickly I was coming to realise that, although I'd always said I'd like to live alone, I had never given the idea of living alone much thought. What do people do? I unpacked a bit, I tried to get the internet working. I turned the television on and off. Eventually I walked to an ill–lit shop on the corner, accidentally bought a bottle of white vermouth, having mistaken it for white wine, and devoted my attention to it as to a strange new friend. Then I opened an old photograph of Joan on my laptop.

I'd first met Joan about eighteen months before, one wet summer afternoon in Dublin, not long after Maeve, my girlfriend of almost five years, broke up with me out of the blue. It did not take long for all the unresolved emotional energy from my side of that relationship to attach itself to Joan. She was someone who stressed the second syllable in 'Nabokov', laughed at my jokes sparingly if at all, and appeared to consider most of what I had to say to be basically preposterous. Yet pretty soon I seemed to matter. For a little while that summer I saw a lot of her, before she went back to Oxford. I was probably not as discreet about it as she would have liked, but nobody died.

Joan was kind of a tough crowd; she had the measure of me at least. She'd had it since one afternoon when, in a quiet pub soon after we met, I'd attempted a live oral translation of a passage from Blanchot's *Thomas l'obscur*, which several weeks before I had copied into my notebook. Joan was as alert to the pomposity of Blanchot as I was incapable of translating him. Still, it should not have been so difficult. Not only had I left university with a French degree, I had also read the passage several times in English before deciding that only Blanchot's original French could suitably adorn the inside page of my notebook. What I was attempting was in fact much less a translation than a recital. Anyway, it felt like a very long time before I'd managed to get through half a sentence, more words skipped over than even guessed at, and Joan told me I should stop, just stop, and I stopped. A silence fell and did not lift until at last she looked at me.

She said: 'Well, that was excruciating.'

She said: 'Do you want another drink?'

We went to the cinema twice that summer. The second time was late September, the weather fine, at that point in the evening when sunlight is still visible only on the highest windows of the city, of Liberty Hall, say, or Hawkins House behind the Screen Cinema, where we sat in the back row of a bad movie to kiss in secret. As the film started rolling it was only us in darkness. Our unspoken plan seemed to be working until, several minutes later, light flooded in through the theatre door, followed by a solitary figure who made his way towards the back, choosing finally our row to sit in, whereupon we had to stop. The film took a long time ending. It starred Casey Affleck as a spurned lover, a wronged fall-guy, something like that. I no longer recall the details. At around this time Joan asked me whether I would have cheated on Maeve with her, had we met a few months earlier. I did not know it then, but this was exactly Joan's style. I said no because I thought that what she wanted to hear was no. As it turned out, it was not.

In the photograph on my laptop, her hair looks a little lighter than usual and, given the circumstances, not nearly as wet as it should. She is in the bath, her face emerging from foam as in Klimt it would emerge from gold. It is 4 a.m. and she is alone. She couldn't sleep, she said. That was not unusual. She said that she could never sleep; but I had seen her sleeping. Shortly after she'd gone back to Oxford, I visited her there; on the last night, I spilt scalding hot coffee over her in a misguided attempt to prevent her from sleeping. I wanted her to stay awake. The next morning, I forgot to pack a pair of socks I'd brought, which I had recently borrowed from a friend Joan did not know. Maroon wool, I remember, with white and I think mustard speckles; really, they were excellent socks. Joan kept them, spoke of them from time to time, toyed even with the idea of posting their owner a photograph of herself wearing them. I'm not sure what she thought might be achieved by this. In any case, she would not give them back. When a few months ago I visited her again in Oxford, she allowed me to wear them once to dinner. Their colour had changed to a sort of chalked mulberry. I guess she has them still.

¶ Iñigo's apartment contained a large bed and a small circular table that was awkward for even one person to sit at. The only window, above the bed, looked into a courtyard so narrow that the room appeared almost as dark by day as it did by night. When I awoke late on the afternoon following my arrival, I had to check the weather online before I could bring myself to go outside in search of a dictionary. Before I left Dublin, I learned a hundred Spanish phrases ('*no puedo quejarse*'; '*no entro, ni salgo*'; '*¿puedo escribirlo?*') but I'd forgotten them upon landing. I was not certain if people still used physical dictionaries, but I felt it was important that I buy one, as a gesture of intent if nothing else. The weather outside was fine: '*8º, despejado*', according to eltiempo.es. By the time I reached the Paseo del Prado, where I thought distantly I could make out the sound of children singing, the weak blue winter sky had darkened and the air had turned noticeably colder. At the Plaza de Cibeles, an enormous stage had been erected for a concert in celebration of Epiphany, the Christian feast that marks the visit of los Reyes Magos to Christ, the new-born Son of God. I stood in a crowd of young families for a few minutes, watched a child haw happily for his parents, then hurried on – I'm no longer sure in what direction. Uphill, let's say. It was a rough couple of hours. I could not find a dictionary. I could not find a bookshop. I could not even find my way home. It is difficult now to imagine the course I walked that night. Memory takes only a sweeping register of things not related to ourselves: the skaters outside the Palacio Real; the fountain at Embajadores; the endless shoe shops near, I think,

Bilbao. The topography of these images no longer makes sense to me.

Not until very late did I pass the Telefonicá skyscraper on Gran Via, close to my brother's old apartment, where I stayed the first time I visited. When, the second time I visited, I tried casually to mention the influence of art nouveau on the neighbouring skyscraper, he responded only that I'd mentioned this the first time. I remember it occurred to me that nobody had all that much to say, and as I walked beneath the same skyscraper months later, my neck craned now towards a starless sky, I recalled my own astonishment when one evening, by way of dissuasion, Joan said that someday she would run out of stories to tell me. I suppressed a laugh: I said she had run out of stories long ago. It is hard to believe she did not know this. She told her stories endlessly, until her life became a part of my mind. Really, you could spend a whole weekend in her company without hearing anything you hadn't heard before, excepting those additional details, the exaggerations and embellishments, sometimes omissions, which everyone, myself included, seemed happy to allow her. I do not know if she was conscious of the subtle but certain way she had of redirecting conversation three or four sentences in advance of an oncoming inconsistency, but I noticed it, admired it even.

I'd run out of stories too. I honestly could not count how many times I'd told her about people I wouldn't even recognise today; or about ex-girlfriends, my various betrayals of each. I don't know whether my decision to leave Dublin arose from some desire to amass a selection of new stories, or if I wanted merely to tell the old ones to new ears. Perhaps neither. In truth I felt happy to repeat myself, omitting whatever I sensed Joan's initial reaction had asked to be omitted next time. Her presence had on me this sort of editorial effect, even in the telling of historical anecdotes. I remember that the second time I related the line Miró delivered following his defection from cubism to surrealism ('I will break their guitar'), I made no mention of defection. She hadn't liked that detail. It had ruined the story for her. She found the idea of artists switching movements, as someone might switch phone companies, distasteful. I think that she did not like groups. What surprised me was how unthinking this process of omission became. I was never conscious of what I would not say until I heard myself not saying it. In the weeks before I left Dublin, I slept with two friends I shouldn't have. I guess I did not feel I owed it to Joan not to. Sure, at one point she'd given me more of her time and attention than she'd probably planned to, and I suppose she had recently as well; but not once was I without the sense that another of her long and unannounced periods of silence, of unanswered emails, no calls to speak of, nothing of her except the voice in my head, was approaching once again. Joan wanted no fucking more than whatever the fuck it was she had. Anyway, I told her about only one encounter; then, with a mixture of satisfaction and regret, I watched as she tried not to appear hurt.

I had been unable to find a dictionary, but thought the night could in some way be redeemed with the purchase of a Spanish newspaper. It is a measure of the ordeal I felt myself already to have endured that I considered it a success to locate a simple corner shop; but when I approached the man at the till with a copy of EL PAÍS in hand, my grasp not only of Spanish but also of basic non-linguistic social conventions, such as queuing or waiting for change, proved so lacking that he could not have believed I was buying the paper for any other reason than to be pictured with it in order to prove that as of 5 January 2015 I was still alive, if clearly not quite all there. As though to redeem my own honour, I started reading as I walked out of the shop, struggling through the first paragraph of the back-page story about the first black baseball referee in the United States. '*Algunos homenajes llegan demasiado tarde*,' it began. 'Too late,' was all I could decipher.

The longer I walked that night, the more reluctant I became to take the metro home. I had worked out that the moment I purchased a ticket – that is, the moment I did what I could and should have done several hours before – the value of each aimless step I'd taken up until then would be reduced to zero. But I was also increasingly aware that at some point the metro would close. I knew I was far from home. At Plaza de España, I bought a ticket, feeling the reduced value of each step not so much in my feet as in my chest. I received in change eighteen single euro coins and a single fifty cent. Roughly half I put in my left back pocket; roughly half I put in my right. Though there were several seats available in the carriage, I chose not to sit down. At the next stop I was joined in standing by an enormously fat old man who, having first raised the echo effect on his amplifier to what I presume was its maximum setting, sang from beginning to end 'Love Me Tender' by Elvis Presley. He was not a good singer, and I cannot say I was in any way impressed by his performance, but not once did I take my eyes off him. He seemed ambiguously present, his echo sometimes very close to his own voice, sometimes very distant. I tried to imagine the day he decided to do this for a living. I wondered if he had first enjoyed a reputation amongst members of his family as a good singer. I wondered if he liked his work, then I wondered about his repertoire. I wondered, did this particular song have any special meaning for him? 'When at last my dreams come true / Darling this I know / Happiness will follow you / Everywhere you go.' I decided that probably it did not. Attached to his amplifier there was a white water cooler cup, now turned miserably to grey. In clumps I removed every coin from each pocket, and when eventually I managed to locate the fifty cent piece, I placed it in his cup and disembarked at Lavapiés.

Back at the apartment, I learned that the Telefónica skyscraper combines a number of architectural styles, of which art nouveau is not one.

¶ I had come to Madrid not long after a serious popular challenge had been mounted against austerity measures implemented during the previous seven years by the country's established political order. There seemed to be protests every week. Some were small affairs: two or three hundred people gathered on a Tuesday evening at the bottom of Calle de Atocha bearing red and white CGT flags in demand of labour reform; or five, six hundred people one Friday morning, fenced into one side of the Calle de Génova, pointing bright orange banners declaring 'YA!' at the unseeing windows of the ruling Partido Popular's headquarters across the street. Other protests, especially on weekends, seemed much more significant. On the final Saturday of January, hundreds of thousands marched from the Plaza de Cibeles to the Puerta del Sol in support of Pablo Iglesias's Podemos, the radical leftist movement and party which many had begun to think could win at the next election. 'We want a historic mobilisation,' said Iglesias, whose ponytail and goatee had the singular benefit of distinguishing him from other politicians. 'We want people to be able to tell their children and grandchildren: On 31 January I was at the march that launched a new era of political change in Spain.' Not me. On 31 January, I was in a dark bedroom on my own, watching Steve Bruce's Hull City take a three-nil thumping at home to out-of-form Newcastle United on a patchy internet stream. Bruce was philosophical in defeat. 'Up until Newcastle scored,' he said, 'I thought there wasn't much between us.'

In a bistro not far from the Museo del Prado, I ate my breakfast every day for a week until I realised that the owner, whose eyes behind their thick lenses resembled the startled eyes of a stuffed bird, was referring to me as *el americano* for the enjoyment of his customers, all of whom clearly despised me. For four mornings straight, I sat on a high stool at the counter and mispronounced my order of *tostada de tomate con jamón y un café solo*. From that vantage, I had a good view of the shrunken old man in the corner, whom I watched each day bent over a farm-themed fruit machine, draped in a brown leather jacket that may or may not have once fitted him, steadily losing everything he had with the utmost grace and calm.

On the fifth day, he was gone, replaced by a not considerably younger man whose leather jacket was not brown, but black. You could tell within a moment of arriving that this guy did not possess anything like the same poise. The crop had failed, his chickens had not hatched. The simple pleasures of pastoral life were obviously beyond him. He started slamming the machine. He started rocking it. He called out in frustration to the owner, expressing an indecipherable sense of injustice. A tension inapt to the hour surfaced as the owner considered the scene in silence for a moment, then disappeared. Though I did not doubt that he would return soon, I flinched to see him do so with a crowbar in his grip. He hopped over the counter and, spearing the crowbar into one of its crevices, he tore the front shell from the farm-themed fruit machine, which, it now became clear, was in fact the property of the not considerably younger man, who collected what he'd reaped into a dirty canvas bag and jingle-jangled down the road. He had not been gone long before the shrunken older man returned.

During the week I taught English for an organisation where, on my first day, I had to sit for most of the morning beside a man like David Brent with black teeth, who in just twenty minutes referred to me as British so many times that eventually I stopped correcting him. If I had a free afternoon, though, after breakfast I would sometimes make my way to the Prado, where more often than not I found myself drawn to the works of Jusepe de Ribera, especially those hanging in Room 9. It was not merely that there is a large bench in Room 9 – though the large bench certainly didn't diminish the room's allure – but that the paintings of Ribera seemed charged with the kind of dramatic intensity I usually had trouble identifying in other Old Masters without first being directed to it. With Ribera, there was no trouble: not with his handsomely bearded Saint Bartholomew, the saint's enormous reach as he holds to heaven the knife with which he is about to be skinned alive; nor with his apelike Saint Jerome, hermit patron of translators, beating his own chest in with a rock; not with Saint Sebastian.

By now one commonplace of emails I sent back to Ireland was that I had never been silent for so long. Of course I knew that this was not the case. Not exactly. It was true I was alone. It was also true I liked being alone a lot less than I'd expected. Most of the time, I didn't know what to do with myself; sometimes I thought of Joan. Still, I was not silent. By day I had little option but to speak to students, and fellow teachers, and disgruntled members of the food services industry. Then even at home I was not silent. Some thoughts I pronounced, some thoughts I did not. Usually what came out were just snatches of speech: often, 'I don't know about that'; sometimes, 'is that so?' It is not clear to me what or whom I was addressing in these remarks, if that is even what I was doing. For the most part, I figured these enunciations were just bits of language cast into the empty room with no purpose other than to mark time, or to remind myself of what I sounded like. Yet lately it had troubled me to notice that, whenever I tried switching to Spanish, as I often did in those moments when I felt shamed by the lack of progress I'd made learning it so far, the first thing I heard was always this: *'estamos aquí'* – always the same, *'estamos aquí'*. 'We are here.' I did not know what to make of that.

¶ On Mondays and Wednesdays I worked in a school way out in a township called Las Rozas. Situated about forty-five minutes outside Madrid, Las Rozas seemed to me a very strange place. Everything felt very far from everything else; and there were never as many people around as you would have imagined necessary for the area's many businesses to prosper as apparently they did. There was little to do in Las Rozas. You could hear footsteps from much too far away. The place had about it the feel of a holiday resort in permanent off-season. The playgrounds were empty, the fountains often dry. The first time I took a walk around Las Rozas, it felt like a cruel joke to discover that all its awful streets had been named after famous writers. Calle Pablo Neruda, Calle Gabriel García Márquez, Calle Camilo José Cela: all those tidily desolate streets with nothing of their namesakes except that they were dead.

During the afternoon, the school I worked in took on the characteristics of its surroundings. Sometimes there would be only two teachers in the centre, each idly waiting for their evening students to arrive before they could teach the class and go home. On one of my first afternoons, the other teacher sat opposite me correcting homework. 'What's wrong with this sentence?' he asked. 'Sometimes it isn't always best to tell the truth.' I had spoken to this teacher once before. He'd come to Spain the previous summer and he seemed not as bad as the black-toothed David Brent. I said something about incompatible adverbs. 'Yeah,' he said, falling silent. The conversation seemed to be at its end, but, as it turned out, it was not. The adverbs seemed beside the point now. In earnest he speculated that sometimes it isn't always best to tell the truth. 'Yeah, like a white lie,' I offered. He shook his head, told me I wasn't listening to him. 'For example,' he said, 'If a pig gets herself all dressed up for a night out, are you gonna tell her she looks terrible?' I was not certain that I understood his meaning. 'Think about it,' he urged. I gave it a second or two. I said that I supposed not. I think he bared his teeth then. 'Thank you,' he said finally, returning to his work. Later, standing on a chair trying to look out a high window, he complained about the downtime. He said he couldn't stand how quiet it got.

On the 7.30 p.m. bus out of Las Rozas most Mondays, an old woman would sit four rows from the front, smelling of the same cream as Joan. Sometimes, especially on Mondays, I would think of Joan. The reasons I'd moved to Madrid were numerous and generally amorphous. Some were plainly material. I didn't have a job in Dublin. I never had any money, and was unable to do the things I wanted to do, like going on the piss every night, eating lunch and dinner in restaurants, or moving out of my family home. Others, such as Joan, were less material, and therefore more difficult to grasp. Initially I told myself I left because I wanted to get away from our semi-romantic situation in which something kept not happening, but happening all the same, briefly, and with an intensity whose consequent feelings of loss and exhaustion did not seem much reduced by repetition. I told myself that since there seemed so little chance that things would change, it was time to leave.

It was not until one Monday evening, on the bus out of Las Rozas, where the smell of Joan had made its way down from row four to row five, that I became dimly aware that until that moment I had not understood my intentions at all. In fact, what I'd wanted to do by leaving was make Joan jealous, I think, of my life. I am not sure why. Possibly I was jealous of hers; possibly for the same reason I'd bothered telling her I'd slept with even one of my friends before leaving: it gave me an unmistakable, though not uncomplicated, feeling of power over her and, perhaps with that, myself. Though I never articulated this desire to myself or to others, I find it is retrievable in clear, if slightly ridiculous, pictorial terms: I'd wanted her to imagine the life I would live in Madrid, a cosmopolitan European city, renting cheaply and within walking distance of several major cultural institutions, through which I would wander, in a manner somehow faintly suggestive of sex having already taken place, with attractive and intelligent Spanish men and women, talking about obscure Spanish painters – no, sculptors – of whom Joan had never even heard, but would no doubt dismiss in much the same way as she dismissed anything she did not know: instinctively, often temporarily.

She showed no sign that she might visit.

¶ Madrid was the first city I had lived in where everyone returned my gaze, a response I did not immediately realise was so automatic as to be empty of all connotation. Some people stared so long I could have sworn they'd caught their own reflection. What struck me as most strange at first was the physical appearance of the streets. It was not that they were longer, or busier, or even more strikingly decorated, than others I had known; they just seemed much wider. Everywhere I went, I was reminded of places I had never been: Miami, Los Angeles, Vancouver. In parts of the city, especially at junctions, the skyline appeared spacious to the point of vacancy. At the Plaza de Colón, where a total of five streets connect, the centrepiece statue of Christopher Columbus seems not only dwarfed by the Pez-dispenser postmodernism of the Torres de Colón to the south, but totally engulfed by the large swathes of negative space to the north, west and east. From a height of over fifty metres, Columbus looked like just another old traffic conductor surveying a city he could probably once conduct. He looked lonely and anonymous now, his figure only further diminished by the appeal it still made to monumentality.

Often I ate lunch not far from Colón, in the Café Comercial on the Glorieta de Bilbao, because I had read that it was there that intellectuals ate lunch. Former regulars included Blas de Otero, Gabriel Celaya and Gloria Fuentes, and although these were names that meant less than nothing to me, I saw the café had a corner named after Antonio Machado. I had at least heard of him. In 1951, as well, Camilo José Cela, the Nobel Prize-winning dedicatee of the street I worked on in Las Rozas, published a novel set entirely inside the Café Comercial. One morning I spent several hours under the high ceilings of the Biblioteca Nacional, reading the library's only copy of LA COLMENA's out-of-print English translation. On the back cover, next to a photo of Cela, one of the blurbs praises the novel – translated as THE HIVE – for what it calls its 'snapshot approach'; but to me its formal qualities seemed closer to cinema than anything else; its narrative panning in and across an ensemble cast of the café's patrons. It is like the opening scene of *BOOGIE NIGHTS*, but instead of a nightclub full of porn stars and pornographers, we have a café frequented by melancholic wise-asses trying to borrow cigarettes from each other. The novel, which makes frequent allusions to homosexuality, was banned under Franco.

Downstairs the café's large, open-plan interior allows you to observe everyone more or less discreetly, but I spent most of my time there trying discreetly to be observed, reading books, large ones, held at such an angle as to place the title in clear view. I didn't notice many noticing. Most of the patrons looked nothing like intellectuals. They looked like people having affairs. Those that did not look like former Tottenham Hotspur managers tended instead to look like Peter Stringfellow. There was, however, one old man of frail distinction who would occasionally sit opposite me correcting what looked like exams and essays. Sometimes, when our eyes crossed paths, he'd smile.

In certain parts of the café, especially near the window where the old man sat, it was possible to tell when a metro was passing underneath by the gentle tremor of its heavy granite tables. I discovered this one afternoon as I sat contemplating a large slice of tortilla that had just been served to me. I have for many years made a point of not eating onion or anything containing onion. It is an absolute refusal that has made many days more difficult for others. My first girlfriend ate a burger once with onion on it. The smell never seemed to leave her breath and shortly afterwards we broke up. Try as I might, I cannot locate an early trauma to account for this aversion.

There in the Café Comercial, at a table near the window, I could see that the large slice of tortilla I sat contemplating contained onion. It definitely contained onion. Not a little onion. Not some onion. Not even a munificent but ultimately removable quantity of onion. The large slice of tortilla I sat contemplating was threaded through with onion. The longer I stayed there, the clearer it became that the large slice of tortilla I sat contemplating was in fact mostly onion. Probably it would not be going too far to say that there by the window in the Café Comercial I sat contemplating not a large slice of tortilla but a large slice of onion. That afternoon I sat there contemplating for such a long time that I began to fear the old man would think I was attempting, by sheer force of my own gaze, to make the large slice of onion, which he would presumably but misleadingly describe as a large slice of tortilla, move. When the table began suddenly to vibrate, I wondered for a moment if it wasn't my doing. The moment passed. I checked my phone, but that was not it either. No one had called. No one would call for some time.

The streets were hot to walk on last September in Madrid. My brother's first serious relationship had just ended and I'd returned to help bring his bags back. Time passed mostly in grim silence that weekend. On the last day, we were sitting by the fountain in the Puerta del Sol, watching nothing in particular, waiting only for our flight time to draw nearer, when a large man dressed all in leather dragged a tiny young woman in front of us. The girl was wearing just a bra and denim shorts. She was blindfolded, gagged and handcuffed, and she was groped all over by the enormous man. At length he struggled to remove her bra and shorts until at last she stood there naked save her handcuffs and her blindfold and her gag. On the inside of her thigh she had a tattoo of an angel whose wings reached up as far as her outer labia, which I looked at for long enough to note were shaven and sweating. Then a camera crew appeared, followed by a director, next a large crowd of onlookers, and finally several police cars. The officers were not impressed by whatever permit the crew waved in front of them. The shoot was shut down, everyone involved harangued, and although the director managed eventually to convince the officers not to arrest anyone, for a few minutes it seemed as if the young woman was going to be removed from one pair of handcuffs only to be placed into another.

I mention this only because it was on my mind as I began at last to eat the large slice of tortilla I had contemplated for so long that it was now completely cold. I finished it in three large mouthfuls, hardly chewing at all; and then I sat watching as the residual trail of half-cooked egg on my plate developed a skin.

I remained there, I suppose, for however long it takes for two people, totally silent, three tables and several decades apart, to develop a relationship requiring each to smile in parting. I tried to fix my hair, which wouldn't sit, and I drank another coffee to wash the cold wet egg and onion from my mouth. I remembered telling Joan about that second trip to Madrid: about the naked woman in Sol, about how long it had taken my brother to collect the stuff from his old apartment. I remembered saying that if I ever had the poor taste to write about the end of my brother's relationship, I had the ending ready. That evening at the airport, I said, my brother briefly and unexpectedly perked up to tell me about something he'd seen weeks before, at the same flight gate, as he waited to board a plane back to Dublin for someone's birthday. A Spanish family was standing next to him, he said, the father carrying two large Burger King bags so full up with food that he had hardly set foot inside the jet bridge before he'd let some fries fall out. My brother could not remember if it was a burger, or a sundae, or a Ranch Crispy Chicken Snack Wrap that fell next; only that the man became flustered. He just kept letting stuff fall, he said, amazed. By the time he reached the door, the tunnel was a horrifying ruin of beef patties, Coca-Cola, Popcorn Chicken, the lot. I said to Joan that here my brother's tone had changed to one of which I had no measure. He said all he had left then was salt.

E

I

INTERVIEW

WITH

MARK LECKEY

THERE IS A PLAYFUL, contrary quality to Mark Leckey's character that is rare in artists of his prominence. When not answering his own critics on YouTube or weighing in on below-the-line debates about his own work on the GUARDIAN's website, he might be found on Twitter reposting the views of his detractors:

> This is an art installation by British artist Mark Leckey. I am not into this sort of thing, but someone will be.
> Just WTF is this? Am I meant to be imprest or something?
> Listening to the guardian long read about mark leckey... #art that I just don't get at all

Neither is his interaction with critics restricted to the virtual realm. Following his Turner Prize victory in 2008, Leckey clashed with the GUARDIAN's Jonathan Jones, whose last-minute volte-face on the merits of INDUSTRIAL LIGHT AND MAGIC was interpreted by the artist as a personal slight. Moments after being awarded the prize, noticeably riled, he snapped: 'I should let this go, shouldn't I?' He didn't.

In part, this captiousness is the consequence of his longstanding sense of distance from the mainstream art world. After graduating from Newcastle Polytechnic in 1990, the same year that he was included alongside Glenn Brown and Damien Hirst in the prestigious showcase for emerging artists Bloomberg New Contemporaries, Leckey stopped making art.

He re-emerged in 1999 with 'Fiorucci Made Me Hardcore', a film collage of found footage chronicling Britain's musical subcultures. The film is now widely revered, and often cited as an influence by artists of a younger generation. Ed Atkins recently recounted his first experience of the work: 'At the time I didn't know who made it, and probably didn't even think it was, you know, "art". I probably thought it was something better. Which it is. Better, I mean.'

Last year's major retrospective, LENDING ENCHANTMENT TO VULGAR MATERIALS, showcased a multivalent body of work exploring the state of the individual within a world directed by popular culture and technology. While the work takes many forms, from Felix the Cat to 3D-printed legs, it invariably addresses what it means to be human. This self-examination is characterised by self-involvement, honesty and self-incrimination.

Leckey's life and art are, therefore, not easily distinguished. His involvement with the online reception of his work feeds back into certain aspects of that very work – including those relating to the status of the individual as professional consumer – and as a result, any critique becomes personal.

———

Q. THE WHITE REVIEW — Before you made 'Fiorucci Made Me Hardcore' you had been living in New York.

A. MARK LECKEY — I went there because I was desperate. When I was in England nothing was ever going right for me, so I just ran away. In about 1992, I had my twenty-eighth birthday in this pub by Goldsmiths. I got very drunk and ended up dancing on a pool table to David Bowie. I just kept putting it on and then getting back up, and upsetting myself in the process. It was an attempt at self-exorcism

I suppose, and after that I managed to scrape together enough money for a flight and I just went.

It was only after I had lived in America for about four years that I became acutely aware of the differences between the States and London. When I first got there it was a release, the horizon changed and felt unrestricted, and by contrast England felt much more compressed. If I hadn't gone to America I don't think I would have become so aware of that, of the many peculiarities of the culture.

Q. THE WHITE REVIEW — And 'Fiorucci' was born out of a sort of nostalgia for those peculiarities?

A. MARK LECKEY — There was a saturation of nostalgia in the Nineties, and I think it was accelerated by the idea of the millennium. There was this weird quasi-hysteria that we were reaching the end of the century, and it made the past have more of a pull. Maybe it was always there, but at that point it just seemed so powerful.

Nostalgia would be the blanket term, but it was more like a heightened awareness that there was something quite particular about England. New York gave me a distance, geographically and intellectually, to comprehend those particularities, and that developed into an obsession. I was obsessed by the idea that I was no longer involved in this unfolding force that had such a unique, specific energy. You would catch glimpses of it, though: you'd hear of Britpop, jungle, the YBAs, all of what was happening at that time.

Having said that, because you were getting it through the media, you could also see that a lot of it was just a copy. I imagine if you were actually in it then it would have felt less like that, but from a distance you saw just how repetitive some of it was.

Q. THE WHITE REVIEW — If you saw it as repetitive and as a copy, then what made you miss it?

A. MARK LECKEY — I don't know if I was missing it, that's the thing. It was more entangled than just missing it. Maybe it was a bit more resentful? I made 'Fiorucci' out of a general dissatisfaction. It was at a time when these nostalgic talking head documentaries were coming about, when that *Mojo* culture that led people to start waxing about the past was beginning. It had always been there, but it became much more prolific.

There's part of me that wants that, there's a *Mojo* part of me, but there's also a part of me that loathes it. So even when I was trying to resolve it, resolve my 'nostalgia', I felt two quite contradictory forces within myself, two conflicting forces.

Q. THE WHITE REVIEW — Aside from this dissatisfaction with the trajectory of culture, can you talk about the creative process that brought 'Fiorucci' into being?

A. MARK LECKEY — One of the things about 'Fiorucci' that has always worried me is that it required a very peculiar set of conditions to evolve. I was asked to make a history of music videos by Emma Dexter, Director of Exhibitions at the ICA. The original idea was that I would make a programme called 'Moments in Love', but the more I worked on it the more I felt uninvolved in it. It felt more like television than I wanted it to, and I was playing at being a TV producer.

From the point of leaving college in 1990 to 'Fiorucci' in 1999, I didn't really make any art at all. I wasn't interested, because I believed that I wasn't able to grasp the ideas that were circulating at the time. Art felt unknowable to me. It was too complex, too intellectual. There was no pleasure there for me at all. 'Fiorucci' only came about because the initial proposal allowed me the opportunity to work within my own compass, and that was all I wanted to do. I thought that if I was operating within the realm of my own experience then I might be able to produce something. I might actually be able to make something rather than choke and feel that my own experience was lacking, that I didn't have enough knowledge, because that's what I felt like at the end of college. I really believed that the knowledge gap was too great, that if I didn't understand Lacan or Nietzsche, that if I couldn't grasp philosophy and critical thinking, then I couldn't make work – or I couldn't make work that was intellectually rigorous enough to be of any interest.

At that time there was just this chasm of lack in front of me. Every day I thought, 'I'll never catch that shit, I'll never get that.' I didn't have that kind of start, so I just gave it up. The process of making 'Fiorucci' taught me how to make art. It taught me that you should always find something within your own boundaries to work with, and then just investigate the shit out of that. There's enough there, you just have to drill down into it.

Q. THE WHITE REVIEW — 'Write what you know,' as it were.
A. MARK LECKEY — That's essentially what I'm saying; I'm just trying to make it sound a bit more interesting. 'Write what you know' has become a hackneyed expression in literature, but it's still true, and it's exactly what was beaten out of you at art school in those times. If you ever tried to make any work from your own experience then it was deemed expressionistic or overly sentimental.

The idea was that if you wanted to make something from yourself, then you didn't understand the notion of false consciousness – that Marxist notion that you have to educate yourself in order to liberate yourself from capitalist ideology. That if you make anything from a state of innocence alone, then all you're really expressing are clichéd phrases that are inherent to the dominant social order. Nothing's being critically or politically dealt with.

Q. THE WHITE REVIEW — Do you think this over-reliance on critical theory is still a problem in the art world?
A. MARK LECKEY — Yes, definitely, and I think it's the biggest obstacle you have to overcome as a student, because if you're making work that's nothing more than an intellectual, critical response, then you're back to the problem of a knowledge gap plus you don't have to invest anything of yourself in what you're making. You are disinterested.

I've got this idea at the moment that art has a viral quality to it, and that it seeks hosts in order to replicate itself. It will *use* you. Art will use you to produce, because it needs bodies, it needs physicality.

Q. THE WHITE REVIEW — So it's a question of whether or not you represent a hospitable host body?
A. MARK LECKEY — Yes, exactly. Critical engagement is just a method. It's seen as the correct method, and in a sense it works, but it's just another one of these host bodies.

The problem with being at art school is that you don't know what to do, or if you do know what to do then it's knocked out of you and you're left in a state of befuddlement. Maybe you've originally gone there because you could draw or maybe you were just interested in painting, but then you are made to engage in this kind of critical thinking. Again, you are encouraged to recognise you own false consciousness and reassemble yourself into this critically engaged adult. It keeps happening over and over again, because in that moment when you don't know what to do, you find this pre-existent model which is freely available to you and immediately accessible. That is the purpose of critical methodology. There's a structure there that you can work into without having to give any of yourself.

You can make work like that if you want to remain quite detached. But ultimately, these kinds of artists are all singing from the same hymn sheet. They just continually circulate the orthodoxy that is spread within art schools and magazines. It's the orthodoxy, it's the focus of interest, and sadly you know that that work will gain a particular kind of critical reception. If your work speaks to speculative realism then you know that it's going to be taken seriously, that people are going to respond to that; but if your work's about Buddhism, then maybe not. That's what I mean about a kind of methodology, you can so easily just acquire it.

Q. THE WHITE REVIEW —— Do you find it strange when critical theory and philosophy is retroactively applied to your work?
A. MARK LECKEY —— No, because I'm influenced as well. I'm just as implicated.

The worst thing is that when I work now, I can feel the voice of the critic in my head, and they'll be saying, 'Leckey's work is investigating a sense of...'

Q. THE WHITE REVIEW —— That's not a good thing, surely?
A. MARK LECKEY —— It's a horrible fucking thing! It's like the voice of Satan. When I read a review of my work I'm always slightly disappointed, because it never says more than what that voice in my head was saying. When I made 'GreenScreenRefrigeratorAction' (2010) I had been thinking a lot about cybernetics and post-humanism – for want of a better word – but I'd also attempted to tackle speculative realism, so there was definitely a little exterior influence there. But now I cringe when I think about that, because the idea that a fridge that talks with a dodgy Scouse accent can embody speculative realism is not a very serious one.

To make interesting work you have to extract yourself from that way of thinking, but it's very seductive, you're always getting pulled into it. It's a little frightening how powerful it is, and honestly I don't really know what produces it. I don't know if it's the result of a certain social pressure or an intellectual insecurity, but you always find yourself willing to succumb to it in some way just to please people.

Q. THE WHITE REVIEW —— I think that particular desire for validation exists in every creative field.
A. MARK LECKEY —— Validation, that's exactly what it is, and I'm no more immune to it than a student is. Maybe I just want to be validated in a more sophisticated manner. Again, there are contradictory forces at play there: part of you is compelled towards it and another part of you is repulsed by it.

That repulsion probably comes from looking at other artists who have struggled out of that conflict, and realising that it's that very sense of escape that gave their work so much power.

Q. THE WHITE REVIEW —— Which artists are you thinking of?
A. MARK LECKEY —— Maybe Frances Stark and Richard Hawkins? I'm not so sure who else I actually like. [Laughs] Mike Kelley is always my touchstone, really. They're all thinking artists. They're still in it, but they're always trying to free themselves, to find a little

sovereignty.

Q. THE WHITE REVIEW — Would you enter into that sovereignty if you could – that artistic utopia that's immune to any kind of critical influence?

A. MARK LECKEY — That's the anxiety, because if you do manage to make it over then you're just lost in a desert. There used to be this idea that you could go to places like L. A. and just vanish, get that free space that you need to evolve your work in solitude. I honestly don't know how to do that. That idea that it's just you, that you're there without any support or any engagement, seems absolutely terrifying to me.

I don't know if it's even possible nowadays anyway – maybe that's my get-out clause. I don't know if it's possible to just get off the grid like that anymore. Pre-internet, you could have done it, but now I don't know. You would have to have an incredible self-discipline to the point of being ascetic, quite monastic. I couldn't be St Jerome or even Agnes Martin.

Q. THE WHITE REVIEW — It doesn't strike me as the healthiest of environments to work in.

A. MARK LECKEY — No, and I know that it's not healthy for me because I've been there. I've been alone, and it's not a place I want to go back to.

Q. THE WHITE REVIEW — You mentioned the increasing influence of the internet on the process of making art, and 'Fiorucci' was made possible by the growing availability of new technologies, of editing software specifically. Was it at that point that you first became interested in the idea of constructing memory from found footage?

A. MARK LECKEY — It definitely begins there. That technology made it possible to synthesise everything that I was into – images, sound, and found footage – and I don't think I would have made work at all if it hadn't appeared. I don't know what else I would have done. It was all very serendipitous.

Q. THE WHITE REVIEW — If we refer to 'Fiorucci' as the birthplace of the art that you make today, what are your views on the work that predates that video? I'm thinking here of the piece that was included in Bloomberg New Contemporaries in 1990.

A. MARK LECKEY — Horrible. It was fucking awful! It's a perfect example of exactly what I was talking about earlier, the idea of art having a viral quality and using fresh young meat as a host. That piece had nothing to do with me; I really don't even know what it was about.

Q. THE WHITE REVIEW — Alongside your lecture series 'In the Long Tail', certain more recent works show how that early adoption of editing software as a creative tool has led to an interest in digital anthropology, and the concept of animism in particular.

A. MARK LECKEY — The word animism started appearing in the collective consciousness as a way to try and comprehend how magical and fascinating and incomprehensible all of these new technological devices are. That's why I started taking an interest in it, anyway, to try and explain how in contemporary culture everything is becoming increasingly responsive. Everything has developed the ability to communicate and we're in the midst of that matrix. For me, that turns everything back to these ancient, pre-literary ideas of animism.

Q. THE WHITE REVIEW — Which leads us into the exhibition that you curated in 2013 for the Hayward Touring Programme, THE UNIVERsal Addressability of Dumb Things.

A. MARK LECKEY —— It's a funny one. When I was asked to curate a touring show by the Hayward I was quite anxious that it could easily become an exercise in taste. That I might end up using it to show how clever I am, or conversely that I would reveal myself to not be that clever or tasteful. I didn't want to do that. I wanted to do something a bit more ambitious and complicated.

Opportunities occasionally arrive in the art world – or outside the art world – that give you a chance to put all your orphan ideas together, all the ideas that you wouldn't want to make an actual work about, and The Universal Addressability was one of those opportunities. I could just shove in all of the things that were in my head at the time and didn't have a place within the greater scheme of what I wanted to make. So it became about everything: animism, cybernetics, autism and so on. The idea of the show was to try and transmit that weird paradox that the more future-orientated we become, the more we bend back into the past, the more we're thrown back into these ancient, aboriginal ways of thinking. I did get very immersed in it in the end because it also became about fetishism. A lot of the objects in that show were fetishistic, and I am a fetishist.

Q. THE WHITE REVIEW —— A fetishist in what sense?

A. MARK LECKEY —— Things, inanimate things, turn me on. They excite me. I'm kind of polymorphously sexual when it comes to things in the world. It's like everything has the potential to be erotic in some way. Not everything, obviously, otherwise I would be walking around in a state of priapic confusion, but I can always allow myself to fantasise.

For me, when you are organising a show like that, it becomes a lot about possession, about the fact that potentially you can *have* these things, and from that you start thinking about the dynamic that we have with objects. I chose things that had a power over me in a fetishistic way. That seemed to possess me and in turn led me to covet them.

Q. THE WHITE REVIEW —— You have talked before about this idea of possession, and it often seems to be tightly bound up with the process of creation. Do you feel more connected with these objects having actually brought them into being?

A. MARK LECKEY —— I guess this is the effect of all that theoretical training. I always felt it was too distant, and what I actually wanted was something much more intimate, much closer to me.

It began when I was making 'Fiorucci', when I was constantly working with this footage and gradually becoming more and more obsessed with it. I felt a desire to be in the image, to enter into it somehow. I suppose that's the ultimate fantasy: that I can be inside it.

Q. THE WHITE REVIEW —— The video-cum-performance piece 'GreenScreenRefrigeratorAction' adopts that idea fairly literally. Am I right in thinking that for that project you directly inhaled the gases from a fridge?

A. MARK LECKEY —— Yeah, that was the idea, to get inside the fridge... It's not that ridiculous when you think about it, it's an actual thing. In the States they call it huffing. You can huff just about any kind of chemical, any kind of gas. People used to do butane when I was a kid and, what's it called... the frothy cream one? Anyway, it had some kind of gas in it that would get you high. It was like doing poppers, but not as good, so you would have to take a lot to get really fucked up. Not like glue. That's just fucking mental. I did glue once. Never again.

Q. THE WHITE REVIEW — Did the refrigerator gases have the desired effect then?
A. MARK LECKEY — A little bit, I suppose. The reason you do these kinds of things is to lose yourself and to stop being self-conscious, to abandon yourself and be lost in a certain environment. That was the idea anyway. In the same way that you take drugs normally, I wanted to lose any self-consciousness and just be present.

I'm reading Maggie Nelson at the moment, and she has this nice idea that to become ecstatic is to be beside yourself, to see yourself as a thing, and to enjoy your 'thingness'. Ultimately, that's what I want out of all this, to not think and just to experience, to experience something without being self-conscious, without being self-aware. I didn't want to be like, 'I am standing in front of a fridge and this fridge means this.' I just wanted to be fridge-like.

I talked earlier about false consciousness, and within that is the Marxist notion of alienation, the idea that as a result of capitalism your experiences are continually being abstracted and utilised.

Q. THE WHITE REVIEW — The principle of estrangement?
A. MARK LECKEY — Estrangement, exactly. You can argue about whether it's Marxist or perhaps even Christian – the idea of original sin and banishment from the 'self' of Eden – but ultimately it's the very same idea of separation, the same state of estrangement.

In life all I want is to know things, to understand things, to encounter things and to be with things, and I'm continually frustrated in that by a sense of alienation. It's the feeling that I can't get close to a thing, that I can't get to that true experience or true emotion because there's so much noise between me and it.

At one point I took up walking. I'd go walking up mountains – mountains are the classic one – but whenever I got to the top of a mountain all I could think was, 'Fucking Caspar David Friedrich!' Do you know what I mean? It's so hard to get to the heart of anything any more, to free yourself, focus and have a 'moment'.

Instead of trying to directly approach this immediacy, you have to mediate towards it, and the more mediated the path is, the more that experience feels true. So instead of going out and hugging a tree, now I stand next to the most technologically up-to-date fridge there is, and then I can feel a bit more like I'm *with* an object. I don't think it's an authentic experience, but that's the point. It's not authentic, it's absolutely inauthentic, but somehow taking that path, making a ritual of that artifice, allows for something satisfying.

Q. THE WHITE REVIEW — Your use of 3D printing in exhibitions like UNIADDDUMTHS (2015) at the Kunsthalle Basel strikes me as another attempt to mediate and indirectly become one with your objects.
A. MARK LECKEY — I had a funny experience with 3D printing recently. I had made a scan of my legs, and when I eventually got them printed they came out slightly smaller than my own, and somehow in that act of diminishing them slightly I began to feel really protective towards them. If they were mine – if they were printed one to one – I think they would have felt too egotistical, too vain, but because they were slightly smaller I entered into a strange paternal relationship with them, with my own legs. In the end they got sold to a collector that I really didn't want them to get sold to and it really fucked me off because now

they're in this collection and I can't bear it. It's like the phantom limb effect. They've got part of me, they've literally got part of me, and it's been really upsetting. Every day I wake up kind of aggravated by the fact that they've got my fucking legs.

Q. THE WHITE REVIEW — Douglas Coupland said recently that 3D printing is 'better than real life'.

A. MARK LECKEY — I'm kind of in agreement. I think if you state it as bluntly as that then it's ineffective, but that alternate world does offer the attractive opportunity to reorganise yourself in a way that isn't alienated. Because how else are we going to resolve that problem? It's quite a postmodern concept, but it makes sense to me, the idea that if you just embrace the 'not real' then it might allow you to feel unalienated and paradoxically more alive.

Q. THE WHITE REVIEW — As an early advocate of art employing new technologies, what are your views on the more recent instances of post-internet art?

A. MARK LECKEY — I think the post-internet thing is a bit of a misnomer. No one wants to own it; no one really wants to be really involved in it.

There is definitely more of a technological element to contemporary art-making today. Whether that's necessitated by the weird technical epoch that we're experiencing or whether we're all just following each other, I don't know, but let's just accept that we're currently living through a strange, very particular type of period. I think its parallel is the turn of the twentieth century, which threw up dadaism and surrealism. Well, and war. It is a transitional moment.

Right now I feel like I'm part-analogue, part-digital, and I feel like psychologically and neurologically I'm being changed. I think that we're being taught a new way of thinking through our newfound interaction with the internet. For me it's a little autistic.

Q. THE WHITE REVIEW — Autistic in what sense?

A. MARK LECKEY — Because as a result of all of these programmes and codes, we're coming to see the world in a rather autistic sense, one that isn't neurologically typical.

To get really hyped up about it, I imagine us moving towards a world without metaphor, because autism doesn't really allow for metaphor, it looks instead for concrete instances. And although I think the internet works through correspondences and analogies, they're not poetic, they're much more concrete.

Q. THE WHITE REVIEW — To return to this question of post-internet art, do you believe that technology is now being utilised in a different way? If you look at certain artists that you are said to have influenced – Ed Atkins, for example – they appear to be driving forward, attempting to craft a new language and a new aesthetic to accommodate it, whereas you tend to introduce technology in order to manipulate the past. Does that make sense?

A. MARK LECKEY — Yes, it does. I go backwards, they go forwards. I worry about my drive backwards into the past. I think it's partly to do with age, and it's partly to do with what I was talking about before, about existing within this transitional epoch where one foot is stuck in the past, the other is being forced into the future, and you end up doing the splits.

I think it's the availability of the archive as well. It's a response to being overwhelmed by that. The internet, technology itself, amplifies everything, including the past. I'm in the middle of something, this semi-memoir that's made completely out of found footage, called 'MyAlbum'.

When I was 15 I went to this club in Liverpool called Eric's and saw Joy Division – I've been able to dine out on that one for years. I can't remember anything of it, it just exists as a kind of anecdote, one of those mythological moments that you carry with you but don't really think about too much. But one night a couple of years ago I was having a drink and going on YouTube – a lot of men my age do this: you pour a whiskey and then look at old videos from your past – and I came across this bootleg recording of that very concert. I started to become fascinated by this idea that somehow I'm in there. Somehow I exist in this crappy, analogue recording, and if I listen hard enough or if I enhance the audio enough then I might be able to find myself.

My fantasy is that I can filter out all the noise, find myself, and listen to the thoughts that I was having at that time. It seems possible in some way, even just in an imaginative but technologically feasible way, that I might be able to reconstitute my 15-year-old self from this poor bit of footage from YouTube. It's the audio equivalent of the Esper machine in BLADE RUNNER that can find information hidden within an image. While it's definitely there, it's not just the nostalgia that fuels these things. It's technology's relationship to the past, and its archaeological ability to unearth and examine this stuff.

Q. THE WHITE REVIEW —— Why do you think that you examine these things? Do you look for your 15-year-old self in an attempt to save that self, or to understand it?

A. MARK LECKEY —— To understand it? To re-experience it? To exorcise it? I don't know why, I don't know what that impulse is.

Q. THE WHITE REVIEW —— Essentially, I'm asking why you make the work that you do, why you make art that looks backwards and looks inside.

A. MARK LECKEY —— Because it's something that obsesses me. I don't know if I could find a reason beyond that. It's just a pathological drive, a fascination.

Coming at it another way: I make art because I'm trying to understand why images have such a power over me. I need to know why certain pictures infiltrate and infect my very soul. I'm frightened by their power over me, their hold. It makes me feel out of control.

Q. THE WHITE REVIEW —— I thought we might loop back to 'Fiorucci Made Me Hardcore', because this idea of archaeology, while being obvious in later works including 'MyAlbum' and the likes of 'Circa 1987' (2013), is also present in that first video. How do you think that your work has developed since 'Fiorucci'? It could be argued that your recent pieces have been a means to a very similar end.

A. MARK LECKEY —— I've definitely gone through periods with 'Fiorucci' when I've thought of it as an albatross, where I've believed that I'll never make anything as good as it again. People loved that film, and to this day I've never made anything else that people have had such an investment in.

At one stage I wanted to kill it, to kill the albatross, but now I've come through the other side and it feels like an extraordinary thing to have done. I've made a cult piece of work, and in the end that's what I wanted to do, because that's all I ever knew. I've furthered that history of cult works just through being interested in cult works, and that's more than I could ever wish for.

So with 'MyAlbum', instead of trying to kill it, I'm trying to confront it a bit more. It comes from the same place as 'Fiorucci', but it's looking for the bits where I'm not dancing.

The recent things that I've made weren't too nostalgic, I don't think. 'Pearl Vision' (2012) wasn't nostalgic, the fridge wasn't nostalgic. My greatest concern is that in this attempt to speak from your own experience alone, you can very easily end up in a trap of sentimentality. I have to watch my own sentimentalism, because that's one of the overbearing drives with all this stuff, and when I say images have a power over me I'm talking about that as well. I'm talking about the fact that I can weep buckets just watching a video. It's something that deeply, deeply troubles me.

HARRY THORNE, MAY 2015

II — IX

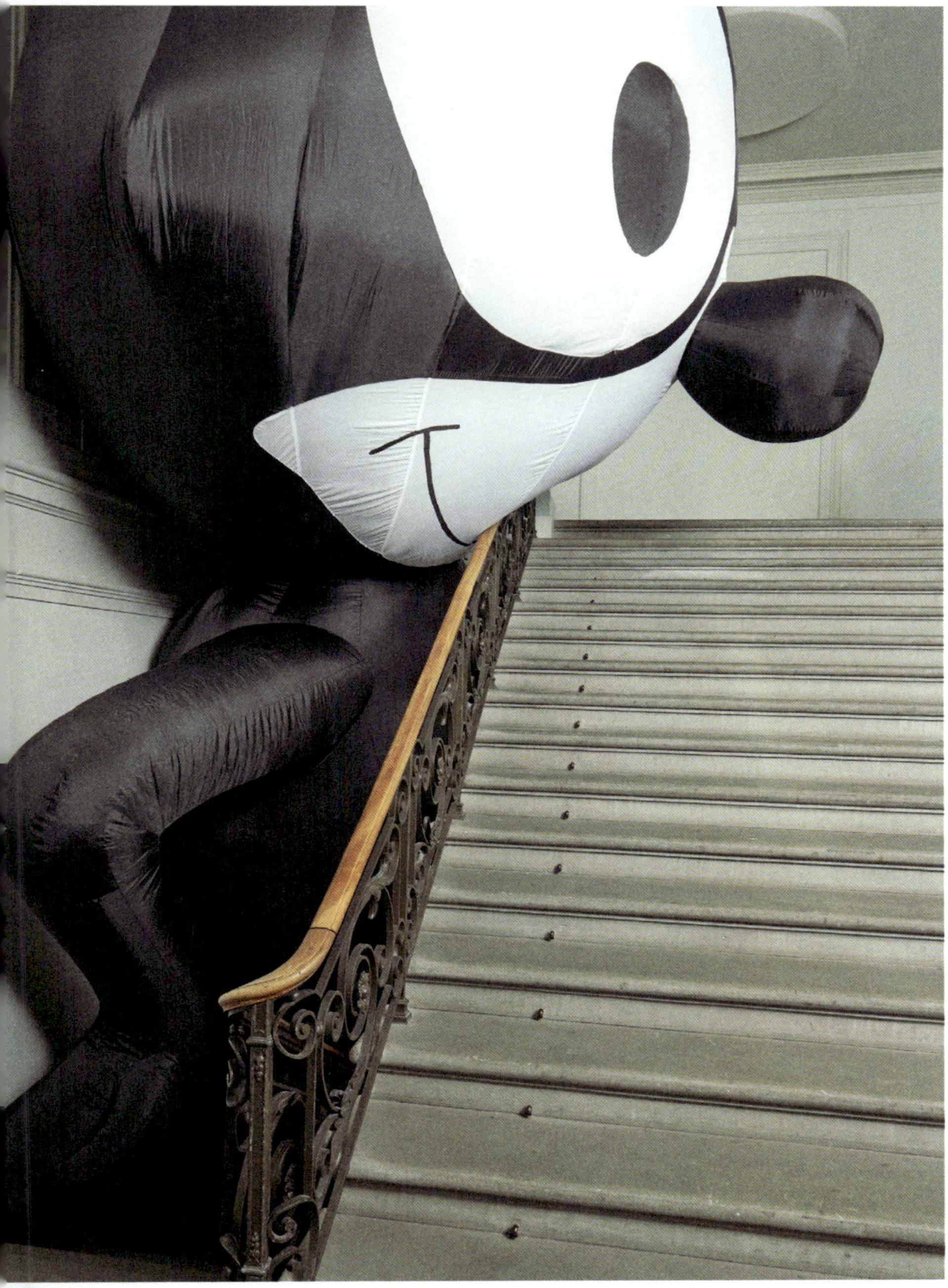

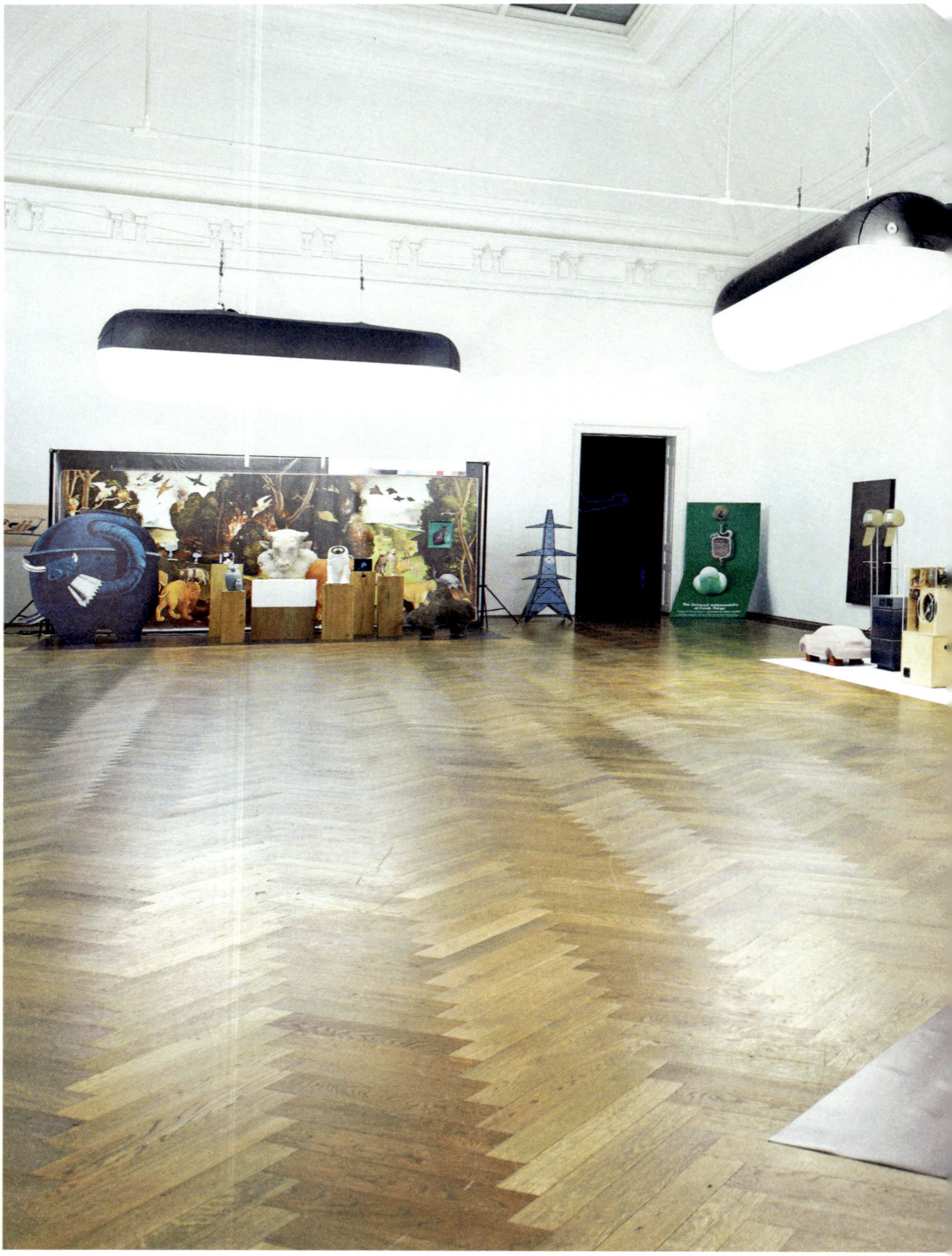

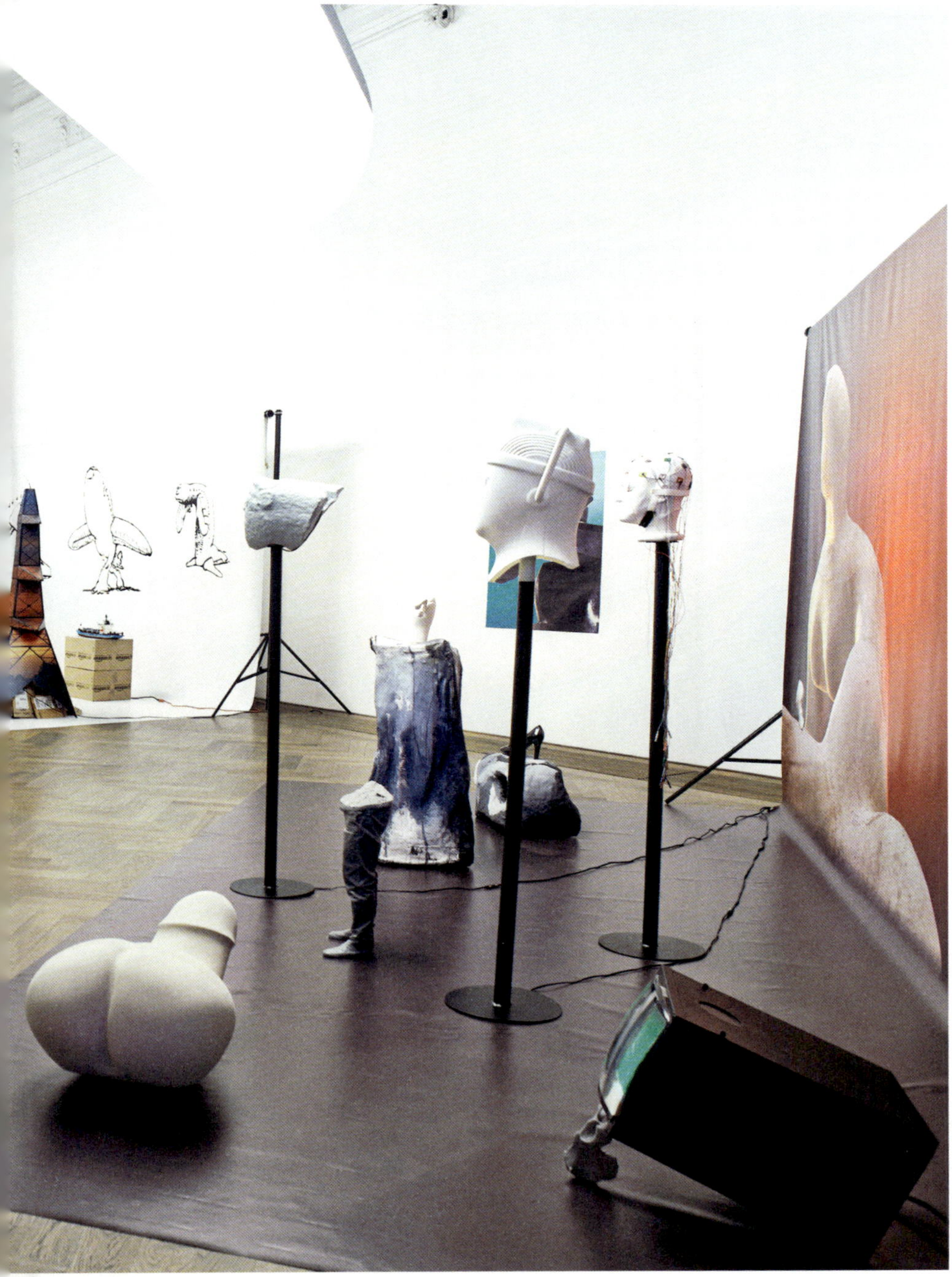

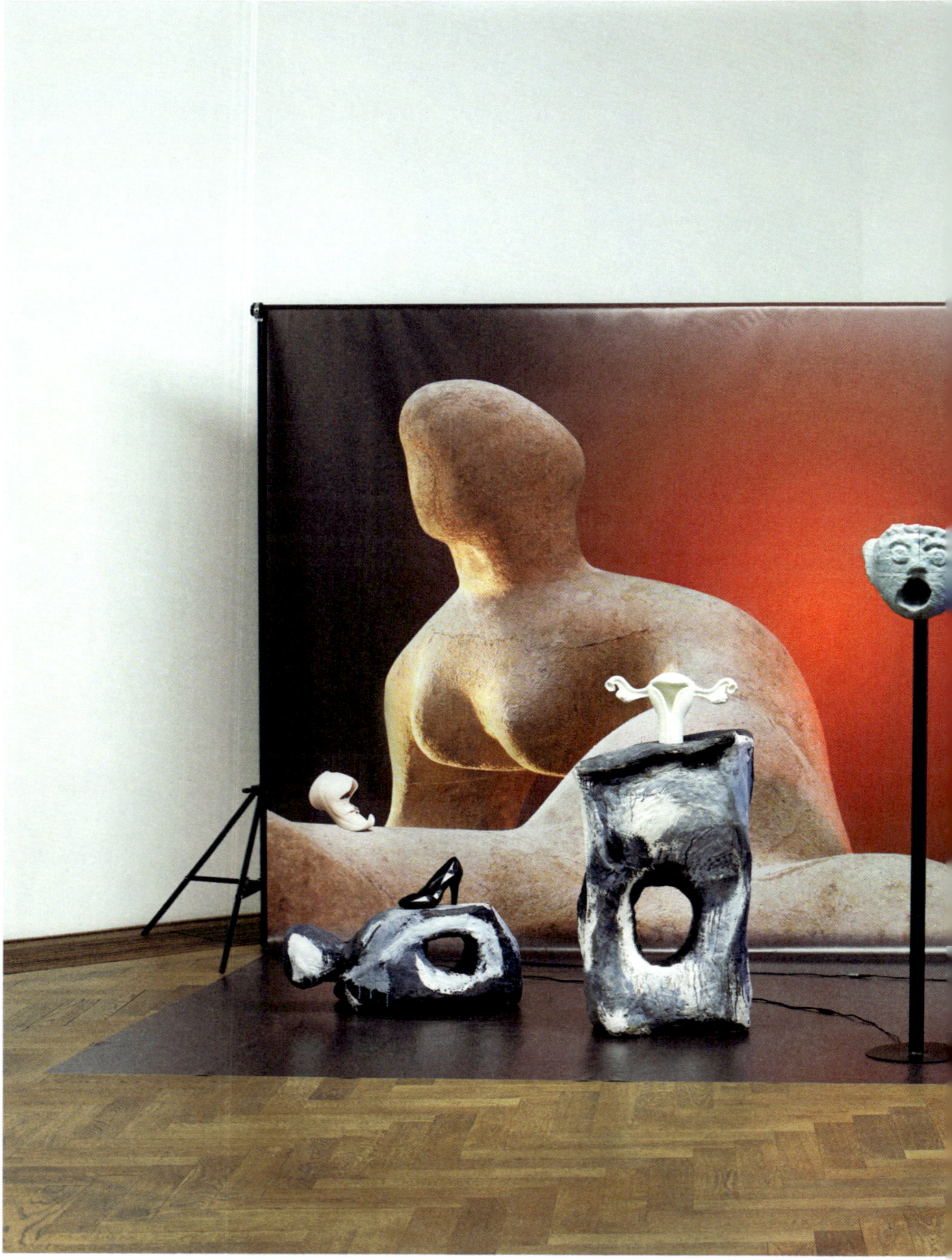

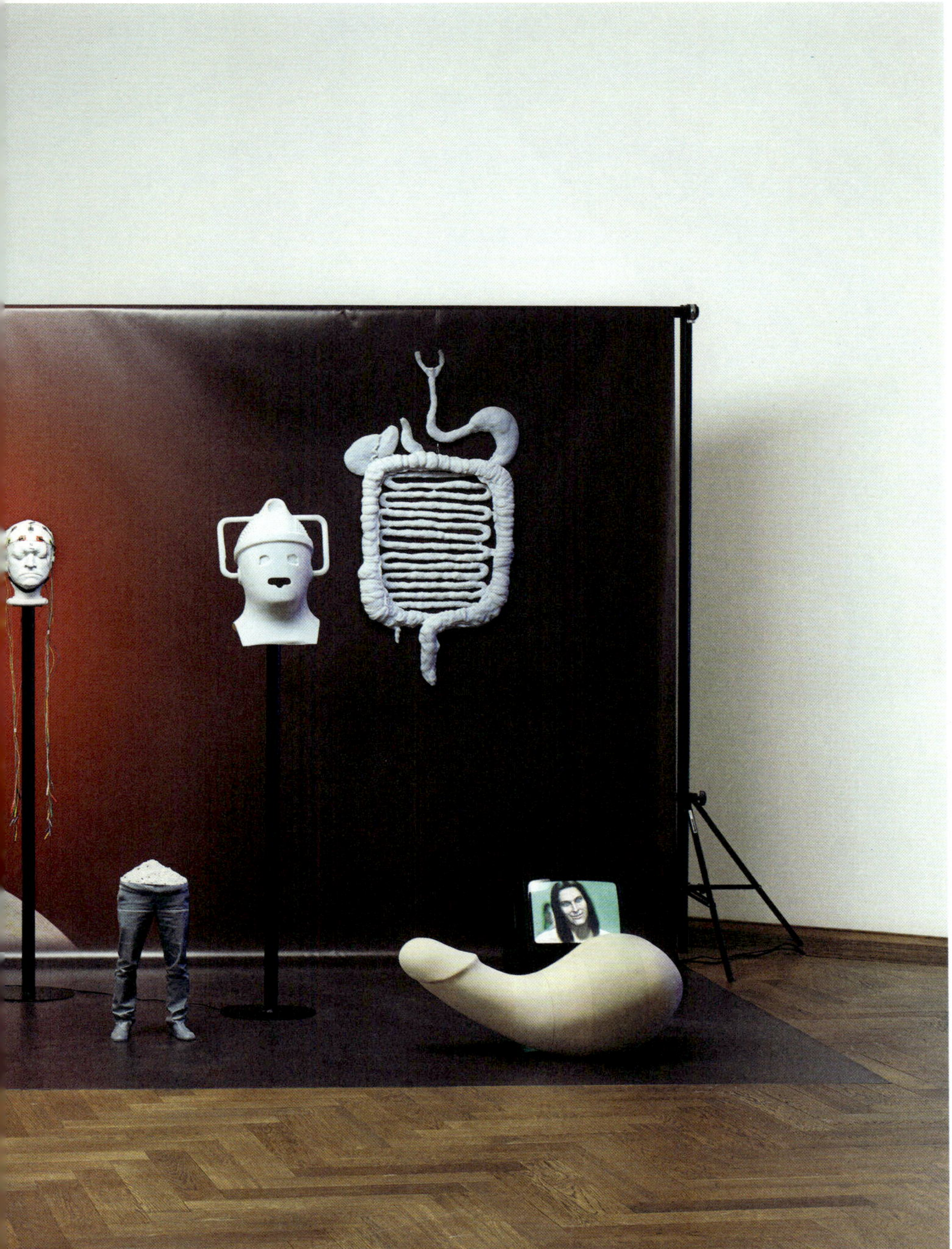

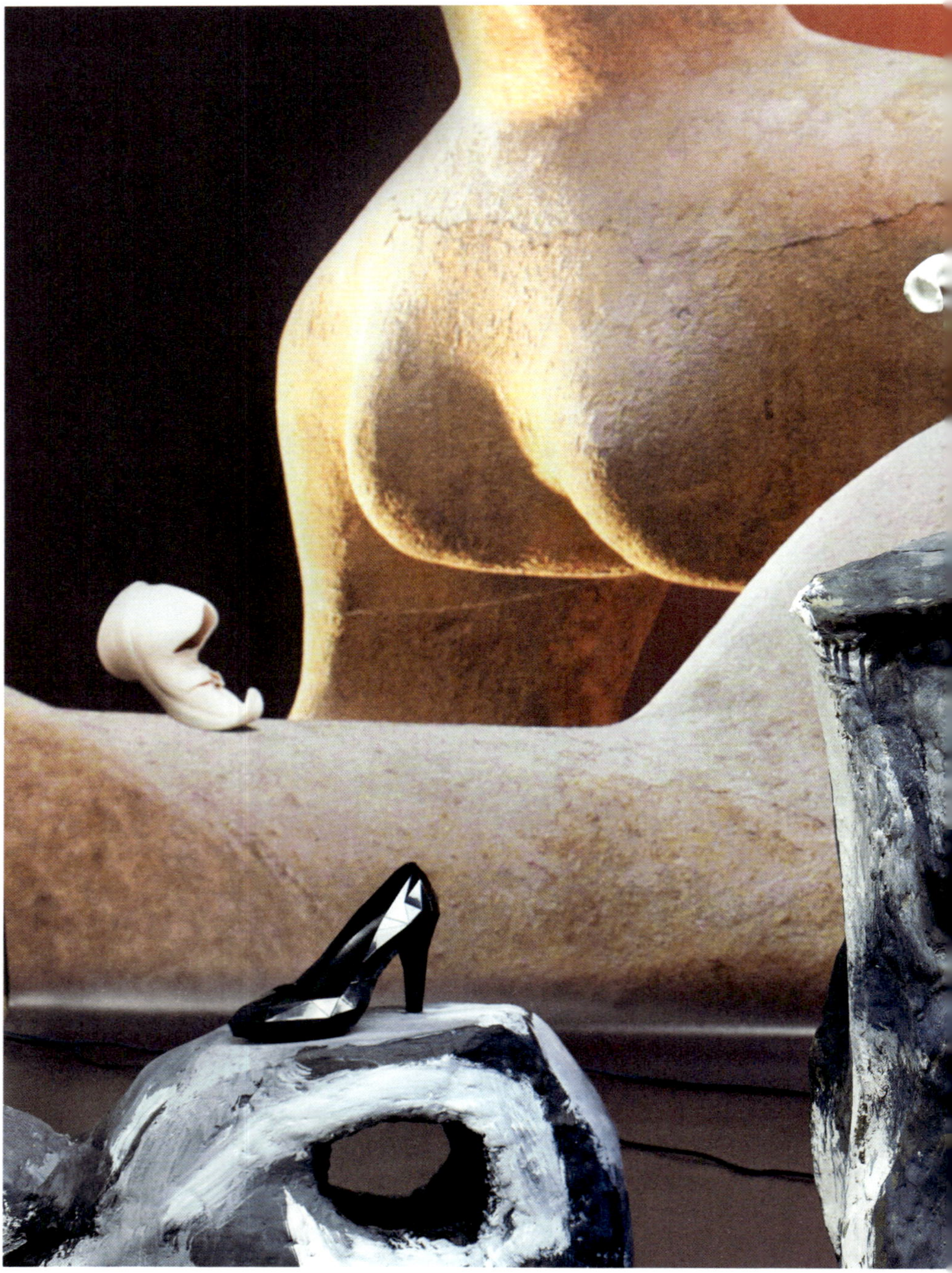

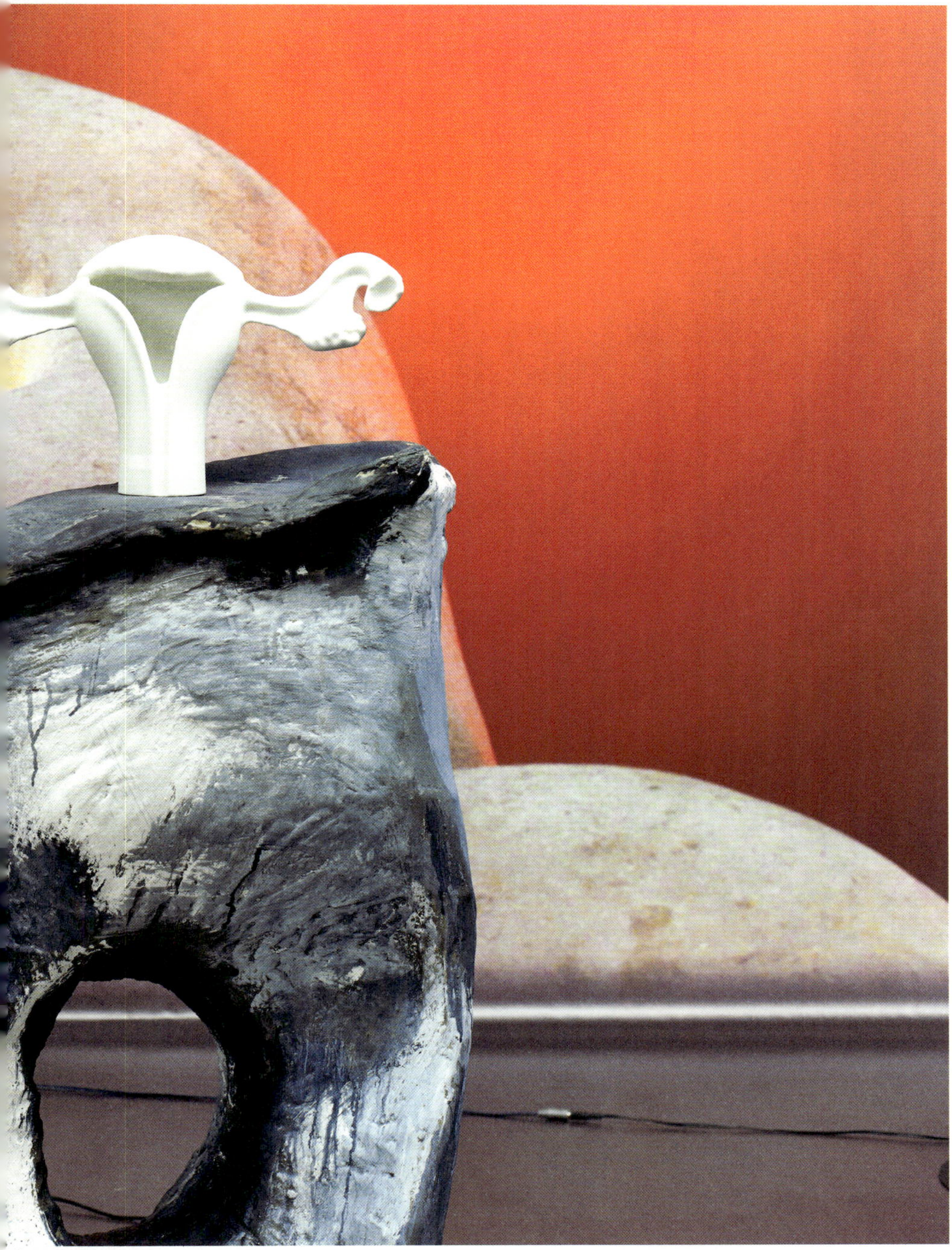

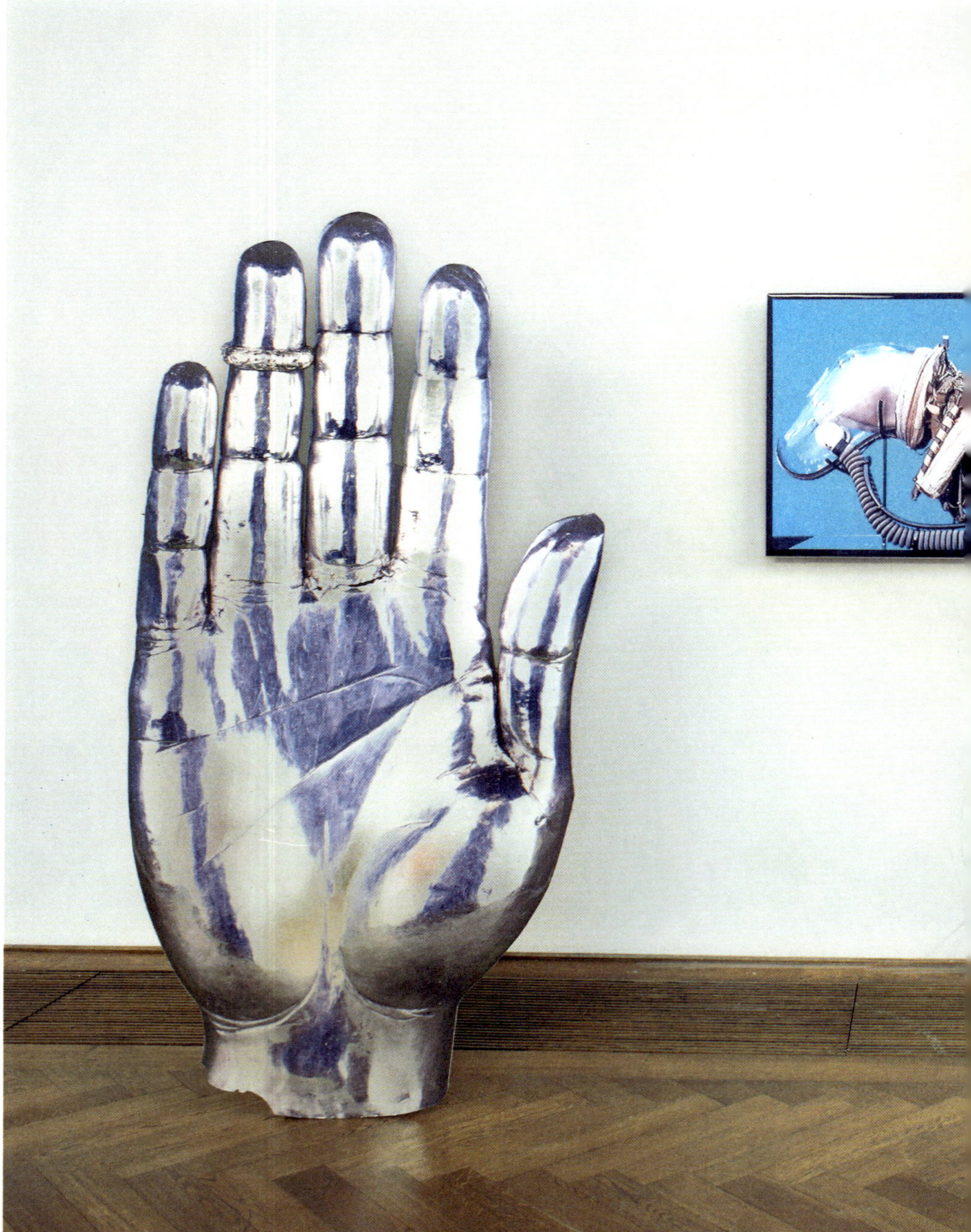

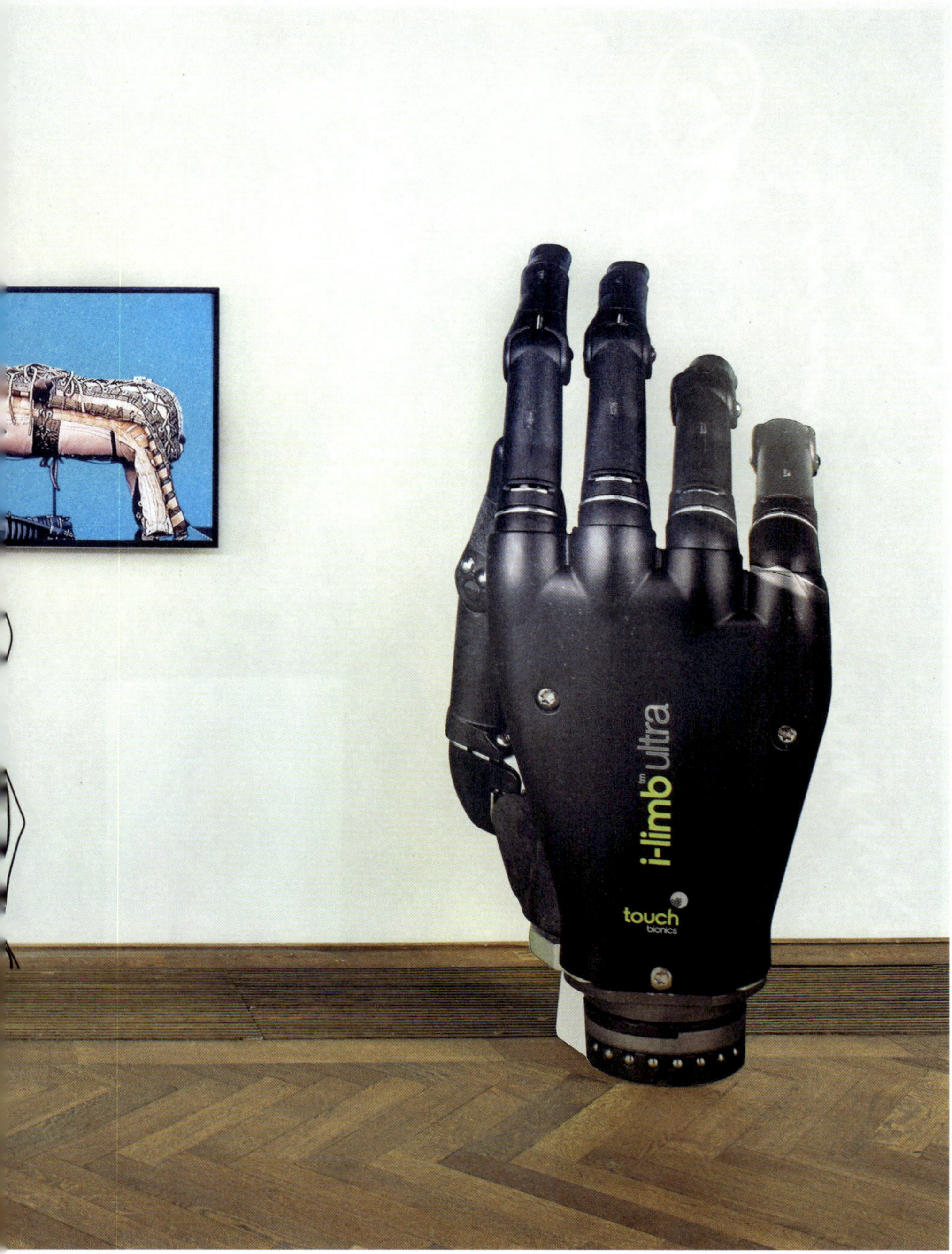
i-limb ultra
touch
bionics

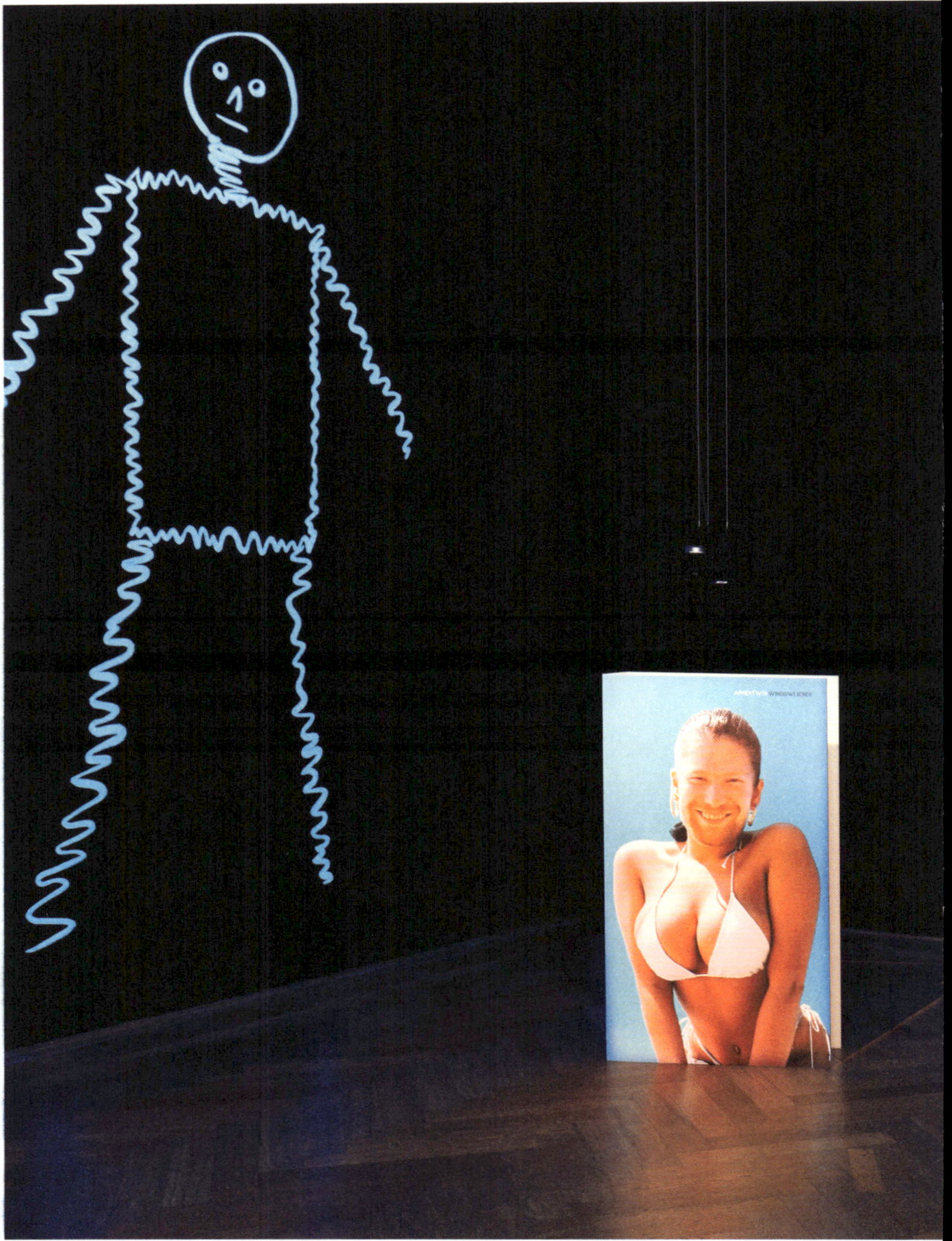

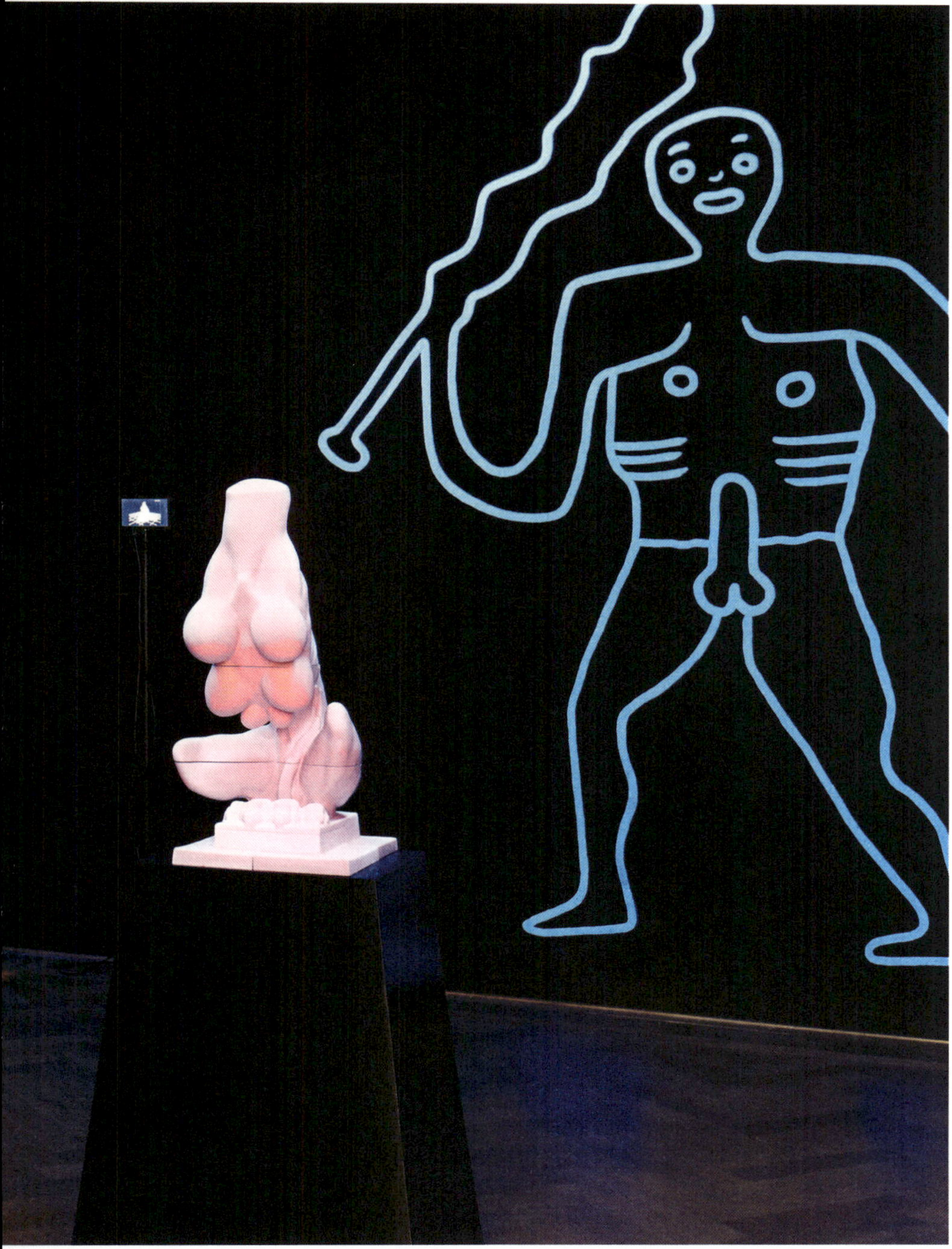

amazon.es
amazon.co.uk
amazon.co.uk
amazon.de
amazon.co.uk
amazon.de

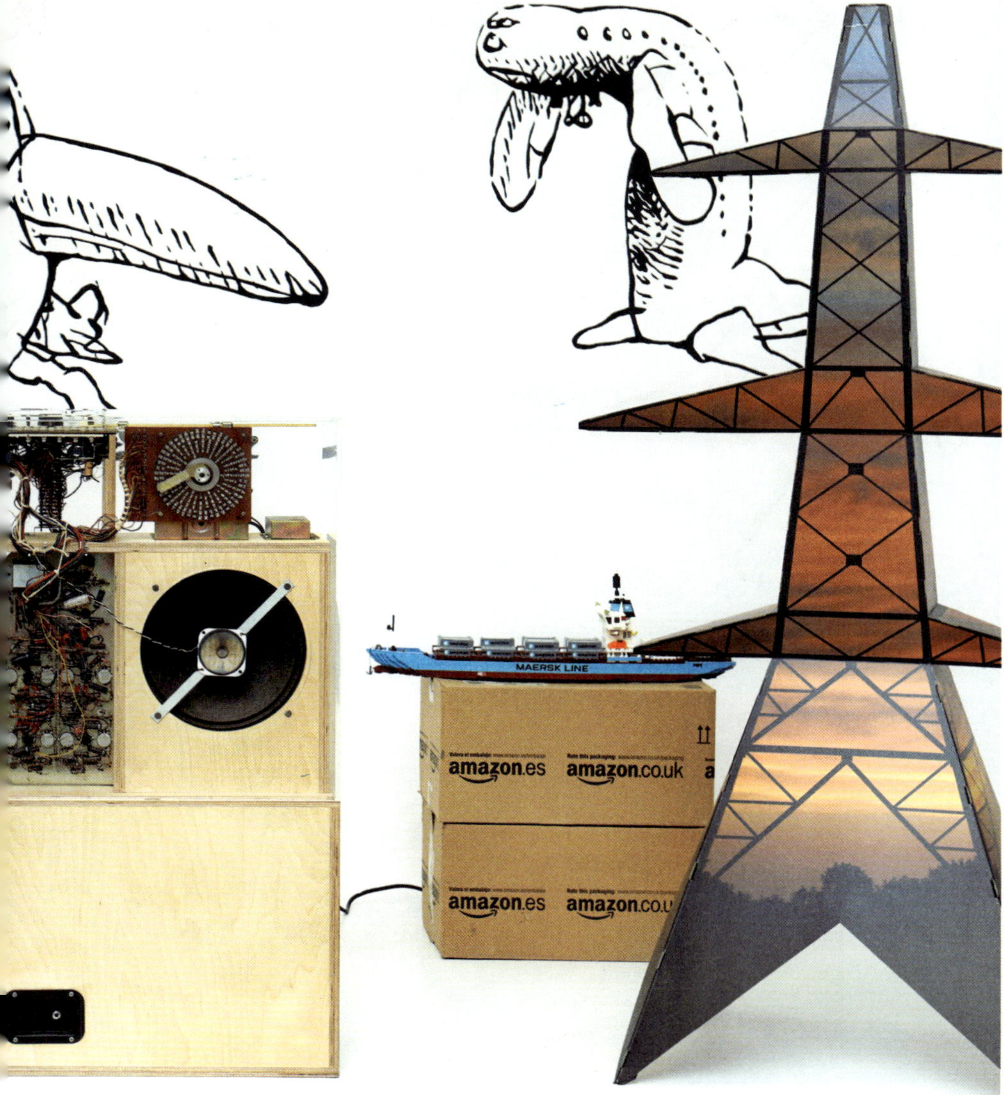
MAERSK LINE
amazon.es
amazon.co.uk
amazon.es
amazon.co.u

amazon.co.uk amazon.de
amazon.co.uk amazon.de
amazon.co.uk
amazon.it
amazon.it

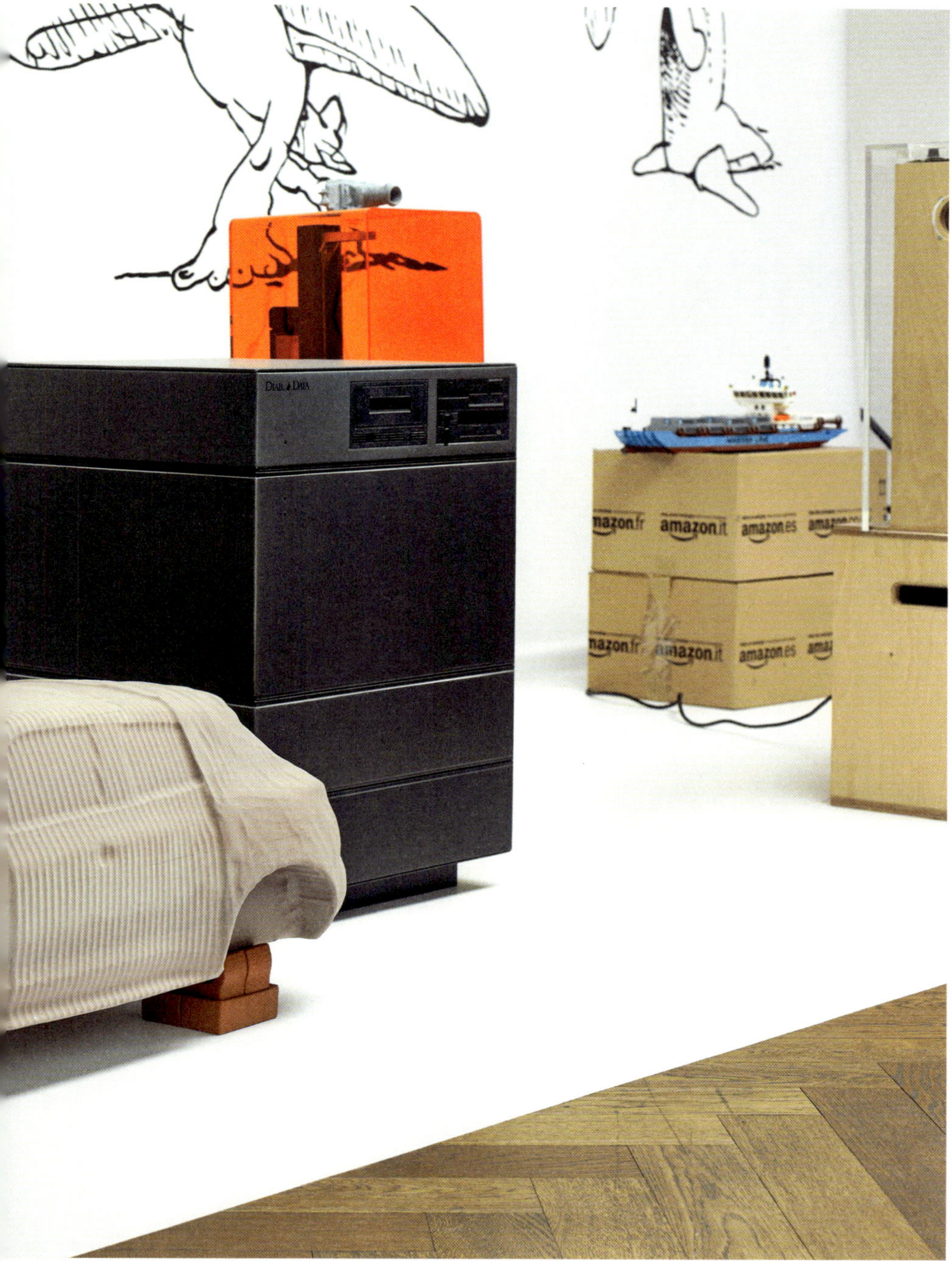
amazon.fr
amazon.it
amazon.es
amazon.fr
amazon.it
amazon.es

INTERROGATIONS

BY

REBECCA TAMÁS

INTERROGATION (1)

Are you a witch?

Are you

Have you had relations with the devil?

Have you

Have you had relations with the devil and what took place?

I kissed him under the tail, it was a bit like soil, a bit like road tar
when it heats up, he was flickering in pleasure, the field would
be just the same when I tongue that, the bird's feathers parting.

What knowledge did the devil give you?

I built a house next to the sea, the roof is red/orange, the sky
is a shaking plate of light peeling you back, there is grass
out the front, some metal bins, you can see a lighthouse. I began
to sleep with the windows open, I began to creep along the bed
to my own globe face in the mirror. Sitting rubbed up in myself
is this fierce fire, it does not come from me, even the stones in
the drive are crackling with it.

What did the devil make you do under his control?

His mother had just died. We ate mint ice
cream by the coffin, he was missing her,
my sock was loose, we kept laughing.

What is magic?

Picture an egg yolk, that huge yellow throw up sun.
Dementedly shining, falling out of itself, birthed and
reverent.

What is magic?

Little cracks coming in, small flaws in the glass,
and the air slapping itself, you stand on a hill,
things are mainly green and breakable,
you think ok I'm not alone, but mainly,
ok I was never alone, on a far off hill the
earth is breaking up against the gas pressure
of the sun, if there was ever anything to miss
this is what you miss, how it's beginning.

What crimes have you enacted?

Love makes me forget myself sometimes.
I am horribly angry, I am sick with it,
my vomit turns black, but this love.
I can't explain it, beyond that it is exactly.

What other witches/sorcerers have you conjured with?

S couldn't eat. The food was poor and cheap but not that.
She had these violet eyes.

Have you taken black mass?

I've wondered why things turn. Rustling and fluttering cells,
the nib of the chest where what you might call soul slides out
and enters a hyena fucking happily amongst the fruit rinds.

What did the devil make you do under his control?

What you should do is go out and get really drunk.

What did the devil make you do under his control?

What you should do is get a sleeper train.

What did the devil make you do under his control?

I can pack everything and I can carry the suitcases up
staircases and along roads. I can go, even though
I am not importantly myself. Some of the things
that are me can go.

Have you profaned holy scripture?

The biggest fear is that reality itself starts to curdle,
stiffens into waxy stops.

Were you born to witches?

Were you

Who have you used spells against in this parish?

I can't say that I've met god directly, but I
can tell you how I think of it. God holding my heart
in a palm as it flexes from blue to green to white.
God being really tired, haar of sea fog.
I've had to decide what it looks like, what it is.
Shiver of the long world, cold feet,
a small, bright, filthy song.

INTERROGATION (2)

How do you do your magic?

How is so balletic, how is like a dance spectacular, getting up
from your seat at the back of the stage and rushing into the
spotlight, rushing into movement, a body doing not exactly
what is 'natural' to it (is dance natural) but what its potential
is, the shapes that flesh didn't command only opened.

How do you do your magic?

If there is a worst word it is nostalgia, the choirs
twisting a larch into a tea towel, if you make it
warm and curling, and so the twitching knowledge
sinks a little, my instinct to stuff leaves into my mouth
recedes, smaller and smaller the incantations and the
freshness.

Have you written your spells down for others to make use of?

aaaaaaaaaaaaaaaaaaaaaaaaaaaaaaaaaaaaaaaaaaaaaaaaaaaaa
aaaaaaaaaaaaaaaaaaaaaaaaaaaaaaaaaaaaaaaaaaaaaaaaaaaaa

Where did you learn your knowledge of witchcraft?

I could pick any woman. i.e Iphigenia i.e Jane Grey
Buy a wife, have a nice and symbolic wedding, take her home,
put your penis in there, make some humans. Sometimes you buy a dress.
Sometimes you are sort of kind and have a blond face, sometimes
you are shit, or drown her with one hand pocketed. Inside that, never.
Inside, a slick web. A field of tubers processed under electric lights.
Please record a million, million, million, million, million ghosts.
Please record a system of language never heard before on the surface of the earth.

What are your plans for treasonous action against the King and state?

If I say the witch knows things, you won't enjoy. I could smash every
dousing crystal, apparition, rune, astrological symbol, bassinet, globe

of silver, dagger, pleated skirt and we would still. Dogs come
singing like well–born ladies on a good day.

How many times have you used your craft for material gain?

There was once a person I led to be killed. In the ballad it
was four roses on a pale cheek, it was wet long hair like
trailing oil. I found myself radicalised. I found the state I was
in unbearable. I found that violence looked pure, all the clean
edges. When the call came. He was quite small for what he'd
done. I never felt less bad. I was. It was freezing, totally freezing.
Everything was a new country, the way you notice things when
you first visit a city, the half open windows, the smell of orange
blossom, the bottle green trams and full skirted waitresses.
Something after all this time had occurred or was occurring.
Not good, existent. Afterwards my lover put a small
kiss on my mouth and said, do you really hate us all?
And I said, obviously.

Have you attempted to draw others into your dark arts?

The best time though wasn't then, all that dry, agonised
scratching. The best time was a Tuesday, we didn't go
into college. We cut up magazines into strange art forms
and listened to the radio. The sun had the touching innocence
of the early 90s, hair bleached a pale lilac at the edges.
There was a little world and it didn't say anything, nor
did it have to perform. No one self–consciously did a
pillow fight in their training bra. Instead, our legs got
warm. Instead we made mothers into a word as easy as
beers in a bowl of ice. We found all the thoughts
there had not been time for in the previous, saw tremendous
fleets of new work flood into the hallway. THE ODYSSEY had
a bit about periods. One new love poem for each asteroid
in the outer atmosphere. Some thawing. All the time I was
thinking, I got it back.

ELIZABETH

She can fuck and stay a virgin, her small cunt is close and apple green, it smells the same, skinned, sharp, those winter mornings when noone is up and the mist pulls the scent of earth into the air and separates it into formal layers. Her mother was a witch and had six fingers. When she was tiny this made her cry, but now it makes her gleeful. Her mother's underwear was always blue and grey like changed skies, her face small and pointed, something like a fruit bat. People ask her stupid questions like 'So how was it seeing your mother beheaded?' She wishes she had. Shoot me into the great dark sun of it. What she remembers: one meal where her mother spat duck bones expertly into the centre of her plate, piles of small velvet shoes, uncomfortable chairs, crying in church so much that she had to be taken out. What she knew of god always made her cry and cry. Both the living and the dead are under her command, she pardons ghosts with a wave, tells graves to vomit themselves up as fresh bodies fall in. Such a silly slut. England is in her head like ground glass, making for periscope vision. She sees everything, her father's fat legs churning against the worms, her mother's soft belly, open mouth, coming and coming against the mounds of earth. Elizabeth eats England, sucks at it, hard. She spits all the little bones into her hand.

IN SEARCH OF THE DICE MAN

BY

EMMANUEL CARRÈRE

(*tr.* WILL HEYWARD)

TOWARDS THE END of the 1960s, Luke Rhinehart was practicing psychoanalysis in New York, and was sick and tired of it. He lived in a nice apartment, with windows facing his neighbours, through which everyone had nice views of each other. He did yoga, read books on Zen Buddhism, and toyed with the idea of joining a hippie commune, but didn't dare. Failing that, he wore bell-bottoms and a beard, which made him look less like a depressed bourgeois than an out-of-work actor. As a therapist, he was resolutely nondirective. If an obese, virginal and compulsively sadistic patient told him whilst on the couch that he'd like to rape and murder a little girl, his professional ethics compelled him to repeat in a calm voice, 'You'd like to rape and murder a little girl?' An elusive question mark disappearing into ellipses. Long silence. The absence of judgement. But, in reality, how he really wanted to reply was: 'Go on, then! If what really turns you on is to rape and murder a little girl, stop boring me with your fantasy: do it!' He held himself back, obviously, from saying such terrible things, but they obsessed him more and more. Like everyone else, he forbade himself from living out his fantasies even though they were more or less harmless – not the sort of thing that got you sent to prison, like his sadistic patient would be if he ever let himself go. What he would have liked, for example, was to sleep with Arlene, his colleague Jake Epstein's wife with the sumptuous breasts, who lived on the same floor in his apartment building. He had the feeling she wouldn't be opposed to the idea, but as a faithful, married man, a responsible adult, he left the thought to bubble away in the backwater of his daydreams.

So his life passed, calm and dull, until the day when, after a particularly boozy evening, Luke spotted a die, a boring old die for playing games, lying on the carpet and suddenly the idea came to him to roll it, and to do what it told him to. 'If it lands on a number between two and six, I'll do what I would have done anyway: take the dirty glasses to the kitchen, brush my teeth, take a double aspirin so I'm not too hungover in the morning, go to bed next to my sleeping wife and maybe knock one out, furtively, thinking of Arlene. On the other hand, if I throw a one, I'll do what I *really* want to do: I'll cross the hallway, knock on the door of Arlene's apartment, behind which I know she's home alone, and sleep with her.'

The die lands on one.

Luke hesitates, feeling vaguely like he's on the brink of something: if he crosses over, his life may change dramatically. But it's not his decision; it's up to the die. And so he obeys. Arlene, who opens the door to him in a transparent nightie, is surprised, but not completely put out. When Luke gets home after two very agreeable hours, he's aware of having well and truly changed. It's not a massive change, but it's more than happens during psychotherapy – as he is well paid to know. He has done something that the normal Luke would never do. A more audacious, more expansive, less limited Luke breaks through the cautious and conformist Luke, and perhaps other Lukes whose existence he had never suspected are waiting behind the door the die might well open for them.

¶ In every circumstance that life presents now, Luke consults the die and, since it has six sides, gives it six options to choose from. The first is to do as he has always done. The other five are more or less departures from routine. Let's say that Luke and his wife are planning on going to the cinema. The new Antonioni film, *Blow-Up*, has just come out, and that's exactly the sort of thing a couple of New York intellectuals like them have to see. But they could also see something *even more* intellectual, an even more boring Hungarian or Czech thing. Or, in the opposite direction, they could see a big generic Hollywood film that a priori they despise completely, or a porno film in a cinema on the Bowery full of tramps, where people like them would never normally set foot. Once under the spell of the die, the most banal decisions, such as which film to see, restaurant to go to, or dish to order, open up if one takes notice of the vast range of possibilities and opportunities to break with routine. Luke, at the start, takes things slowly. He chooses safe options, not too far removed from his typical choices. Little sidesteps, which spice up life without completely turning it on its head, like swapping sides in the bed or trying new sexual positions during intercourse with his wife. But soon his options become more audacious. He begins to see everything he's never done before as a challenge to be taken up.

Going to the kind of place he would never normally go, entering into relationships with people he would normally have nothing to do with. Attempting to seduce a woman whose name he found at random in the phonebook. Borrowing ten dollars from a total stranger. Giving ten dollars to a total stranger. Venturing into a gay bar, getting chatted up, doing a little flirting himself, and – why not? despite being totally straight – going to bed with a man. With his patients, being direct, impatient, despotic. To someone with low self-esteem, who thought of himself as worthless, exclaiming suddenly: 'And what if the truth is that you actually *are* a piece of shit?' To the failed writer: 'Instead of slaving away on your shitty book, why not go to the Congo and join a revolutionary movement? Why bother looking back over your shoulder? Sex, hunger, danger?' And to the extreme introvert: 'Why not have it off with my secretary? She's ugly but she's up for it. On your way out of my office, make a move, jump her bones, the worst she'll do is give you a slap – what do you have to lose?' He pushes his patients to abandon their families or their jobs, to change political or sexual orientation. The results are disastrous and his reputation suffers, but he couldn't care less. What turns him on, right at this moment, is to do the exact opposite of what he would normally do: salting his coffee, jogging in a tuxedo, going to his office in shorts, pissing in flower pots, walking backwards, sleeping under the bed instead of on it... His wife thinks he's weird, obviously, but he says he's conducting a psychological experiment, and she lets herself be convinced. Until the day he gets the idea to initiate the children.

Oh yes, he knows very well that it's dangerous, very dangerous, but it's a fact that all conceivable options, even the terrifying ones, must eventually be submitted to the die and, sooner or later, come to pass. And so, one weekend, when their mother is away, Luke has his little boy and girl play a seemingly innocent game: they write down on a piece of paper six things that they would like to do, and let the die choose one of them. At the start, everything goes nicely (it always goes nicely at the start); they eat ice cream and they go to the zoo, but then the boy gets his courage up and says that what he'd like to do is smash in the face of a friend at school who annoyed him. 'OK,' says Luke, 'write it down,' and that's what ends up being rolled. The boy expects that his dad, with his back to the wall, won't follow through, but no, Dad says, 'Go for it.' The boy goes to find his classmate, punches him in the face, comes home, and, eyes glowing, asks, 'Where's the die?'

This makes Luke stop to think: if his son adapted so easily to this way of being, it's probably because he hasn't yet been completely alienated by the absurd assumption of parents, and society in general, that it's good for children to develop a coherent personality. What if, for a change, we raised them otherwise, valuing contradiction and perpetual change? Lie all you want, little darlings, be disobedient and unreliable, stop this pernicious habit of brushing your teeth before bed. We tell ourselves that children need order and points of reference – what if the opposite is true? Luke seriously considers making his son into the first man entirely subject to chance and, in so doing, releasing him from the tedious tyranny of the ego: a child according to Laozi's philosophy.

At that point, the mother comes home, discovers what has happened while she was away, and, not finding it the least bit funny, leaves Luke, taking the children with her.

There's our hero relieved of his family. It saddens him, because he loves them, but the die is a master as demanding as Jesus Christ: he too asks us to give everything away in order to follow him.

¶ Luke next abandons his job, after an evening with the who's who of New York psychoanalysis. The roadmap that the die had given him (it has to be said that he was pretty high that night when he made his list of options) was to change personality every ten minutes. The six roles he had to alternate between over the course of the evening were: an experienced psychoanalyst (the one he was before the die), a retard, a disinhibited nymphomaniac, a Jesus freak, a left-wing activist, and a far-right activist, giving aggressively anti-Semitic speeches. Scandal ensued, followed by psychiatric internment and a hearing before a disciplinary committee. Luke takes this unexpected forum as an opportunity to broadcast to the world what he presents as a revolutionary kind of therapy. His colleagues are horrified: this revolutionary therapy is the systematic destruction of individual identity. That's exactly right, acknowledges Luke, but isn't that the best possible outcome? What we call individual identity is nothing but a straightjacket of boredom, frustration, and despair. All therapy aims to do is tighten the straightjacket whereas freedom would be to obliterate it altogether, for people to no longer be prisoners of themselves but instead to be able on a whim to become someone else, to become dozens of other people… 'What do you really want? Everything, I guess. To be everyone and to do everything.'

After this declaration of faith, the visionary is exiled from his professional community – just as another visionary, Timothy Leary, the apostle of LSD, had been chased from his. No family, no job, no ties, Luke is free, and feels the full dizzying force of freedom. He has discovered, and tested on himself, something that initially spices up life, but whose logic of one-upmanship calls its very possibility into question at every turn. To begin with it was like marijuana, pleasant and amusing, but now it's like acid, huge and exultant, with the power to destroy everything. In order to give a personality's repressed tendencies a chance, we go from transgression to transgression. This becomes a form of asceticism, no longer hedonistic or fun at all. The last barrier to fall is the pleasure principle. For he who takes the path of the die initially does the things he would never dare to do but has always dreamed of, more or less secretly. Then the day comes when the die makes him do not just things he would never dare to do, but things he doesn't even *want* to do, because they are outside of his tastes, desires, even personality. But that's just it: personality, miserable little personality, is the enemy to be vanquished, an indoctrination from which one must be liberated. To no longer be a prisoner of oneself, one must agree to pursue desires that one doesn't know, or even have at all. Take sex: one starts by changing habits, to the satisfaction of both husband and wife, and then one sleeps with a different woman entirely, and then one leaves his wife (or, in Luke's case, she leaves him), and then one sleeps with every attractive woman who crosses one's path, and, then – to expand the horizons, to be slightly less in thrall to one's boring preferences – one moves on to women who aren't attractive at all – the old, the fat, those you wouldn't have looked twice at in the past – and then to men, and then to little boys, and then to rape, and then to sadistic murder, AMERICAN PSYCHO-style, why not?

¶ No serious die follower can avoid, at one point or another, the possibility of murder being an option for the die. It's the supreme taboo, and it would be cowardly not to transgress it. Luke, when the die instructs him, imagines two sub-options: killing someone he knows, or killing someone he doesn't. He would like, of course, the second of the two, but, no, it's the first that is ordered, and he finds himself obliged to devise a list of six potential victims, on which he bravely includes his two children. Fortunately for him, he is spared this test, just as Abraham is saved from murdering his son Isaac. Instead, the die orders him only to kill one of his former patients.

If you believe his autobiography, he didn't chicken out. He went ahead with it. Certain commentators have doubts and, fifty years on, it seems unlikely the matter will ever be resolved. What does seem to be beyond doubt, however, is that, having completely trashed his career, his family life, and his social standing, Luke was primed to become a kind of prophet – and did.

In those years, in America, when from coast to coast the most paradoxical kinds of therapies thrived, a die guru had every chance to be a hit. And so that's how the infamous Centre for Experiments in Totally Random Environments, where one signs up of one's own accord but cannot leave until the experiment has run its course, was born in a sleepy New England town. Beginners hone their skills by playing emotional roulette, choosing six strong emotions and expressing them as dramatically as possible for ten minutes. The more advanced students move on to a role–play of varying duration, which consists of listing six personalities, say, philanthropic or cynical, hardworking or slacker, normopath or psychotic – these possibilities exist within each of us – and then staying within the one chosen by the die for ten minutes, an hour, a day, a week, a month, a year (the die decides how long). Living in the skin of a psychotic as an experiment for a year, if you're not already psychotic, is pretty tough. The boldest, at the end of the course, attempt total submission, for an equally variable time, to someone else's will, someone who will not only throw the die but also choose the options. This is how Luke himself became the slave of a totally neurotic girl, imaginative enough to have him live for a month in a sadomasochistic delirium during which he claims to have learnt more about himself, and life in general, than in the forty years previous.

Among the recipients of the therapy, there are some who went mad. Others are dead or in prison. Some, it seems, reached a state of stable happiness and enlightenment, not unlike Buddhist nirvana. In any case, within only a year or two of existence, the Centre created by Luke became as scandalous as the communities created by Timothy Leary. A chaos school, the conservative press wrote, a threat to civilisation as serious as communism or Charles Manson's Satanism. The end of the adventure is shrouded in mystery. It's said that Luke was arrested by the FBI, that he spent twenty years in a mental hospital. Or that he died. Or that he never existed.

¶ Everything I've just told you is from a book, THE DICE MAN, published in 1971 and translated into French the following year. I discovered it when I was sixteen, at the same time as I was discovering the paranoid and deranged masterpieces of Philip K. Dick, and it almost made as big an impression on me. I was an adolescent

x

with long hair, an Afghan jacket and little round glasses, horribly shy, and for a time I walked the streets with a die in my pocket, hoping it would give me the confidence I lacked with girls. It worked more or less (more less than more), but regardless THE DICE MAN was the kind of book that offers not just pleasure but rules to live by, a subversive manual that one dreams of actually following in real life. Was it fiction or autobiography? It wasn't clear, but its author, Luke Rhinehart, had the same name as the book's hero and like him was a psychiatrist. He lived in Majorca, according to the publisher, and Majorca or Formentera was the place where MORE, the Barbet Schroeder film about drugs, which starred the marvellous Mimsy Farmer and featured the haunting music of Pink Floyd, was set: the perfect hiding place for a burnt-out prophet who had just escaped the shipwreck of his crackpot community.

The years have passed and THE DICE MAN has remained the object of a minor but enduring cult, and every time I would meet someone who had read it (almost always a stoner, and often a believer in the I CHING), the same questions would come up: had it really happened? Who was Luke Rhinehart? What had become of him? Later, I began to write books that centred on this desire to have multiple lives. We are, each of us, horribly trapped within our own little selves, contained within our habits of thought and behaviour. We would love to know what it's like to be someone else, or I would at least, and if I became a writer it's in large part because I wanted to imagine just that. This is what drove me to tell the story of Jean-Claude Romand, who spent twenty years pretending to be someone he wasn't, and that of Edouard Limonov, a man who has lived ten lives. Several months ago, I was talking about this to a friend who countered what I said about this desire for multiplicity with the stoic tradition, the goal of which is instead coherence, loyalty to one's self, and the patient cultivation of a personality as stable as possible. Given that we can never take every road in life, my friend suggested, the wise thing to do is to stick to one's own, and the narrower it is, the less forked, the greater the likelihood it will climb high. I agreed; with age my thinking had tended in that direction too. But I thought back to Luke Rhinehart, the apostle of dispersion, the prophet of the kaleidoscopic life, the man who said all roads must be taken at once, even if they lead to dead ends. A ghost of the daring and dangerous 1960s, when people believed in living it all, trying everything. I once again asked myself where he was, this ghost – did he still exist, somewhere?

In other times, faced with such a question, I would have had to rely on my imagination, but today there's the internet, and after an hour of browsing online I had learnt more about Luke Rhinehart than I had in thirty years of lazy speculation.

His real name is George Cockcroft and he's getting on a bit, obviously, but still among us. He has written other books, but none replicated the success of THE DICE MAN, which, more than forty years after its initial publication, is more than ever a cult book. There are dozens of websites dedicated to it, and many legends about the book circulate. Ten times it's been discussed for adaption for cinema, with the biggest Hollywood stars – Jack Nicholson, Nicolas Cage – fighting over the role of Luke, but mysteriously the project never got off the ground. Communities of dice followers exist all over the world. The mythic author, meanwhile, leads a reclusive life on a farm in upstate New York. No one has seen him for three decades, and a single photo of him circulates, which shows, under a Stetson, a gaunt and sarcastic face, which strikes me as bearing a resemblance to that of another magnificent ghost: Dennis Hopper in THE AMERICAN FRIEND by Wim Wenders. I start to realise that there might be a piece to write out of this, so I pitch it to Patrick de Saint-Exupéry, the editor-in-chief of *XXI*, describing Luke Rhinehart as a mixture of Carlos Castaneda, William Burroughs and Thomas Pynchon, a radically subversive icon transformed into an invisible man. Patrick, of course, is sold.

¶ This should have tipped me off: my invisible man himself has a personal website, which I used to contact him. I received a good-natured reply, the sort you don't expect from a recluse, within the hour. I wanted to come from France to interview him? What a great idea! And, with the details of my visit arranged, he told me kindly that he hoped I would not be disappointed. Setting off in search of Luke Rhinehart, I was going to meet George Cockcroft, and George Cockcroft, by his own admission, was 'an old fart'. I took this warning as an affectation.

Stopping in New York on my way, I invite out to dinner a dice follower with whom I'd made contact online a few weeks earlier. This young man of thirty, Ron, dresses like a conceptual artist and urban pirate, and leads a community of 'dice people' who get together monthly for what, under the cover of New Age jargon, seem to be good old-fashioned gang-bangs, where a die decides, in the main, who will be on the top, who will be on the bottom, and which orifices will be filled. Nothing like that, I'm a little disappointed to learn, is planned during my visit, but the urban pirate seems very impressed by my nerve: knocking on the door of Luke Rhinehart! Taking the tiger by the tail! This is really going over to the dark side of the Force. I reply that he seems, from our correspondence, like a nice old man. Ron looks at me, thoughtfully, a little pityingly: 'A nice old man... Perhaps, after all. Perhaps the die instructed him to play a certain role for you. But never forget that the die has six sides. It shows you one, but you don't know the others, or when it will choose to show them to you...'

From Penn Station to Hudson in upstate New York is two hours by train through charming countryside. The man waiting for me at the station is wearing the same Stetson as in the one photo of him online, he has the same gaunt face, the same faded blue eyes, the same slightly sardonic smile. He's very tall, stooped, and, with a certain amount of theatre, one could find him disturbing, except that when I put out my hand, he reaches out and hugs me, kissing me on both cheeks as if I were his son, and introduces me to his wife, Ann, who proves to be equally easy-going and warm. The three of us climb into their old estate car and drive through the peaceful town. White wooden houses, verandas, and lawns: this isn't DESPERATE HOUSEWIVES suburban America, but a much older America, more remote, more rural. Don't get the wrong idea, says Ann, in spring it's beautiful but four months out of twelve all of this is covered in snow, the roads are often blocked. To live here all year round takes a stockpile of supplies. As we drive through the woods and orchards, I think to myself that this scenery, in its winter incarnation, is that of one of my favourite novels, ETHAN FROME by Edith Wharton, and when I tell my hosts this, they're thrilled by the reference. It's one of their favourite novels too, and George often taught it to his students. To his students? He's not a psychiatrist or psychoanalyst? 'Psychiatrist? Psychoanalyst?' repeats George, as surprised as if I had said 'astronaut'. No, he never was a psychiatrist, but an English teacher his whole life, in high school. Really? But in his author's note on the back cover of his book... George shrugs his shoulders, as if to say: editors, journalists, they say all sorts of nonsense...

We leave Hudson an hour behind us, George driving with an abruptness in contrast to his good-natured manner, and the way he has of making his wife laugh – the sort of affectionately mocking laughter reserved for the tics of those who are dear to us. It's moving to see how much they love each other, the two of them: every look, every gesture between them is tender, affectionate, carrying the suggestion of the long habit of each other's company. This is real life Philemon and Baucis, and when Ann tells me they've been married for fifty-six years, I'm not surprised. But, at the same time, this doesn't square – seriously, not at all – with, on the basis of his book alone, the Luke Rhinehart I'd imagined.

The house is an old farm fitted out for the harsh winters, on a gentle hill leading down to a pond where ducks swim. It'd be very expensive these days, but they were lucky enough to buy the property forty years ago when it was within their means, and they haven't left it since. Their three sons grew up here, and two of them live in the area, where they are a local carpenter and house painter. The third son still lives with them: he's schizophrenic, Ann tells me without embarrassment, and at the moment things are good, he's not having any episodes, the only thing is I shouldn't worry if I hear shouting coming from his room, which is next door to the guest bedroom they have prepared for me for the weekend (I've invited myself for the weekend, but I sense that if I wanted to hang around a week or a month, it wouldn't be a problem).

Ann serves tea and, armed with our mugs, George and I settle down on the terrace to do the interview. He's swapped his Stetson for a baseball cap and, since I ask him to tell his life's story, he starts at the beginning.

¶ He was born in 1930 in a town located a few kilometres from where he lives today, and where in all likelihood he will die. Member of a semi-rural 'middle class' put to the test by the Great Depression, he nevertheless recalls quite a happy childhood and adolescence. Good at maths and translation, not in the least bit adventurous, he says he reached the age of twenty without experiencing the slightest creative inclination. But the courses he enrolled in at college (in order to become a civil engineer like his father) bored him and he switched to Psychology. It's the early 1950s, and Psychology, such as is taught at universities, isn't Freud, or Jung, or Erich Fromm, it's tedious experiments on rats, and he realises that he might be better off reading novels – something that had never occurred to him until then. Thus, whilst interning as a night guard at a hospital in Long Island, he devours Mark Twain, Melville, and the great Russians of the nineteenth century, and begins to write a novel set in a psychiatric hospital (ah, after all!), in which the hero is a boy admitted because he thinks he's Jesus, and among the staff members is a doctor named Luke Rhinehart, who practices therapy with a die (again: ah, after all!). The name Luke was chosen in homage to the disciple, which I'm very pleased to hear – as is George when I tell him this – having just written a long book about him. As for playing with dice, it's a hobby that George picked up at high school as part of a group of friends. They used them on Saturdays to make plans for the evenings (there wasn't a great deal of choice in any case: hamburger, drive-in...). Sometimes they would give each other dares – to do a lap of the block hopping on one foot, to ring a neighbour's doorbell – nothing particularly naughty, and when, full of hope, I ask George if as an adult he ever pushed the boundaries further, he shrugs his shoulders and smiles kindly, an apologetic expression on his face, because he can tell I want to hear something juicy. 'No,' he confesses, 'what I asked the die were things like, for example if I was bored of working, whether I had to stay at my desk an hour or two longer? Or whether I could go for a walk?'

'What are you talking about?' asks Ann, coming out onto the terrace to offer us the blueberry crumble that she'd just taken out of the oven. 'Don't you remember at least one important decision the die made for you?' He laughs, and she does too, the two of them moving as ever together, and he tells me that at the hospital he noticed a very attractive nurse, but that he was shy and couldn't bring himself to say a word to her. The die had made him approach her: he'd offered her a lift home, taken her to church but the church had been shut, and so he'd invited her to play tennis with him. The comely nurse was Ann, of course.

Ten years later, they had three little boys, and George, who had become an English teacher, applied for a position at the American high school of Deia in Majorca. This expatriation was the great adventure of their life. Majorca in 1965 is a dream, but they know nothing of what had fascinated me in *More*: George doesn't do drugs, is faithful to his wife, and socialises with a circle of teachers like himself. But, nevertheless, he doesn't totally miss out on the zeitgeist, making a point of reading books about psychoanalysis, antipsychiatry, eastern mysticism, Zen Buddhism – all the counterculture of the 1960s, the big idea of which, in so many words, is that we have been conditioned and must free ourselves from this conditioning. Under the influence of this reading, he suddenly realised the revolutionary potential of what up until that point he had believed to be a childish game, more or less abandoned after adolescence. Despite having completely abandoned the idea of writing books since getting married, he then furiously began what would become THE DICE MAN. He would take four years to write it, faithfully supported by his wife all the while – something which surprised me because, whilst both Ann and George are very open and tolerant people, they are, at heart, also quite virtuous and domestic. The book, however, is monstrously transgressive. Today, still, it remains shocking. I ask Ann, 'Did you not find it troubling to read? To discover that your husband, the father of your children, has these horrors in his head?' With a tender smile: 'No, it didn't bother me. I trust George. And I liked the book: I was proud of him.'

¶ In her candour she was right: right to be proud of him, right to trust him. An American editor bought the book, to their great surprise, for a lot of money, and the film rights sold to Paramount. Then it went out into the world, erratically and unpredictably. There was success in Europe – but not the US, following a curse that seems to befall the great eccentrics, from Edgar Allan Poe to Philip K. Dick – the book was reprinted regularly, and its cult status was re-established ten years ago by the internet. There were disappointments: the film, for unclear reasons, was never made, with Paramount sitting on the rights while dozens of independent film-makers dreamed of making it; and none of the other books George wrote subsequently ever had any success, leaving him the author of a single unclassifiable masterpiece. But that's at least something; life hadn't been bad to him, to them. The sale of the rights of THE DICE MAN had allowed them to buy this beautiful house, on the land of their fathers, and to grow old in peace, George writing and Ann painting, the two of them looking after their sick eldest son and worrying only of dying before him.

That day happens to be Mother's Day, and the two other boys have come to celebrate with their parents. They are good Americans in checked shirts, drinkers of Budweiser, trout fishermen, settled in life. Their schizophrenic brother briefly comes out of his room and, despite a little lethargy, doesn't cut a bad figure. All three tell Ann that she's been 'a terrific Mom' to them, and I'm sure it's true. After dinner, we finish the evening at one of the boys' houses nearby, also in the countryside, and, in an outdoor jacuzzi, George and I keep boozing, looking up at the stars, so much so that I don't remember exactly how I got back to my room. I wake with a start around three in the morning. My throat is dry, all that's visible through the window is the dark and heavy mass of the forest, which surrounds the house, and a monotonous, croaky voice a few metres away is chanting phrases I don't understand. A ray of light comes through the crack of the door separating my room from that of the schizophrenic son. I am momentarily frantic, but take a moment to calm myself, and, as is often the case, it is the world of culture that saves me from fear. I think back to all the stories of visits to old reclusive writers in their houses in the woods on a hill – the classic of classics in this domain being *The Ghost Writer* by Philip Roth, in which a young Nathan Zuckerman discovers that the enigmatic secretary is none other than Anne Frank, who has actually survived. I think to myself: it's strange what we can project onto a photo. That one of Luke Rhinehart had made me imagine a life like a novel: a dangerous, intoxicating life of excess, of total transgression, of all kinds of nonconformity. Many dangerous women, lots of drugs, at least one or two suicides. Mexican brothels; lunatic communes in the Nevada desert; demented, consciousness-expanding experiences. And this face, the same face with strong bone structure and steely eyes, is in reality that of an adorable old man with his adorable wife at the end of a gentle cushy life, the only hiccup of which had been to write this terrifying book, which has meant that in his old age he has to explain gently and kindly to people who come to see him because of it that they mustn't mistake him for his work, that he's merely a novelist.

In reality? But what did I actually know about reality? I recalled Ron, the urban pirate, warning me: what you see there, the lovely old man, is only one side of the die. It's the face the die has ordered him to show you, but he has at least five others in reserve, and perhaps that night he will change it. Perhaps tonight it will be the Stephen King option that appears. The pretty farm with the white picket fence, the tender life companion who makes blueberry pies, Mother's Day, the powwow in the Jacuzzi – all of that will reveal its dark side. The looming silhouette, the silhouette of an ogre if you think about it, is on its way to the barn to get the chainsaw...

¶ It was obvious at breakfast that George was afraid of disappointing me. At that moment, maybe he had: I was asking myself what the hell I was going to write. So he took me out onto the lake, and with our two kayaks drifting gently over the calm water, he told me the story of one of his disciples. Because what George was content to imagine, others had done, for real. Take the extravagant tycoon Richard Branson, the guy who founded Virgin and made headlines for travelling around the world in a hot air balloon or, on losing a bet, worked as an air hostess on one of his aeroplanes. He tells anyone who'll listen that all of his choices, in life and in business, he has made thanks to the die, and under the influence of Luke Rhinehart. He refers to him the way others refer to Laozi, Nietzsche, or Thoreau: a great liberator, a teacher of freedom. The readers of a trendy London magazine, *Loaded*, have the same opinion: in a poll, they declared *The Dice Man* the most influential novel of the twentieth century. This gave the editor-in-chief an idea for a piece, which he assigned to the most gonzo of his journalists: for three months, following the example of Luke Rhinehart, entrust all decisions to the die, and record what happens. The funding for this was, if not unlimited, at the very least enough to be able to make *almost* anything happen: taking an aeroplane halfway around the world, ending up in a fisherman's hut, renting the penthouse of a palace, hiring a hit man, or having to pay an exorbitant bail... The journalist, one Ben Marshall, took the experiment sufficiently seriously, it seems, and wrecked his emotional and professional life, disappearing for several months without a word to anyone.

'A funny guy, Ben,' George tells me, 'You can see him in *Dice World*, a documentary made by a British channel in 1999.' I knew nothing about this documentary, and so I asked George if he had a copy on DVD, and if we could watch it together, and just like that he got embarrassed. He says the documentary isn't great, that he's not sure if he has a copy. I insist so much, however, that before long, the two of us find ourselves sitting on the couch in front of the widescreen TV, remote control in hand, the opening credits rolling: he was right, it isn't great, a little abrupt, with tiresome editing techniques, but, sure enough, there's Ben Marshall, who volunteered to play out his life according to the die, a young guy with a shaved head and unblinking eyes, gesturing nervously, who explains in a very convincing way how he stopped himself before going insane because it can make you insane, doing this, it's the most exciting thing in the whole world, but people should know that it really can drive you to insanity. He has the air of someone returned from a long way away, one part paradise, ten parts hell. And just after him, whom do we see? We see his inspiration, our friend George, or rather our friend Luke, as he was fifteen years ago: the Stetson, the gaunt face, the piercing stare, very handsome, but not at all in a way that resembles the nice-looking grandfather that I know. In a deep, insistent, hypnotic voice, he says, staring down the barrel of the camera: 'You lead an empty life, the life of a slave, a life that doesn't satisfy you, but there is a way out. The die is the way out. Let it happen, submit yourself to it, and you will see, your life will change, you will become someone you could never imagine in your wildest dreams. Submission to the die will finally set you free. You will no longer be a nobody, you will become everyone. You will no longer be you, you will finally be you.' He has the air of a charismatic televangelist as he speaks, or of a crazy preacher in a Flannery O'Connor novel, of a cult leader being filmed just before his followers commit mass suicide. He's scary. I turn towards the man sitting next to me on the couch, this friendly retiree in slippers holding a mug of herbal tea, and he looks back at me with an embarrassed smile, an apologetic smile, as if butter wouldn't melt in his mouth, and says that it's Luke we're watching on television, obviously, just an act that the director had asked him to put on. He, George, wasn't really up for it, but the director had insisted, and George hadn't wanted to be difficult... Ann, who's listening from the kitchen, breaks into laughter: 'Are you showing him the film where you play the bogeyman?' And he echoes her laugh, a metre away from me. Nevertheless, when I see him on screen, I find him terribly convincing.

¶ I met other followers of the die online: one in Salt Lake City, one in Munich, one in Madrid. All men: I don't have any explanation for it except that dice are a boy thing, like westerns or sci-fi. The Münchner told me, 'In order to write an article that is worthy of the *dice life*, the only solution is to become a *dice man*.' Strangely, that scared me. So much so that I didn't even dare to entrust the die with a decision as benign as where to go: once I'd ruled out Salt Lake City, I picked Madrid over Munich for the contemptible reason that I prefer Madrid to Munich.

Oscar Cuadrado, who came to pick me up from the airport, is a young guy: pudgy, sociable, and very nice. As we drive to his place in his 4x4, he tells me a joke that I'm beginning to be very familiar with: 'I seem nice right now, but you don't know what the die has in store for this evening, maybe I'm a serial killer and you're going to end up chained to a radiator in the basement.' He lives with his wife and his little girl in a pretty suburban house, on the lawn of which we consult the die without further ado: do we have a drink straightaway, or do we wait until we've finished the interview? Three options against three options – we may as well have been flipping a coin. The response: right away. And now it's, do we drink a beer, or table wine, or the fancy bottle that I'm saving for my little girl's eighteenth birthday? Two chances for the beer, three for the table wine, one only for the fancy bottle because even though he would open it willingly, without questioning the die, still... In the end, it's the table wine – but it's not bad at all – with which Oscar initiates me into his way with the die. He's not a lover of lofty philosophical or perverse thrills. Like everyone, he's heard stories of people who've trashed their lives by giving themselves extreme orders, like leaving their family overnight, travelling to the furthest corner of the world never to return, having sex with animals, or killing a total stranger at random in a crowded Indian train station. These sorts of stories are passed around on websites dedicated to the die – starting with the one that Oscar has run for the past ten years – but they don't interest him. Lacan used to say that psychoanalysis wasn't intended for fools or scoundrels, and Oscar would be the first to say that the die wasn't intended for the suicidal or crazy. He advocates a hedonistic use of the die, which makes life as fun and surprising as possible. For this he says, there are three rules. The first is to *always* obey, to *always* follow the orders of the die. But obeying the die is ultimately obeying oneself because one sets the options oneself. Which brings us to the second rule, relating to the decisive step of setting the six options. Because finding six ways to react to each of life's daily solicitations forces one to use one's imagination, to investigate oneself, to try to know what it is one really desires. It's a sort of spiritual exercise, at once about knowing one's self better and becoming more aware of the almost limitless possibilities presented by the material world. One must, according to Oscar, keep only the pleasing options, but – and this is the third rule – at least one of the options must be a little difficult, something that flies in the face of hesitation and forces habits to be overturned. It has to be something that one would not normally do. It must be surprising and even coercive – but nicely, tactfully so, which is a matter of dosage and self-awareness. The moment the die is cast, desire must overshadow apprehension.

Ever since he first stumbled across a Spanish translation of THE DICE MAN at seventeen years old, these little challenges he sets himself have become second nature to Oscar. When it comes down to it, he's a tax specialist, like his father, but it's not much fun being a tax specialist, so on top of that he's become, thanks to the die, a wine importer, a website host, a Go teacher, a regular visitor to Iceland, and the publisher of the Mauritian poet, Malcolm de Chazal. How so? Well, first of all, he'd thought that it would be good to make ties to a foreign country, preferably one faraway. Six continents, six options. The die fell on Europe, and then, when he narrowed it down, on Iceland. Very good. Now, by what means of transport should he visit Iceland? By foot, car, hitchhiking, boat, bike, or skateboard. He was afraid that if he rolled skateboard he would chicken out, but he rolled bike, and went through with it even though he'd never learnt to ride a bike. He learnt, toured Iceland by bike, and even convinced the young woman who would become his wife to come along. It was during this escape that the die had ordered him to pop the question, which had received an affirmative response. For their honeymoon, the young couple headed to Mauritius – although this, Oscar admits, was a gift from his in-laws, not the die. Over there, he made up for it. He was looking for something to read, an author with a connection to Mauritius, either who was Mauritian or who had written about the country. His list comprised Bernardin de Saint-Pierre, Le Clézio, Baudelaire, Conrad, and the poet Malcolm de Chazal. Bingo: Oscar fell madly for Malcolm de Chazal, a sort of Creole surrealist with whom people like Michaux, Paulhan and Dubuffet had been infatuated. It hadn't escaped him that Malcolm de Chazal hadn't been translated into Spanish, and so upon his return he started a publishing house in order to remedy this. He knew nothing about publishing, no more than he had known about how to ride a bike, but he goes to get the books from his library and I understand why he's proud of them: they are magnificent. He continues: 'It's via Luke that I got to know Malcolm and, now that I know you, you. It's funny, no?'

¶ At this point, with the help of a second bottle of considerably less average wine, we've become very good friends, me and Oscar, and I'm just about to confess my anxiety about what his Bavarian counterpart had said to me: in order to write about the *dice life*, one must be a *dice man*. I'm not a *dice man*. Because my life suits me? Because of a philosophical conviction? Or just because I don't have the balls? It doesn't really matter why, the fact is that for two months my life has centred on this story and I haven't once dared to take the plunge myself. 'Try,' says Oscar, taking a die out of his pocket and placing it on the table between us. I panic, as if within five minutes I might find myself gormlessly forced to massacre my family with a machete, or, in a milder turn of events, to scale Mount Everest in flip-flops. But, no, what Oscar is proposing is simply to let the die choose where we go for dinner. My idea was to take him to a nice restaurant in the centre of town. 'Very well, noted, that's our first option.' Another is that he takes me out to dinner. A third, to go to the most expensive restaurant in Madrid and roll the die again when the bill comes. A fourth, staying home. A fifth, staying home, but I cook the dinner myself. Oscar smiles, seeing that I've taken to the game. I rack my brains, searching for a final, more extreme option. I say, 'The sixth is that we take the car and go to dinner, the two of us, in Seville.' Oscar nods: '*Bueno*, now roll.'

I'm suddenly very afraid of rolling a six, because if I do, I know that we're *really* going to get up, get in the car, and drive to Seville, which is at least 400 km away, and it's close to 10 at night and we've already knocked back two 14 per cent bottles of red. I roll, and, phew, it's a five. Now, I'm not going to try to convince you that the hours that followed were a major transgression or a deliberate derangement of the senses, but the fact is that to find oneself in a stranger's kitchen, glass in hand, stumbling around, opening the cupboards, throwing together in a pot whatever is within reach, is a pretty funny experience. When I came out of the kitchen with my steaming beef stew, ten times too spicy, the entire family was waiting for me at the table, places set. They complimented me on my culinary skills, and we agreed that this kind of role-playing was a good way to break the ice at times when the situation was a little tense. Perhaps it could be the inspiration for a new way to resolve international conflicts; it would be interesting to see how successful it might be in Ukraine. In passing, I noticed again how many of the dice followers' spouses tolerate their partner's hobby with equanimity. Susana Cuadrado, in any case, didn't seem any more afraid than Ann Cockcroft that an addiction to randomness might put her family on a slippery slope of trials and tribulations. Each of them, no doubt, was right to be so trusting. But, as far as I was concerned, I continued to think that I'm right to be wary.

When I got this email, I was, in this order, astonished, sad, moved. I had only spent

Dear friend,

We have the pleasure of informing you of the death of Luke Rhinehart. He wanted you to know as soon as possible so that you didn't worry if your email went unanswered. For several years his online friendships have mattered a lot to him. He would have loved to not die in order to continue them, but fate decided otherwise.

Luke wasn't afraid of death, even if the idea made him a little nervous. He saw it as a new experience – something like a trip to a foreign country, or the beginning of a new book or relationship. He liked to laugh about it – but he liked to laugh at everything. He thought that we take life too seriously. He was expecting, once on the other side, to send us a report describing in minute detail what he had found. He was hoping that this report would reassure us and make us laugh. To this day, unfortunately, we still haven't received anything.

Luke's final days, for those who are interested, weren't so different from his final weeks, his final months, or really from the last thirty years of his life. For someone who worshiped randomness and perpetual change, he was true to himself in a way that might have been discouraging. The people who came to see him on the basis of his books were often disappointed to discover him so attached to his habits. Even when he rolled the die it was always more or less to do the same things.

'It's not bad in and of itself,' he would say, 'to always do more or less the same things. The question is to know if you like it. Most people, unfortunately, do things that they don't like, and it was always with this in mind that I wrote about the die. But, I'm OK with that.'

His wife, Anne, stayed by his side until the end. At the start of last week, he said to her: 'I'm dying.'

'Ah,' she said, adjusting his pillows to make him comfortable.

'I find it interesting. This has never happened to me until now, you see.'

'But it's happened to lots of people.'

'I know. It's a comforting thought. All those people waiting for me on the other side that I'm going to be able to meet them.'

'Unless they don't feel like it.'

Luke looked at the ceiling, thoughtfully: 'That would be boring.'

'Typical, always afraid of being bored.'

'Are you going to miss me when I'm dead?'

'Oh, listen, I spent almost sixty years whining that I had to put up with you all the time, and now I'm going to whine because I won't have to put up with you: that's that.'

'That's also a comforting thought.'

'Of course I'll miss you.'

two days at George's and his wife's house, but I felt affection for them, truly. So, since I had their telephone number, I called Ann to offer my condolences. When she answered, she was as cordial as ever, happy to hear from me but curt, and she said she'd put me onto George. I wondered if she'd lost her mind, or if I had, and mumbled something about the email I'd just received, and she responded, like someone used to small inconveniences: 'Oh, the email! Of course... But don't worry, it's not George who's dead, it's Luke.'

George, when he took the phone, confirmed this: 'Yeah, I'd had enough of Luke. I'm getting older, you see. I still love life, looking out the window to see what the weather is like when I wake up, gardening, making love, kayaking, but I'm less and less interested in my career, and my career, essentially, was Luke. I had written that letter for Ann to send to my correspondents once I was dead. I'd kept the file in store for two years and then one day I told myself, it's time to send it...'

Ah, I see, OK. I asked two more questions. The first: before hitting send on the email, which after all was something pretty unusual, had he rolled the die? Had it been the die, in the end, that had decided the death of Luke? He seemed genuinely surprised: 'Oh, no, I hadn't even thought of that. The die is useful when one doesn't know what one wants. But if we know, what's it good for?'

Second question, now: aside from me, how have your correspondents taken the news? A little muffled, mischievous chuckle from the old prankster: 'Well, there were a few who found it to be in bad taste. Some thought: George has lost it. And the others thought: that's Luke all over! What do you think?'

E

HENNING BOHL

XI —— XV

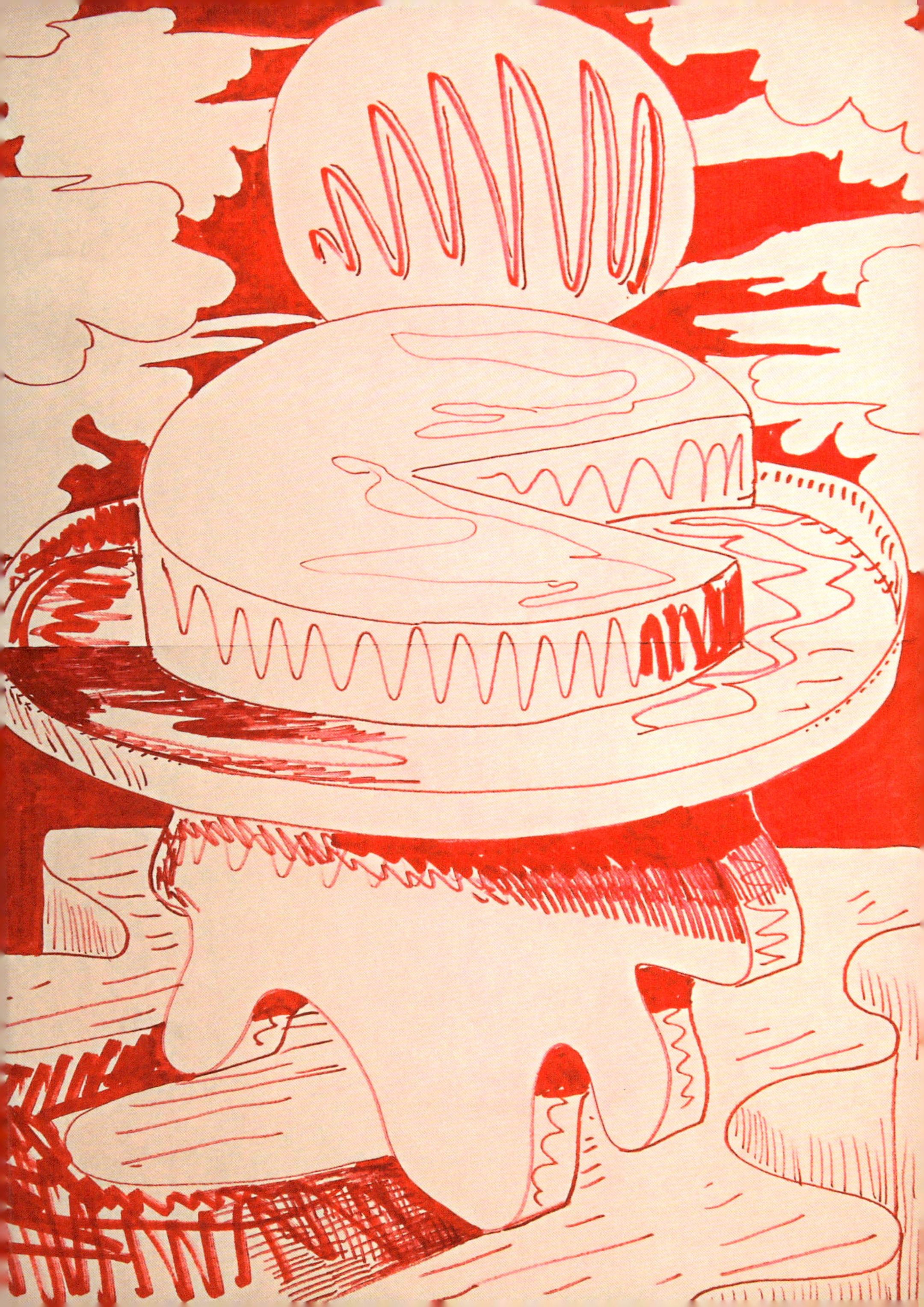

Seite 18　　　　　　　　　　**Ingenieurwesen/Technik**　　　　　　　　24./25. September 2011　ALPHA

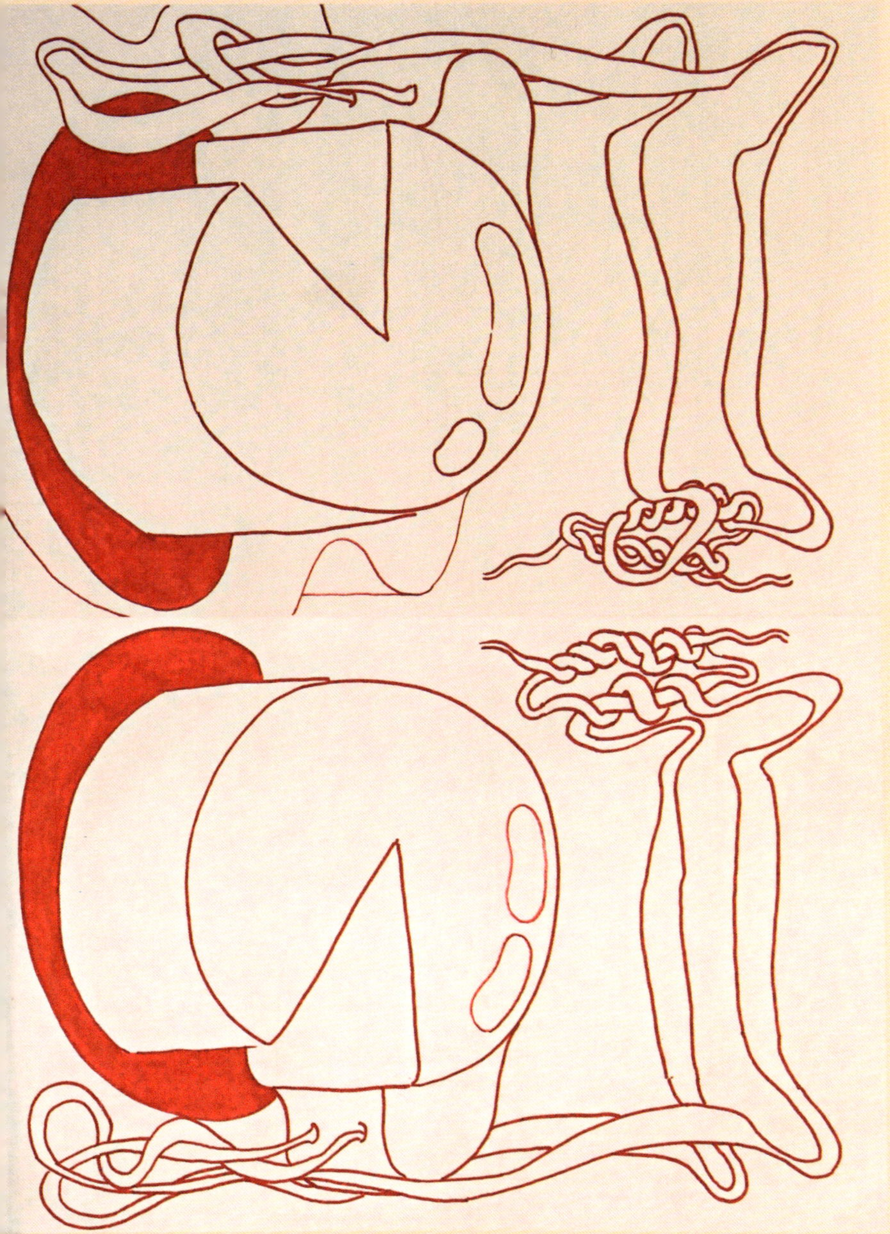

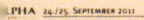

Kundenberatung/Verkauf

Marketing/Medien/PR · Kundenberatung/Verkauf

Gesundheitswesen/Medizin - Diverse Berufe

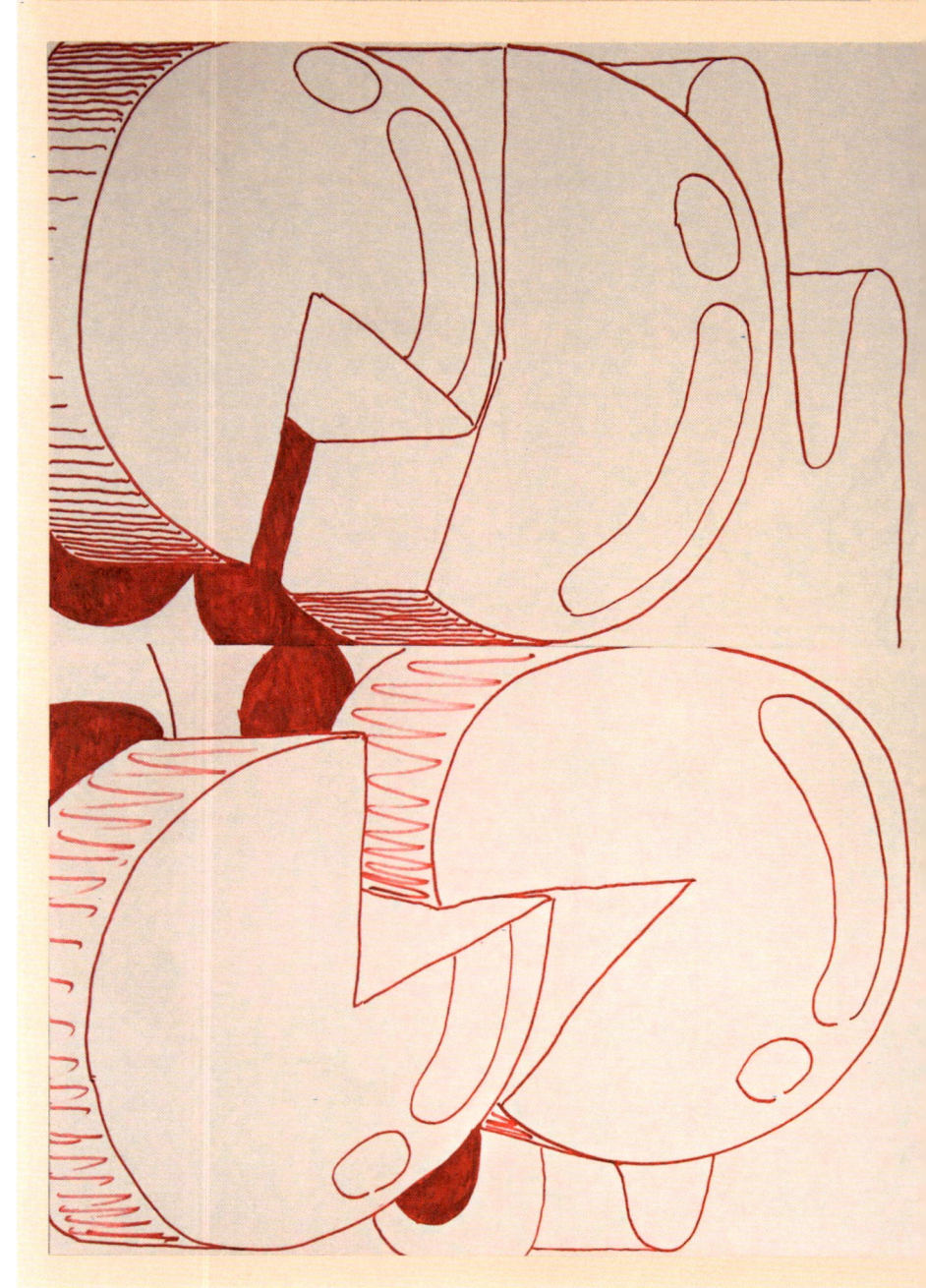

Ingenieurwesen/Technik

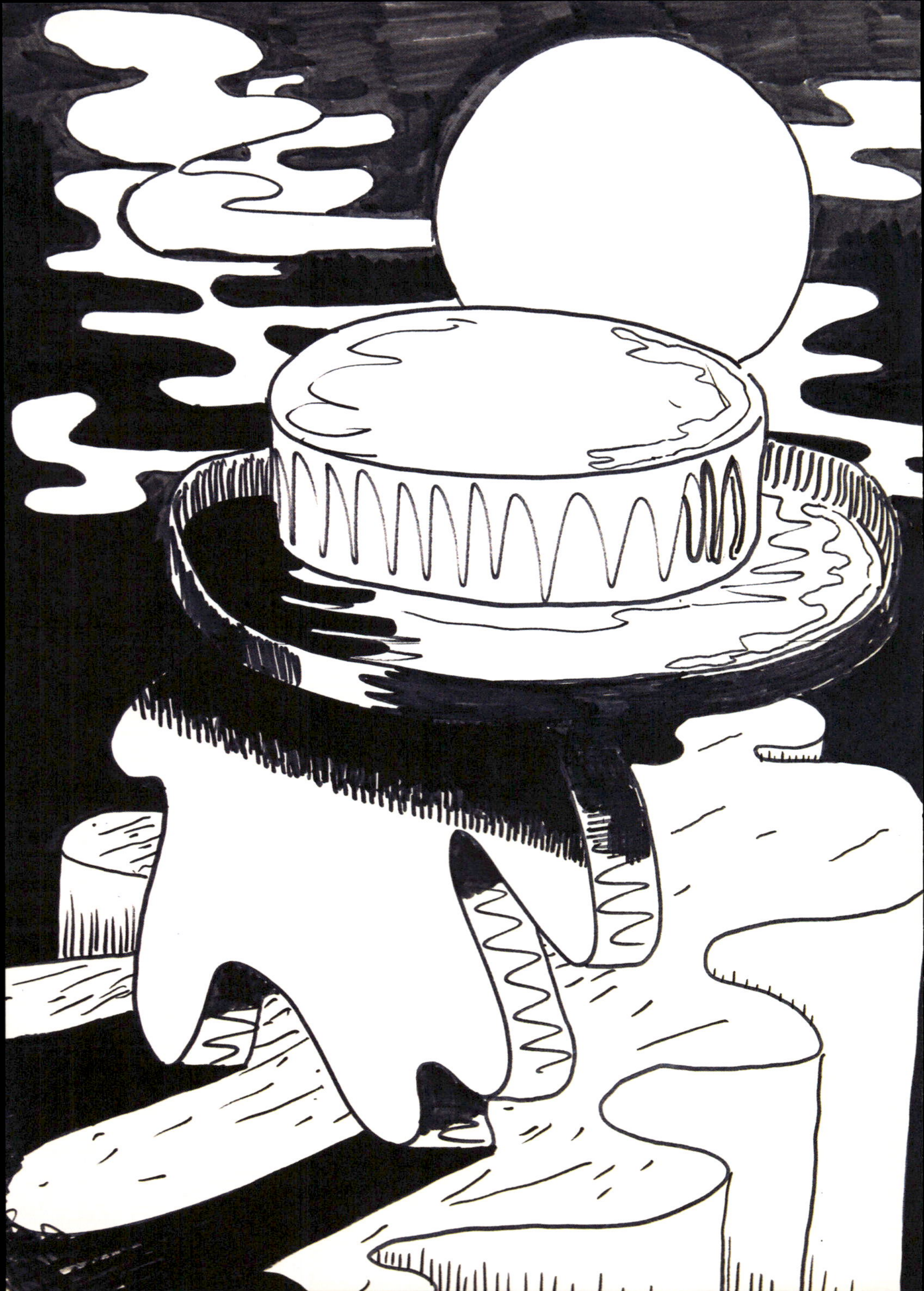

INTERVIEW

WITH

HAL FOSTER

HAL FOSTER'S WORK FOLLOWS in the tradition of the modernist art critic–historian, a public intellectual whose reflection on, and synthesis of, contemporary culture is informed by a deep commitment to history and its writing. His influence is considerable, reaching well beyond the disciplinary boundaries of modern and contemporary art into architecture, literature, and critical theory – all arenas in which Foster is an authority. His formidable powers of analysis and explication are deployed, more often than not, in the service of disruption and destabilisation, and his work is as polarising as it is revelatory. Foster was one of the key critics in the 1980s debate over postmodern art, for example, a debate that turned on redeployments of historical art practice, principally appropriation, and made fierce by art's role in the culture wars and the inflating art market.

Intellectually formed in the heady theory days of late 70s New York, Foster has spent his career exploring the power, promise, and limits of critique. His art historical writing covers the bifurcated twentieth century, focusing acutely on pre-war avant-garde practice and its recuperation in the decades after World War II. Psychoanalysis looms large in his writing. Nevertheless, there is no dogma in Foster's approach. While his sympathies are decidedly Marxist, and key passages from Freud, Bataille, and Lacan are recurring touchstones, critical theory is always for him both methodology and object of history. As he says in THE RETURN OF THE REAL (1996), 'when it comes to critical theory, I have the interest of a second-generation initiate, not the zeal of a first generation convert. With this slight distance I attempt to treat critical theory not only as a conceptual tool but as a symbolic, even symptomatic form.'

In addition to his art historical writing (COMPULSIVE BEAUTY (1993), DESIGN AND CRIME (2002), PROSTHETIC GODS (2004), THE FIRST AGE OF POP (2011), THE ART-ARCHITECTURE COMPLEX (2011), BAD NEW DAYS (forthcoming, 2015)), Foster is a regular contributor to ARTFORUM, THE LONDON REVIEW OF BOOKS, and OCTOBER, where he has been an editor since 1991. Editorial work – some of which we discuss in this interview – has a prominent role in his cultural analysis. A notable example, The ANTI-AESTHETIC, his first edited volume, mapped the uncharted terrain of postmodern thought, and has since become required reading for students of postmodernism in any discipline. I was one such student, and was fortunate to have Foster as my graduate adviser at Princeton University, where he is the Townsend Martin, Class of 1917, Professor of Art and Archaeology. This interview took place as a tracked-changes document exchanged via email –the same format we employed for my dissertation drafts a few months earlier. Foster and I were both between Princeton and New York when the interview took place, but this seemed the most appropriate method (among other things, it allowed him to continue to correct my punctuation).

Q THE WHITE REVIEW — Your most recent book of essays, BAD NEW DAYS, will be published by Verso in the autumn. In recent years you've published THE ART-ARCHITECTURE COMPLEX (2011) and THE FIRST AGE OF POP (2012), as well as numerous essays for exhibition catalogues and essays and reviews for ARTFORUM, the LONDON REVIEW OF BOOKS, and the journal OCTOBER, where you are also an editor. You're a productive writer by any measure. Can you talk a little bit about your process? Do you keep to a strict routine?

A. HAL FOSTER — Life is too hectic for a routine, and I don't think I'd like one in any case; I don't have a process either. What I do have is a compulsion; I'm not comfortable unless I have a text in the works. (Ideally two – one short-term, critical or polemical; one long-term, historical or archival.) The worst is to be between projects, the best is to have the initial idea, the actual writing is mostly misery (I don't believe those who claim otherwise). That said, if I weren't happy in my life, I wouldn't be productive, so I suppose I owe my productivity to my wife and kids.

Q. THE WHITE REVIEW — You studied Comparative Literature as an undergrad and then fell in with a theory crowd as a Master's student at Columbia, correct?

A. HAL FOSTER — Comp. lit., English and Art History at Princeton in the mid-1970s, a classic education in the Humanities at a university not much troubled by the 1960s, though hints of theory did come to us, mostly from Yale. Harold Bloom visited soon after he published THE ANXIETY OF INFLUENCE, and I was taken by his idea of a tradition that young writers wrestle with and revise somehow – how could that fierce Oedipality not appeal to an ambitious student interested in literature? Then I came to New York to delve into art and theory; I was drawn downtown by brilliant critics like Susan Sontag and Rosalind Krauss and uptown by Columbia professors like Michael Wood and Edward Said. I learned a lot about critical writing from Michael, and Edward was generous about theory: he taught everyone from Vico to Gramsci and Benjamin to Foucault and Derrida. I also fell into his seminar on Orientalism just before his great book was published; it was exciting to witness a new discourse in the making. Said was charismatic but aloof: for all his engagement in politics, he was old-school in style. Sylvère Lotringer was different, a hipster theorist we could hang with, and he introduced us to his Paris pals like Baudrillard. In those days Jonathan Crary, Michel Feher, Sanford Kwinter and I were inseparable. When the Odeon opened downtown in 1980, we commandeered a table as our office, and our conversations there led to ZONE magazine, which later morphed into Zone Books.

Q. THE WHITE REVIEW — We could do the whole interview about the origins of ZONE. I'll resist. But can you situate the project? You arrived in New York after 'Schizo-Culture', right? Were you involved with SEMIOTEXT(E)? Was that the model for ZONE? Or was ZONE a departure?

A. HAL FOSTER — No, the 'Schizo-Culture' conference occurred in 1975, and I came to New York in 1977 (though I visited often in college). And, no, I wasn't involved in SEMIOTEXT(E), and ZONE wasn't modelled on it – we were more Foucauldians than schizoanalysts, or at least my compatriots were. To be honest, they led the way; though we identified with each other, my intellectual sympathies were a little different. More Marxist, I would say – that was my reflex reaction to the rise of Reagan and Thatcher, but I was also drawn to the Frankfurt School. Jameson was an important influence at the time, especially his POLITICAL UNCONSCIOUS (1981) – what an acrobatic troping of the anti-dialectical French for his own dialectical thinking that book is! In fact, I was on the editorial board of SOCIAL TEXT with him in the early 1980s. ZONE was pitched both as alternative to SEMIOTEXT(E) and as alien to OCTOBER, though I harboured a not-so-secret affinity with that project too, as became obvious enough when I joined the board a decade later.

Q. THE WHITE REVIEW — And THE ANTI-AESTHETIC emerges from these conversations?
A. HAL FOSTER — All those conversations: that book includes a great range of thinkers. Said is there, Baudrillard too, and Jameson (with his first version of his famous essay on postmodernism), but so is the OCTOBER crew – Rosalind Krauss, Douglas Crimp, and Craig Owens. Habermas is included with his critique of Lyotard and his reaffirmation of 'the project of modernity', so you have the late Frankfurt School represented, and Kenneth Frampton is there with his Arendtian position, because postmodernism had a different inflection in architecture. In a way I'm surprised the book was so influential – it's such a smörgåsbord. But then these theorists were in conversation, directly and not; they shared similar questions if not objects – problematics, as we used to say then. That's why the book worked.

Q. THE WHITE REVIEW — Who introduced you to Lacan? It wasn't Edward Said, right? I guess what I want to know is how you came to a psychoanalytic approach? Did that interest predate your work with Rosalind Krauss?
A. HAL FOSTER — It was feminist artists and critics – Laura Mulvey, Mary Kelley, Jane Weinstock, Barbara Kruger, Silvia Kolbowski, Craig Owens too – we were editors together at ART IN AMERICA from 1981 to 1987, and we did lines of theory like it was cocaine. In a way I worked through psychoanalysis in reverse: the Anglo-American take on French feminism first, then its critique of Lacan, then his re-reading of Freud, finally Freud, and then on to other schools (Klein and Winnicott especially). Rosalind didn't influence me here – if anything it was the other way around – but psychoanalytic criticism was almost a lingua franca in my sector of the 1980s.

Q. THE WHITE REVIEW — Is it fair to say that you were interested in critical theory before you were interested in art? Why art?
A. HAL FOSTER — No. Even as a kid in Seattle I wanted to be a writer, and my best friend, Charles Wright, who later became the transformative director of Dia, had advanced art in his home. As a teenager I'd stand, often stunned, in front of works by Mark Rothko, Roy Lichtenstein, Robert Morris, and others. Oddly, minimalism and Pop were my entrées into all of art, but later this grammar allowed me to think back in time, to abstraction and 'the painting of modern life', as well as forward, to institution critique and appropriation art. Already in college I sensed that my interests in writing and theory could intersect in art criticism.

Q. THE WHITE REVIEW — What's the difference between art criticism and contemporary art history?
A. HAL FOSTER — Contemporary art history is now a field of its own, but it remains an oxymoronic category. When does a practice become a 'thing of the past' and for whom? Appropriation art, the work of my generation, isn't a historical object for me, yet it is for others. In my view it's a mistake to historicise art prematurely: you never know what the present will drag back in (witness the old performances re-enacted in museums today). In a roundup on 'the contemporary' I assembled several years back, Richard Meyer relayed several questions to his students that remain pertinent: 'Why are you studying Art History if what you really want is to write about the current moment? Where are the archival and research materials on which you will draw

– in the files of a commercial gallery, in a drawer in the artist's studio, in the works of art themselves, in a series of interviews that you intend to conduct with the artist, in a theoretical paradigm that you plan to apply to the work, or in an ideological critique of the current moment? What distinguishes your practice as a contemporary art historian from that of an art critic? And how does the history of art matter to the works you plan to write about and to the scholarly contribution you hope to make?'

Q. THE WHITE REVIEW —— Can you explain what 'critical' means today? Can you parse the 'critical' in 'critical theory', 'critical art' and 'art criticism'?

A. HAL FOSTER —— Mostly it means what it has since Kant: reflexive thinking about what different forms of inquiry can and can't do, including forms of art. Sometimes, however, that inquiry turns into prescription, and the attention to form becomes formalist; ideology critique is then a crucial corrective. Yet that critique has its problems too, such as its arrogance about its own authority, and so it has to be questioned in turn. As indeed it was – by deconstruction, discourse analysis, the refusal of power in feminist, queer, and postcolonial theory, and so on. This story is familiar enough; I rehearse it here simply to underscore that critique is always incomplete: it remains a *project*, and that project remains, as in the Greek root *krinein*, to separate and to decide, to articulate and to judge. In different ways that project is active in all theory, criticism and art worth the name; in large part it is what makes us modern, and it can't be wished away.

Q. THE WHITE REVIEW —— Some of your more recent work calls for a return to critique, or laments a post-critical turn in cultural analysis of the last couple decades. How do you reconcile this apparent crisis of criticality with the proliferation of progressive journals (TRIPLE CANOPY, JACOBIN, N+1, to name a few) alongside novel outlets (often online) for critical reviews of exhibitions?

A. HAL FOSTER —— I understand the fatigue with criticality, even the aversion to it, that many express today, for when it hardens into a value in its own right, its function is mostly lost, and it can feel oppressive in its correctness when not defeatist in its negativity. That said, I have nothing good to say about the post-critical turn in contemporary culture (I make this clear enough in my new book), and it heartens me to see those journals flourish.

Q. THE WHITE REVIEW —— What about this phenomenon that some writers – often white male writers – bemoan as the neo-political correctness of internet 'call out culture'? Isn't our era marked by a plurality of active, powerful (if anonymous) critical voices?

A. HAL FOSTER —— Sure, but sometimes that plurality of voices is a plethora of opinion at best and a miasma of bile at worst. The blogosphere is not a public sphere as I understand it; as least in principle (and that may be all it is) the public sphere is a shared space where different arguments can be articulated and assessed – it needs to be both common and focused. Too often the internet is a cyberspace filled with rhetorical drones that, however targeted, blindly collide or shoot past one another.

Q. THE WHITE REVIEW —— Is there some nostalgia for agonism in your calls for criticality?

A. HAL FOSTER —— Why 'nostalgia'? Is agonism altogether gone? If so, then criticism is too, because it depends on agonism, just as democracy depends on *dissensus*. As usual Baudelaire had it right: 'To be just, that is, to justify its existence, criticism should be partial, passionate, and political.' In the early years of neoliberalism critical theory was deemed a drag to the art market, so it had to be jettisoned. Critics were pushed to the sidelines, and collectors and dealers called the shots. Today, with such a vast art market few successful artists want to risk their niches, and with such a cacophonous art world few critical artists can be heard.

Q. THE WHITE REVIEW —— Whose side is the critic on today? Or maybe, who does or should the critic serve?

A. HAL FOSTER —— Is there a subject of history today in the Marxist sense? Some say the neoliberal 'precariat', but others no longer believe in any such dialectic; it was simpler in the days of 'the author as producer', or even, not so long ago, during the rise of feminism, the queer movement, postcolonialism – then the committed critic might know what side or sides to be on. Put as simply as possible, I think the critic is always on two sides at once: on the side of *the idea* in the work – its concept must be clarified – and on the side of *the conjuncture* of the work – its situation must be explained. Years ago Perry Anderson argued that modernism had three primary conditions of possibility: political revolution (the Russian above all), technological transformation (new forms of transportation, reproduction, and so on), and the art academy as antagonist (as a prime agent-symbol of bourgeois culture). Contemporary culture can also be triangulated – by neoliberal deregulation, technological transformation (digital of course), and the all-dominant market. To be critical today art must somehow reflect on those preconditions – not only or even directly, but one, two or all three of these aspects must be engaged.

Q. THE WHITE REVIEW —— I ask that question, in part, because there is so much money in certain corridors of contemporary art. There is so much money in art and there is so little money in publishing – critical or academic. What does art money mean for the art critic?

A. HAL FOSTER —— The media talk obsessively about the money in the art world, and the numbers are mind-blowing, but it only affects the 1 per cent directly, or really the 0.1 per cent. That is not to downplay its importance: it has effected a structural change both in the production of some work and in the presentation of much more. Yet the market is not new – modern art is coeval with it. Who pioneered the one-person show if not Courbet and Manet? (And in some ways conspicuous consumption in art today is more in keeping with the historical norm of art used as a prize in prestige wars.) Should the money be redistributed somehow? Sure. Will it? Not likely in this political order. But there is a little solace in this: like salon art of the past, market art in the present will wash out over time. The likes of John Currin will go the way of Bouguereau; if they remain on museum walls it will be as markers of artistic blandishment and bad taste.

Q. THE WHITE REVIEW —— Bad taste? The phrase still exists in this future you're imagining? We've found our way back to judgment (or we never lost sight of it, the Kantian in you suggests). Although you describe them as inseparable, hasn't contemporary criticism jettisoned judgment (particularly questions of taste)?

A. HAL FOSTER —— There's no getting around taste. My generation of critics upheld a moratorium on terms associated with connoisseurship and authority. We wanted to shift from 'object' to 'practice', for example, and from 'judgment' to 'conjuncture', say. But that was

Q. THE WHITE REVIEW — What kind of future do you think art history – your art history – anticipates?

A. HAL FOSTER — Serious art anticipates the future as much as it reflects the present. By the same token serious art history is driven by the present as much as it is informed by the past. That is to say, 'my' art history takes its cue, in part, from contemporary practice: for example, twenty-five years ago feminist art concerned with sexual difference led me to think again about the sexual unconscious of surrealist representations, and our extended period of emergency today prompts me to look back on the twentieth-century avant-garde at times of political crisis, particularly in the aftermaths of the two world wars (that is my long-term project now). Such work has value as history, I hope, but it is also a small offering to the present and the future. Another pittance is the criticism I do – as thoughtful a witnessing as I can muster of the contemporary practice that interests me ('thoughtful' is not opposed to 'partial, passionate and political').

Q. THE WHITE REVIEW — Your book COMPULSIVE BEAUTY (1993) is that rethinking, indebted to feminist art, about the sexual unconscious of surrealist work. One of its many contributions to the field is the recuperation of a lost version of surrealism – a version that links up with postwar art and theory; a version, perhaps, recruited to fight alongside contemporary art and theory. Yet there are no women artists in this recuperation. When approaching the past using the tools of a present struggle is there any danger that those tools are misappropriated (in this case, to rescue a heterosexist past)?

A. HAL FOSTER — It's difficult to be a privileged subject of an art practice when you are its primary object. Of course there were women who were surrealists, but as such they were in a bind – personal, aesthetic, social, political. I also didn't take them up because 1) others (like Whitney Chadwick) had, and 2) 'my' art history is about rethinking a canon more than expanding it. I don't see the past as ammo for present battles; I see present debates as an entrée to the past.

Q. THE WHITE REVIEW — What is the use value of history to art today (at least the art that interests you)?

A. HAL FOSTER — As Jameson and others have long argued, consumer capitalism is an amnesia machine; this is structural, not incidental, to its operation – it requires us to forget so that the next shiny commodity will always look new to us. Against this enforced presentism many artists have developed an 'archival' practice (this is another subject of my book); in this respect history has all kinds of use value for artists. Of course, history is also embedded in art history, and such history is extremely valuable for practitioners as well. Baudelaire (to cite him again) once called painting 'the mnemotechny of the beautiful'. If painting is extended to art, and the traumatic is added to the beautiful, that motto still works for me. The artists I most admire – one is Richard Serra, another is Richard Hamilton – have the most partial-passionate-political understanding of art, of how its history informs, indeed sustains, their work. With Serra one can talk deeply about many problems in sculpture and architecture, and Hamilton was brilliant on the twinned development of easel painting and new media.

Q. THE WHITE REVIEW — The traumatic is added to the beautiful? Or does the traumatic replace the beautiful in your telling? Is there beauty in traces of trauma?

A. HAL FOSTER — In a sense the traumatic is our version of the sublime – the trauma of modern history, of contemporary history – and like the old sublime it doesn't replace the beautiful, though there are instances when the one cuts into the other. There's a traumatic dimension to the beautiful abstractions of Gerhard Richter, for example, just as there's a weird beauty to the traumatic silkscreens of Andy Warhol. I think the two complicate one another in some work by many contemporaries I love – Louise Lawler, Cindy Sherman, Robert Gober, Charles Ray, James Casebere, Thomas Demand, Sarah Sze...

Q. THE WHITE REVIEW — The new terms in your lexicon are 'emergency' and 'precarity' (trauma remains). It seems artists who engage your preconditions of contemporary culture directly ('neoliberal deregulation, technological transformation, and the all-dominant market') must adopt precarious materials, personae, and practices to do so – Thomas Hirschhorn is a key figure for you in this regard. Precarious art can rescue culture from structurally-enforced precarity?

A. HAL FOSTER — Not 'must adopt' – I'm not prescribing – and not 'rescue' – would that it were so easy! Such work exposes the fact that our political bond – whether we call it the social contract or the symbolic order – is always tenuous, and now, after years of neoliberalism, more fragile than ever. This work (I think not only of Hirschhorn but also of Isa Genzken, Rachel Harrison, many others) foregrounds its own schismatic condition, its own lack of shared materials, meanings, and motivations, redoubling social instability with artistic instability. In this way, paradoxically, the precarity can become a ground for art, and an affliction can be turned into an appeal.

Q. THE WHITE REVIEW — Appeal for what? Shared meaning and motivation for the most vulnerable despite (in celebration of?) heterogeneity, plurality, division, even atomisation? Neoliberal capitalism thrives on difference and instability, and security is offered up daily from banks, insurers, governments – 'securitisation', it's called, and it is the establishment of precarious ground. Don't we need an alternative terra firma?

A. HAL FOSTER — It's not an appeal for solid or even common ground; it's an address that is less political than ethical perhaps, and thus more limited – but also more direct. Almost a face to face encounter, with all the attendant risks that it will be missed somehow, along the lines that Judith Butler traces in her essay 'Precarious Life' on Levinas: 'To respond to the face, to understand its meaning, means to be awake to what is precarious in another life or, rather, the precariousness of life itself.'

Q. THE WHITE REVIEW — The face-to-face encounter distributes our shared precariousness? Add precarious materials to such an encounter and you might get an artwork like a tent city. Like an occupation. Occupy had an ethics of encounter. But it also had a politics of change – of alternative.

A. HAL FOSTER — A tent city is no model for an artwork. My new book ends with a caution about formlessness; it doesn't necessarily open up the work or animate the viewer or do many of the things associated with participatory or indeterminate art. Occupy was extraordinary, but it was also too attached to its own informality. Not all authority is authoritarian.

Q. THE WHITE REVIEW — What is the status of 'theory' today? Is it still the bad word it was a couple of decades ago?

A. HAL FOSTER — Alas, poor 'theory', you have become a scare word, an idiot reification. In the 1970s critical theory was the avant-garde continued by other means, but it took a beating during the culture wars of the 1980s and the 1990s, in which the Right triumphed, and the situation during the terroristic Bush-Cheney years was even worse. To this day not only journalists but also critics love to bash it – in the name of anodyne ideas of beauty or expression or whatever. But I sense a renewed taste for theoretical reflection among a lot of artists and writers; witness artists like Sam LeWitt and Cheyney Thompson and writers like Rivka Galchen and Tom McCarthy, to name just a few.

Q. THE WHITE REVIEW — You were on the editorial board of OCTOBER though parts of that turn away from theory and now the turn back. How has the journal changed, aside from adding editors?

A. HAL FOSTER — There was never a turn away from theory in OCTOBER! On the contrary, it came to embody, for many people, that blue meanie itself. Do a search for OCTOBER – or, even better, 'Octoberites' – in the NEW YORK TIMES, THE NEW YORK REVIEW OF BOOKS, or THE NEW YORKER, and that's how it figures: as a figure for 'theory'– as obscurantist, ultra-leftist, power-driven, or whatever other bad fantasy the writer is possessed by. Like any journal it has its good stretches, when it's in focus, and its weak periods, when it's not very relevant. It is very hard to establish these publications these days, so unlike modernist journals, which were almost proud of their short life spans, we soldier on.

Q. THE WHITE REVIEW — You haven't done much curating, which I suppose makes sense, since you aren't a curator. But it seems everyone is a curator today – artists, writers, critics. Why not you?

A. HAL FOSTER — I have advised on shows for both artists and curators (like my friend Leah Dickerman at MoMA), but in the contemporary field there is now a divide between serious curating and spectacular exhibition-making. I don't want to be no cultural impresario.

Q. THE WHITE REVIEW — Do you have an art collection? If so, how does it compare to your book collection?

A. HAL FOSTER — We have a group of works by friends but no art collection per se. As a young critic I didn't want to touch the commercial side of things, and as some friends rose on the art market I shied away from writing about them (today my writing doesn't affect their value greatly). I also didn't have much money. I bought a few things cheaply – once for a book cover, a few times when a friend needed cash more than I did. More recently I have sometimes traded, but that is more gift exchange than tit for tat, text for object. I'm not pure, but I also don't feel corrupt. As for books, I don't collect them. I see them as tools – often beautiful ones, to be sure, but tools nonetheless. I fetishise things as much as the next person, but I try to spare books.

Q. THE WHITE REVIEW — What about the formation of new critics and historians? The academy no longer offers shelter for young writers – dwindling tenure lines and stiff competition mean little room for truly challenging work. There's no money in writing or editing anyway. Where do young critics come from? Where do they go?

A. HAL FOSTER — When I began one could still hope to be an independent critic. Then the market moved in, and that space – in the interstices of magazines and journals, museums and galleries – shrank dramatically. That's when I retrenched to the academy, where critics are now often born and bred. I think that continues (the situation is not quite as dire as you say), and with historians even more so, of course; that's one reason why teaching remains important to me. But there have to be other outlets as well. Alienated young people in search of alternatives will find these openings. They have to; as Said used to say, there are no alternatives without critique.

Q. THE WHITE REVIEW — That's probably a good place to leave it, though I'm curious to know, are you reading anything good at the moment?

A. HAL FOSTER — I'll just tell you what's next to the bed, all of which I'd recommend: SATIN ISLAND by Tom McCarthy, THE HISTORY OF ROCK 'N' ROLL IN TEN SONGS by Greil Marcus, EXTRA-STATECRAFT by Keller Easterling, SIX DRAWING LESSONS by William Kentridge and UNDOING THE DEMOS by Wendy Brown. There's also HUCKLEBERRY FINN. Charles Ray just did an extraordinary sculpture of Huck and Jim, commissioned by the Whitney Museum; they backed away from it, however, and the Art Institute of Chicago also refused to put it in a truly public space during his current retrospective. Why isn't this a scandal? We all remember that book fondly, but it's searing about this country. It makes for instructive reading after all the police shootings and the massacre in Charleston.

CHRIS REITZ, JUNE 2015

A SHADOW

OF A SHADOW

OF A SHADOW

BY

JOHN DOUGLAS MILLAR

ON 13 MARCH 2015 KENNETH GOLDSMITH – conceptual poetry's most visible proponent – took to the stage at Brown University to read a lightly-edited version of the autopsy report on the body of Michael Brown, the black teenager whose fatal shooting at the hands of white police officer Darren Wilson led to days of protest on the streets of Ferguson, Missouri. As is typical of his practice, Goldsmith maintained that his reading rendered the legal report literature. In the days that followed a furious reaction spread across social media. Goldsmith was accused of appropriating black suffering for the advancement of his own artistic career, of enacting white supremacy and of perpetuating a racist fetishising of the black body. While what follows is not addressed specifically to those claims, I do see it as part of the same debate around the limits of a retrograde avant-garde posturing that embeds certain modes of privilege and ignores other voices. Goldsmith's reading represented the moment when a light Warholian posturing flew into something much heavier than it seemed to recognise existed.

¶ Conceptual poetry's relationship to its claimed theoretical, art historical and institutional inheritance is complex, and much of the difficulty coalesces around the question of the kind of work the words 'conceptual' and 'poetry' are doing in the rubric. The term points towards the twin genealogies from which conceptual poetry emerges: 1960s art world conceptualism and the school of poetry that emerged from the journal $L=A=N=G=U=A=G=E$ in the late seventies and early eighties. Avant-gardes never arrive fully formed from the head of Marinetti; hybridity is ingrained, which means that the critical mode of inquiry itself must be hybrid, able to traverse the histories and theories of both art and literature without ignoring the specific historical conditions that pertain to the critical development of each.

In critical discussion of conceptual poetics, a variety of theoretical positions with regard to the avant-garde are restaged, re-enacted and in some cases disavowed. Talking to Francisco Roman Guevara, Kenneth Goldsmith said that: 'After finding [John] Cage, I became devoted to that kind of thinking, which led me to embrace anything having to do with the avant-garde.' The critic Brian M. Reed, by contrast, has rejected the term 'neo-avant-garde' in relation to conceptual poetry altogether, instead positing the movement as an authentic avant-garde in its own right. Conceptual poetry's 'gestures', he writes, 'are profoundly political in inspiration, calculated attacks on the institutional norms and practices that not only shape literary careers but also preside over the formation of obedient, well-disciplined neoliberal citizen subjects.' Reed's statement (in NOBODY'S BUSINESS: TWENTY-FIRST CENTURY AVANT-GARDE POETICS (2013)) follows the German literary critic Peter Bürger's model of avant-gardism insofar as it embeds the claim that 'neo-avant-garde' art is not 'political in inspiration'.

E

Bürger's influential *Theory of the Avant-Garde* (1974) presents a narrative of avant-gardism that is based on 'authenticity'. The European and Soviet avant-gardes of the pre- and immediately post-First World War period (constructivism, Dada, futurism, and particularly surrealism) are 'authentic', in his account, because they are committed to a radical, anti-institutional practice of 'art–into-life'. For Bürger those practices that emerged in America in the aftermath of the Second World War and which appropriated certain traits of the pre-war, or 'historic,' avant-garde were 'inauthentic' because they allowed the political and social efficacy of avant-garde strategies to be neutralised by bringing them within the sphere of the institution. He coins the term 'neo-avant-gardism' to signify a belated mimicry even further removed from the possibility of political and social transformation that he holds to have been the promise of the historic avant-garde: '[A]ttempts are made to continue the tradition of the avant-garde movements. But these attempts, such as the happenings, for example, which could be called *neo-avant-gardiste*, can no longer attain the protest value of Dadaist manifestations.'

To the extent that it continues the avant-garde project, the neo-avant-garde does so in the very context the historic avant-garde sought to obliterate the institution. On these terms, the historic avant-garde is viewed as having been retrospectively absorbed by modernist high-culture. 'Avant-garde' and 'modernist' are, therefore, synonymous.

We might note that the development of conceptual art contains a movement from the context of experimental literature towards art; that is reflected in conceptual poetry's movement from conceptual art towards literature. Bürger's account helps us to map conceptual poetry's development from Language poetry's position of 'resistant autonomy' to its apparent opposition to a certain model of the institution of literature. While the methods of the Language school appear to be diametrically opposed to those of conceptual poetry (the former prioritising composition, the latter production), many of those who practice and proselyte conceptual poetics were also either part of the Language poetry coterie or favourable critics: Susan Howe, Charles Bernstein and Marjorie Perloff among them. Although different in form, Language poetry is nonetheless the condition of possibility for conceptual writing, much as autonomy in art is for the emergence of the historic avant-garde.

Language poetry evolved from within the Comparative Literature departments of the 1970s where, as Hal Foster maintains in *The Return of the Real* (1996), 'critical theory served as a secret continuation of modernism by other means ... to the extent that it retained such values as difficulty and distinction after they had receded from artistic form.' In the work of the Language poets, difficulty and distinction are returned from the realm of theory to that of artistic form. In Language poetry one can see a working-through of Jacques Derrida's critique of the philosophy of presence, of

Michel Foucault's chains of discourse and of Roland Barthes' dying author. The lyric self, if present at all, is shown to be a feather-light but chained construction constituted by the devastating force-fields of ideology, social conditioning and biopower. The complex syntax and new coinages are designed to force the reader into a kind of agency; the reader becomes writer, building meaning like Jean Marais in Cocteau's ORPHÉE, receiving and reconstituting garbled messages from the underworld. Perloff lists the central claims of the Language school as follows: (1) poetry is not speech-based but a form of writing: it cannot represent the full presence of the spoken voice; (2) poetry is not a species of referential discourse, designed to 'say' something, but a complex trace structure of shifting signifiers; and (3) poetic discourse does not 'belong' to the author who antedates the text but to the reader who constructs it. Two examples:

> Symbiosis of home and prison.
> Then, having become superfluous, time.
> One has to give to.
> Taste: the first and last.
>
> I remember the look in.
> It was the first time.
>
> Some gorgeous swelling feeling that.
> Success which owes its fortune.
>
> —from Bob Perelman, 'Chronic Meanings' (1993)

> at the end of delight, one
> who or that which revolves
>
> more than chests have
> to heave '... where gold,
>
> dirt, and blood flow
> together'!: margins
>
> the family, not personal
> fallibility leads
>
> to instrumentality
>   in self-restraint
>
> —from Diane Ward, 'Limit' (1989)

Conceptual poetics takes up the anti-palliative element of the Language school and its disavowal of the authorial sovereignty of the poetic subject, but it drops the formal difficulty, replacing it with a Warholian, productivist model that enacts an overblown mimesis of contemporary modes of labour. Works such as Kenneth Goldsmith's *Day* (2003), a transcription of a single issue of the *New York Times* published as a limited edition 900-page book, or *VIA* (2005) by Caroline Bergvall, a transcription of the first tercet of every English-language translation of the *Divine Comedy* in the British Library, clearly engage in questions concerning language. They are, nevertheless, examples of what Reed has called the 'spectacle of wasted labour'.

Conceptual poetry cannot be held up as avant-garde according to Bürger's model because, rather than operating outside of the institution, it makes critical attacks on one institution (literature) from the relative safety of another (art). The question might be: is this the only way to survive and enact critique, given that there is no longer an outside position from which to operate? Let us then examine Hal Foster's defence of the neo-avant-garde and assess whether it might offer us a more adequate model.

In his *Return of the Real*, after accepting that any serious work on the avant-garde must contend with Bürger's work, Foster writes that

> [Bürger's] description is often inexact, and his definition overly selective ...
> Moreover, his very premise – that one theory can comprehend the avant-garde,
> that all its activities can be subsumed under the project to destroy the false autonomy
> of bourgeois art – is problematic. Yet these problems pale next to his dismissal of the
> post-war avant-garde as merely neo, as so much repetition in bad faith that cancels
> the pre-war critique of the institution of art.

Taking up the terminology of Michel Foucault's 1969 lecture 'What is an Author?', Foster maintains that the innovators of the historic avant-garde are best viewed as 'initiators of discursive practices'. Foucault uses the term to refer to the authors of foundational texts of a particular discursive genealogy – in his case, Marx and Freud. For Foucault, on Foster's reading, a critical reading of such texts need 'not be another accretion to the discourse'. Not merely the piling up of academic footnotes and vacuous repetition but the opening of a genuinely fresh and radical discursive space through a return to the foundational text.

We can see the direction of the argument Foster is lining up here: just because an artistic practice restages or reuses certain avant-gardist tropes, it does not mean that it is automatically conservative or mannerist. It may in fact be a reconnection with a lost practice 'in order to disconnect from a present way of working felt to be outmoded, misguided, or otherwise oppressive'. For Foster, the neo-avant-garde acts on the avant-garde in ways that only become recognisable in the present, ways that were unrecognisable to Bürger. Foster's model could be seen to mimic Walter Benjamin's concept of the dialectical-image, the image that allows a sudden awareness of a different order of time outside what he termed 'victor history'. Though Foster does not mention Benjamin, the latter's 'victor-history' could be mapped onto the defeatist historicism that Foster sees as detrimentally endemic to art history. It is, says Foster, 'this persistent historicism that condemns contemporary art as belated, redundant, [and] repetitious'.

In *Neo-Avantgarde and Culture Industry* (2000), Foster's OCTOBER colleague Benjamin Buchloh presents the relation of the neo to the historic avant-garde as 'a dialectic in which the mutually exclusive forces of artistic production and of the culture industry as its utmost opposite can still be traced in their perpetual interactions. These range from mimetic affirmation (e.g. Andy Warhol) to an ostentatious asceticism (e.g. Michael Asher).' To propose an avant-garde, then, is as Webber suggests: 'to occupy a position that must be provisional, prone to be overtaken as soon as it is marked out ... a lifting or suspension of the canonical authority of tradition.'

In relation to conceptual poetry this seems a more adequate – yet still flawed – formulation. Conceptual poets re-enact avant-gardist tropes but reframe them within the context of the literary institution and the digitised network. In this sense they are returning to the avant-garde as 'initiators of discursive practices'. However, by taking up a position on the inside of art and the outside of literature, conceptual writing is able to tactically traverse both, thus ringing in a trickster space that is resistant to full recuperation, something like a *hacker* space. Nick Thurston, himself a conceptual poet and academic, offers a compelling characterisation of the conceptual writer as funambulist. On one side of the tightrope the conceptual poet is exposed to what Thurston describes as a 'collapse into defenceless alienation that completely accepts the realism of capitalism and the obedience of literature to a business ontology'. The institution of literature presented here manifests as the Man Booker prize and the ever metastasising discourse of 'creative writing'. It is the version of literature upon which conceptual poetics – with its claim to be against expression and the 'lyric I' – presents itself as oppositional critique.

On the other side of the rope, Thurston describes 'an infinite movement against that collapse; a movement whose energy is closer [to] rave culture and computer hacking than it is to [the] "proper" autonomy of the *littérateurs*.' Where in this reading is conceptual art? The suspicion grows that the legacy of conceptualism is a paternal discourse that conceptual writing is trying to shake off.

The poet Craig Dworkin – in his short introduction to an archive of conceptual writing that he assembled for Kenneth Goldsmith's UbuWeb project – presents conceptual writing as a term the primary function of which is to evaporate genre distinctions. Conceptual writing signifies a 'theoretically based art that is independent of genre, so that a particular poem might have more in common with a particular musical score [or] sculpture than with another lyric.' Secondly, he contends that conceptual writing stands in opposition to the 'caricatured and mummified ethos of romanticism'. If romanticism is being caricatured, then Dworkin himself is responsible.

In an essay entitled 'The Fate of Echo' in the subsequent anthology AGAINST EXPRESSION (2010), Dworkin reiterates the genre-flipping intention behind the coinage – however, here the category of literature, which had not been mentioned directly in the UbuWeb essay, comes into play. Indeed Dworkin writes that the new volume is an 'inversion and expansion' of the original genre-evaporating premise:

> The inversion comes about because instead of drawing indiscriminately from various disciplines or creating a new critical environment in which to juxtapose poetry with pieces from other traditions, this volume keeps its focus – with a few deliberate exceptions – on works published or received in a literary context. Posited as literature, these works take their part in an open dialogue with the cultures, conventions, and traditions of literary institutions.

Moving the critical reception from an art context towards a literary one allows Dworkin to make a series of critical claims about conceptual writing as institutional critique. This move is made, I think, in recognition that there are problems with the theoretical and art historical claims Dworkin makes in the original online introduction. Firstly, Dworkin fails to acknowledge the genealogical inheritances that conceptual art carries within itself. The legacy of Fluxus, happenings and performance, avant-garde and concrete poetry (artists like Vito Acconci, Dan Graham and Carl Andre self-identified as poets well into the 1960s and regularly published their work in experimental poetry journals alongside New York School poets such as John Ashbery),[1] the experimental musical scores and writings of musicians such as Erik Satie, John Cage and György Ligeti, and modernist works of literature such as those of Samuel Beckett and Alain Robbe-Grillet, all have an acknowledged place in the development of conceptualism. In other words, conceptual art already contains and, to a degree, acknowledges the broad avant-garde church that led to and fed its own emergence. To make a claim for genre fluidity in such a context seems both anachronistic and redundant.

[1.] The relationship between poetry, score and performance is exemplified by this quote from Vito Acconci, published in AVALANCHE in 1972: 'My involvement with poetry was with movement on a page, the page as a field for action ... [to] use language to cover a space rather than uncover a meaning ... I consider that work a series of scores for more current work: I can consider my use of the page as a model space, a performance area in miniature.'

Further, Dworkin's characterisation of romanticism fails to acknowledge its complex relation to modernism, avant-gardism and contemporary art both poetically and philosophically. In his ANYWHERE OR NOT AT ALL (2013), Peter Osborne provides a radical and critically productive reading of Schlegel's ATHENAEUM FRAGMENTS (1798) with LeWitt's SENTENCES ON CONCEPTUAL ART (1968) that helps in thinking through the relation of romanticism to conceptual art – but also, by extension, the relation of romanticism to conceptual poetry – and which destabilises certain claims made on behalf of conceptual poetics.

Osborne sets up the reading by acknowledging that the ATHENAEUM FRAGMENTS and LeWitt's SENTENCES might appear an 'idiosyncratic and arbitrary conjunction' but appeals to Walter Benjamin's aforementioned concept of the 'dialectical image' as the 'experimental method of montage as the means of production of historical intelligibility'. As David S. Ferris writes in THE CAMBRIDGE COMPANION TO WALTER BENJAMIN (2004), 'in the dialectical image past and present meet and form a constellation only viewable from a certain position ... History no longer appears linear and progressive.' This reconfiguration of historical time Benjamin describes as 'dialectics at a standstill'. In Osborne's reading then, the FRAGMENTS and the SENTENCES produce 'an image of romanticism as conceptual art, and an image of conceptualism as romantic art'.

Osborne then clarifies that the philosophical romanticism he is referring to is a precise period of philosophical production, that in Jena in the second half of the 1790s, an era from which derive 'many of the ideas central to the understanding of modern and contemporary art ... not only the *fragment* and *project* but also the ideas of *the new*, of *collective* (*anonymous* or *pseudonymous*) *production*, of the *dissolution* of genres into an artistic process of *infinite becoming* and, finally, *the incomprehensible*.'

Here we have the central categories for an understanding of contemporary art and contemporary poetics: *the new, dissolution of genre, production*. Indeed, these are effectively the categories under which Dworkin writes 'The Fate of Echo' and they apparently emerge from 'caricatured romanticism'. Nonetheless, conceptualism and romanticism do not, on the surface, appear to be happy bedfellows. The characteristic of romanticism Dworkin really has in mind, of course, is the romanticism that represents a 'valourisation of the creative genius of artistic subjectivity'. Conceptual art and conceptual writing both pose as anti-subjectivist practices but, as Osborne writes, the appearance of opposition is misleading because 'the productive infinity of the subject has merely been withdrawn from the realisation of the work back into its *idea*.' So that Sol LeWitt's SENTENCES and the vast majority of rule-based conceptual poetry is 'made up of a particular relation of the subjective (the choice of the rule) to the objective (the mechanical process of developing the series or poem) by applying the rule.' The artist cannot become a machine: conceptual art and conceptual poetics *nuance subjectivity* but they cannot obliterate it. Here is Osborne again, writing on

LeWitt's *Sentences*, but we might replace them with any of the schematic and serialist poems produced by conceptual poets:

> It is the priority of the process over the object or result here, which is the consequence of the ontological priority of the idea of the work – the virtual infinity of possible actualisations – that LeWitt's conception of art in his *Sentences* approaches an early romantic one most closely. Each involves the dissolution of genres into an artistic process of infinite becoming, and thereby a change in the fundamental status of works from 'objects' to 'projects'.

Dworkin's desire for an anti-subjectivist art, an absolute art of the automaton, is shown to be undermined by the very thing that it sets itself up in opposition to. This was partially recognised by Goldsmith when he said, in conversation with Francisco Roman Guevara, that 'my books are tied to the notion of the author with a capital A', and Marjorie Perloff's description of conceptual writing as 'unoriginal genius' perfectly encapsulates this complex dialectical relation between romanticism and conceptualism. Ultimately, however, conceptual writing's critical positions are tactical: it takes up what it needs in the moment and on the fly. It is, as Thurston maintained, a hacker activity. When its critical claims are held up to theoretical scrutiny they tend to dissolve, a wisp of smoke.

¶ When we talk about conceptual writing we are, in a sense, talking about something historical, something already past. In his *Uncreative Writing* (2011), Kenneth Goldsmith recognises that the practices he has been utilising and proselytising have already lost something of their iconoclastic potency (if such they ever possessed). He himself now teaches 'uncreative' writing on the 'creative' writing programme at Columbia University in New York, and has also given readings and workshops at the White House, dressed in his faux-bohemian paisley suit and sporting his Ezra Pound beard. Indeed, Goldsmith's 'look' is symptomatic of conceptual writing as a whole, a re-spun, po-mo version of the avant-garde; a virtual avant-garde with a virtual politics, an opportunist discourse. When you are teaching uncreative writing strategies to Michelle Obama in the Oval Room something has gone either very wrong, or very right. Goldsmith himself would have us believe he has brought the avant-garde right into the heart of darkness, fear and loathing in Washington. It's an empty gesture.

In its zombie re-enactment of the avant-garde, conceptual writing ultimately points to a long and unfolding series of failures; the failure of the avant-garde, the failure of institutional critique, the failure of the techno-utopianism that greeted the early years of the web, the failure of a discernible politics, the failure, perhaps, of a mode of art criticism too.

It is also symbolic of another problem with the conceptual writing movement; its Warholian desire for visibility and self-promotion. Goldsmith talks up the fact that there are no stakes in poetry, there's no money: nobody is looking so we can do what we like. But people are looking. The contemporary art world has made poetry its new *cause célèbre*. FRIEZE magazine recently ran a front cover stating that 'ART HEARTS POETRY'. The embrace of the art world is double-edged: welcome to a whole new slipstream of funding, say farewell to the critical ecologies that sustained you. Sometimes, in Goldsmith's hands at least, conceptual poetry seems like a brand, a funky e-start-up trying to attract as many constituencies as possible. But really, these are surface gripes.

The real problems for conceptual writing are structural and theoretical. It is an opaque, confused discourse. It makes claims by suggesting that it stands in opposition to 'traditional' poetry with its apparently hackneyed self-expression and 'the Lyric I'. However, the strategies it inherits from conceptual art share a common root in the romanticism that it claims to oppose and anyway, as Marxist poet Keston Sutherland maintains in his 'Theses on Antisubjectivist Dogma':

> There is no such thing as 'traditional poetry' and there is no such thing as 'the Lyric I'. The use of the first person pronoun in poetry is as various and complex as the use of language itself ... Conceptual poetry does no conceptual work toward defining the 'subject' whose rejection is its principal dogma. Poetry dismissed by conceptual poets as romantic, subjective, expressive etc. often does a great deal more of that conceptual work than 'conceptual poetry' does.

This points to a recurring problem with conceptual poetry's critical claims. It fails to give adequate models of the things it claims to oppose. If this is true of poetry as a history, practice and discourse, it is also true of 'literature' as an institution. Conceptual poetry fails to give an adequate account of what 'literature' is, or at least the model of literature that it opposes. We can assume that the model proposed is a humanist, liberal, Leavisite conglomeration but this is never sufficiently articulated, and again, such a model has not been found in its pure form in literature departments since the theory wars of the seventies and eighties. It is another straw man.

Conceptual writing is defined as much by what it claims to disavow as by what it takes up, and nowhere is this more apparent than in its tortured relationship with conceptual art. In its early critical manifestations it was depicted as a continuation of conceptualism. Later it claimed to be an inversion of it. Where conceptual art was about dematerialisation, conceptual writing was about re-materialisation; where conceptual art made words to look at, conceptual poetry produced screeds of words it claimed should be ignored. But was it ever so simple? Binaries rarely are. The whole edifice rests on a series of critical misrecognitions and caricatures. If conceptual writing was anything, it was a depleted version of conceptual art masquerading as an institutional critique of a literature it could not define. A shadow of a shadow of a shadow.

Conceptual writing does point towards a problem that criticism needs to explore. What is contemporary literature? Contemporaneity is a category attended to in recent work within the field of contemporary art, as Boris Groys, Peter Osborne and Terry Smith have attempted to define the term. Future work in literature will need to centre on new categories and terms. Instead, literature seems preoccupied by the death of the book and the slow strangulation of publishing houses by the internet. It is here that perhaps literature can learn something from contemporary art about how to build liveable ecologies through self-publishing and strong theoretical responses. The broader question remains, though, of how to think about practices that do not fit within the narrow confines of the publishing industry but which retain a desire to do justice to the model of literature that Derrida articulated in 'This Strange Institution Called Literature':

> The space of literature is not only that of an instituted fiction but also a fictive institution which in principle allows one to say everything ... To say everything is [to] break out of prohibitions. To affranchise oneself in every field where law can lay down the law. The law of literature tends, in principle, to defy or lift the law. ... It is an institution which tends to overflow the institution.

OLIVER OSBORNE

XVI — XVIII

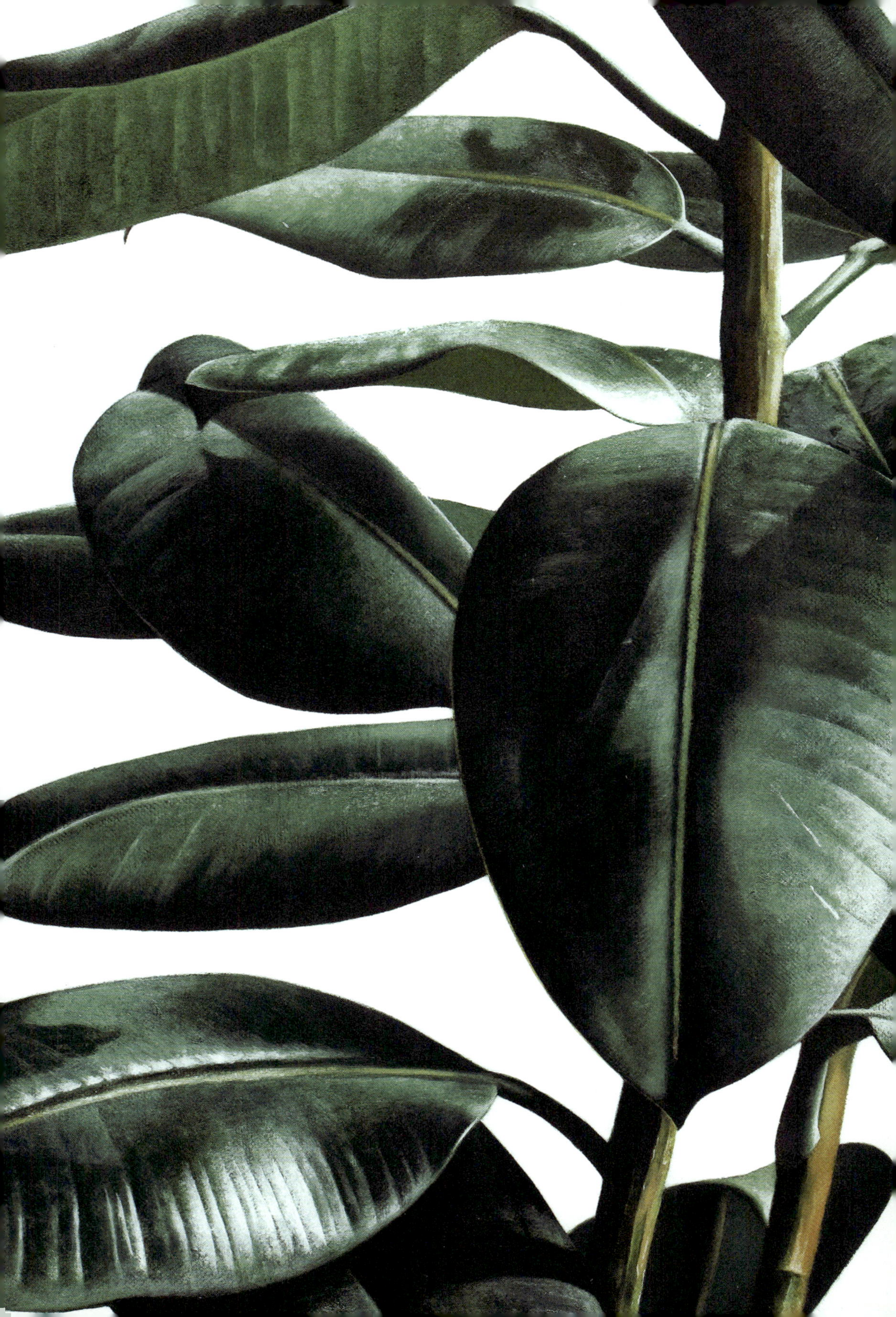

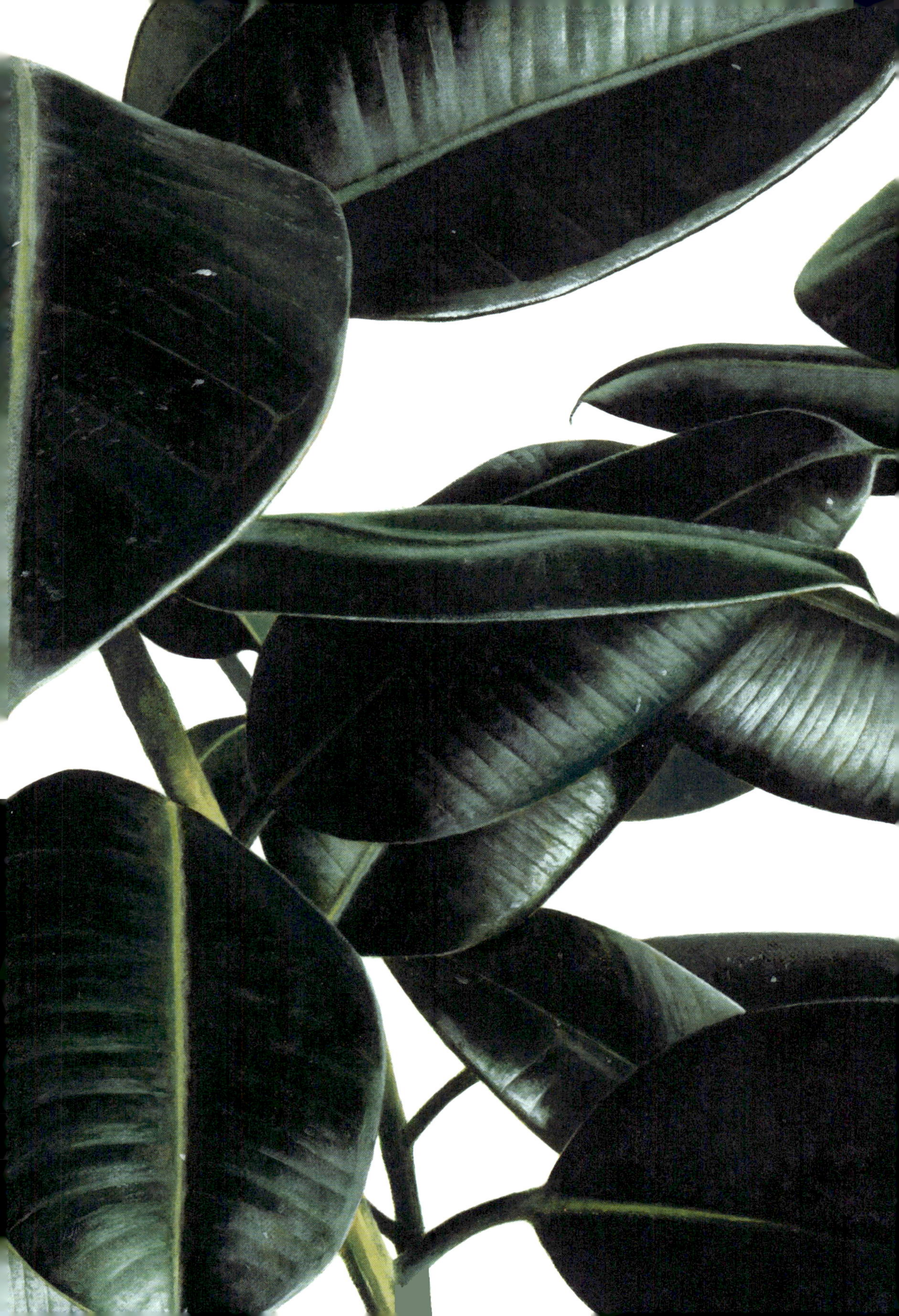

+49

He could not deny it, +49 was beautiful.
He stood at the porthole studying the ship pulsing in the light.
The craft. Black. Huge. Hanging like a lizard hibernating in oil.
Its belly intricately overlaid – dark tiny scales throwing a chrome
washed glow, soft, almost invisible; its skin translating starlight
           into ancient psalms of the spectrum.

Again the blue light shot off her stern.
Arcing wide. Drawing in before shooting out into the distance
like a beacon from a lighthouse. Every hour or so a pod emerged
from her hull, each pod identical in shape. The crafts hung beneath
+49, surrounded by the thin mist – silver pearls at first glance
           glowing with the indifference of death.

There was a deep philosophy in +49's presence.
From the quiet image he saw – he knew the horrific soughs
it threw when the blue light turned grey. The chaos before the silence.
Every thought falling away to cease. In the craft's wake – a faint
rainbow peeled off its scales. The light, a wet black slough
           beneath the wings of this unholy giant.

P

THE PROPOSAL

He watched the pink balloon rise high above the park.
His head cushioned on the mat. The raised birthmark
below his cheekbone throbbing – a red fleshy island
the shape of Uganda. On Faro's finger, bright sparks
of imprisoned sunlight burst out of a yellow diamond.

A bare cedar stood behind them, quiet like a sentinel
rooted to its post. Their eyes locked to each other's,
rheumy and red. *So if she has your grandmother's
nose – Tishani, but if she has my grandmother's, we'll
call her...* Then they came. A procession of soldiers

dragging their heels past the picnicking couple. Youths –
dazed. Heads bowed to the earth, their worn boots
scrapping over the scorched turf. An unnamed patrol.
Hawk flashes on their shoulders. *Freedom and Truth*
scrolled on dirty berets. Crude smells of coal, petrol

and creosote lingering in their wake. The old wage
of war. Lives of men and women paying the sum
that billowed and echoed in the mountains. Bombs
louder than all the waves of the oceans rocked the stage
of the world, ancient cities buried in simple tombs

> I could not open my mouth because I smelled something terrible. I heard my daughter snoring in a terrible way. When crossing to my daughter's bed, I collapsed and fell.
>
> Joseph Nkwain

Lake Nyos, Western High Plateau, Cameroon – 1986

I. FOREST MIRROR

i

When the moon's eye shifted deep over churned waters,
        forest and grassland rolled wet with nocturnal songs flowing
    white with myth, a curse from the lake's depth, an ancient breath freed to rise.
The gates had parted beneath the water, snapping back with fire from deep underworlds.
          The thunder ball exploding – rising silently. A wave
      snuffing all life in its path, its hypnotic wake too quiet
           and stark to believe, a white shroud
              from molten lungs. The faulted rock asleep in the arms of the devil's soul.

ii

And the emerald air seals the mountains' humid shadows.
        Moonlight, cool on simple paths, linking villages to the maar.
     White long-horned cattle low above black volcanic turf: hoof, dung, ancient glass.
The forest sings thick with the sorcery of the earth. The witchery of the pale sky
          turning shadows into shadows, beasts to humans, then air.
       Where harvest masks rest, millet bowls sit empty –
            all without ceremony or wine,
         the soft tongue of the moon rolling silently through these sleepy plains.

iii

Here is the altarpiece off water: the moon dissolving to milk.
         The spirit's breath. The spirit, thin and white, pale and almost whole.
    Here is the deviant priest rising to fall from the mirror's divine eye –
a heavy shade, a rushed whisper slipping off a mute's tongue.
          Each dark breath shaped with troubled promises
      turning to wire in our veins. So we slept.
           Our faith woven into the peace
        of a sleep too intimate and sweet to foresee, or ever come back from.

II. SUBUM

In a flat effortless way, the body gives into the freefall.
The eyes calmly close. Each wet collapse robbed of grace.
Pots and crockery ring loud, the steel-clang – communal.
Windows blacken. Embers suffocate in the fireplace.

Door to door, ugly snores. Guttural gasps, rubber breaths
above mist-beaded floors where sweating women stood
locked stiff above fufu pots – the air drawing their blood
black, the moon's billowing veil ushering in their death.

Then, the jagged starry absence echoed loud with light,
each village poisoned by the lake's secret, the tall grass-
fields bowing where scythes had sparkled with the rite
of life – where harvest flutes spindled out notes of glass,

spinning the air with rain falling like grief into the maar.
The dead were dead. And the hours recoiled as a red sun
rose silently above the compound. The steaming dawn
thinning out, rising dryly beneath the sky's terrible stare.

III. RÊVES. MUSIQUE.

In this dream
        we are loosely rising,
our feathered shadows unable to wake,
            knotted to the uptake like dew
on the rise off the dawn's tongue,
              a music envisioned by air.
        The moon will sing,
and the spirit will simmer somewhere,
              leaving us with a breath of wings
                  sprayed with fiery phlegm.
            In this dream we are rising through the darkest ascent
          where our screams know nothing of our faith in sleep,
                our minds neither believing in,
                    nor questioning,
                      breath.

IV. RETURNING

i

When the rain comes, the flies go
with that heavy, sickening noise
that rings wild over tangled limbs –
pale wine from blisters and burns
blessed black by hoards suckling
eagerly from the dead's swollen
eyes. Cavernous jaws, once busy
with the dark orchestral echoes of
flies now stand brimmed with water.
This rain flushes out odours and
cleanses split flesh. Thick sheets
of loud saturated air shroud each
veiled dawn with rushed dreams
washing fast through lives almost
broken by the *Bad Lake's* curse –
a wall of wet light bridging heaven
and earth with legends of ancestry
and myth. When the rain comes,
it sings off thatch – sings off tin.
Songs sung over body and earth,
the eternal rite of new beginnings.

Through dense canopies, rain breaks. The air sluiced with sound.
    Rivers feed miniature tributaries veined over mud-cracked ground.
Streams rumble red, busy with dead insects and leaves flushed out with the current.
        Then silence composes vistas and valleys, rolling hills.
            The air flushed with death slipping wet over slippery paths.

ii

Sun over moon recycles the moon over the sun. Empty huts.
    A quietness lingers in the air with the bitter taste of human salts,
the faint smell of abandonment hovers flat where doors crumble beneath lintels
        sagging into shadows
    where the dead once stood, where
            the dead now sing in the constant hold of our hearts.
  Sun over moon. Bitter salt of the heart.
           Enter now.

iii

"First things first: I am neither
shadow nor words – only flesh
could fill these bundled folds of
grief, these torn faded clothes
you once loved, that now make
me question what I must look
like now. Your daughter says
I slip into the night and sing
your name when I'm asleep –
I say that's bullshit. She's never
met you. And I know only grief
from these hills, these red hills
painted wild with absences
I could never have expected.
Now every thought fails the old
practices of this deserted place,
this house, these rituals of loss
sweet in the ache of time falling
sweet off the rote of each breath.
The years have aged me – hoary,
brittle boned. Walking up from
the valley, dawn rose, dew bells
dripping off blades of grass, the
grass sharp at my skin, cutting
shins scarred as my daughter's

*shins now – mine bleeding less.
And I return because I am lost,
return for the shadowed sunrise,
the shadowed dusk. And walking,
I am afraid, and remember your
fingers slipping neatly into mine,
the red broken road burning with
the sun behind us, burning with
youthful promise. Who we were
then was the mystery to unfold
and draw us back into a dream
only I would wake from, silence
ringing heavy and loud, heavy,
and loud... Soft pulses of sunlight
drip through rotting thatch, ant
 mounds pregnant with life stand
pressed into the walls. And I am
here, alone, exhausted by chance,
alone with a daughter who dreams
of you, but will never know who
you are. We stand by the door.
And I set my knee to the ground.
My eyes lost in the empty hearth."*

V.

And if there was an eve of something,
                              it was in how the sun set.
                                       The air liquid and quiet.
And if there was a quiet fold in the dark,
                              it came as the way things were. The way children cried.
                                             The way the moon rose.
                                             The lake silver without a pulse.

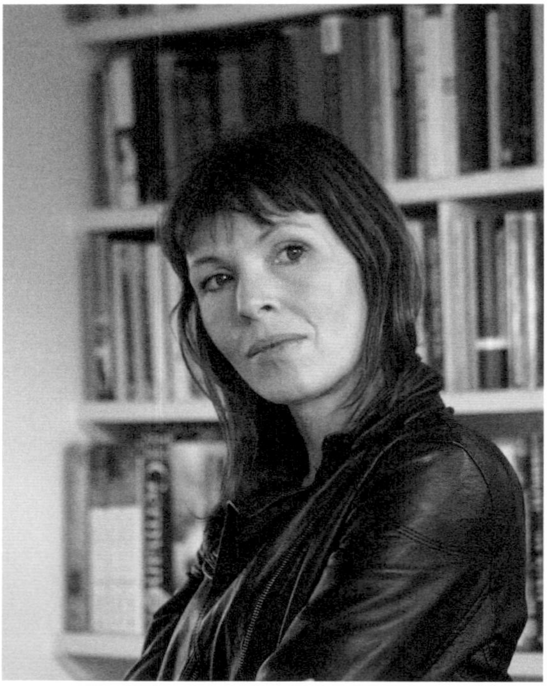

INTERVIEW

with

RACHEL CUSK

IN RACHEL CUSK'S EIGHTH novel, OUTLINE, a character named Anne, who has just suffered a violent attack, explains why she considers it important to speak about her experience. 'If people were silent about the things that had happened to them,' she asks, 'was something not being betrayed, even if only the version of themselves that had experienced them?' Cusk's work – fiction and non-fiction – is imbued with the same defiant honesty to which her characters aspire. Her non-fiction books – especially AFTERMATH, a raw, elliptical response to her 2009 divorce, and A LIFE'S WORK, a memoir about the bewilderment of first-time motherhood – have attracted vitriol from readers who balk at the candour with which she writes about personal subjects; praise from those who admire her determination to question herself, her refusal to conform to established female roles.

Cusk's career has, on paper, been conventional and glittering. Her 1993 debut, SAVING AGNES, won the Whitbread First Novel Award when Cusk, like her characters, was fresh from university; her third novel, the Wodehouse-esque comedy of manners THE COUNTRY LIFE, earned the Somerset Maugham Award. She was named one of Granta's Best of Young British Novelists in 2003, and her latest novel, OUTLINE, was shortlisted for the Bailey's and Folio prizes; soon after we meet, its cover could be found adorning posters on the tube. Her work seems to follow the trajectory of a life: four years on from A LIFE'S WORK, Orange Prize-shortlisted ARLINGTON PARK (2005) featured an array of desperate housewives, suburban mothers who contemplate child-murder as they negotiate coffee-mornings and dinner parties. In THE BRADSHAW VARIATIONS (2009), Tonie has had enough, and goes back to work, guiltily leaving her husband at home with their daughter. By OUTLINE, the protagonist is divorced, her children grown: Faye is in Athens to teach a creative writing course, mirroring the details of a British Council tour Cusk herself embarked on in 2012. Far from being self-revelatory, Faye is an unknowable narrator, her name only revealed towards the novel's end: OUTLINE accumulates the stories she hears from the people she encounters – her neighbour on the plane, her lunch companion, her students – but never tells her own.

Many of Cusk's female characters find themselves listening rather than talking; Cusk, however, having gained a reputation as a chronicler of the personal, is constantly pressed to talk about herself, yet simultaneously chastised for doing so. A review of AFTERMATH criticised the book for not revealing enough juicy details about the divorce. Indignant – and imperceptive – reviews of A LIFE'S WORK accused her of hating her children. Her retaliation is subtle and satirical: she is currently writing a version of Euripides's MEDEA for the Almeida Theatre. We met in an airy North London gastropub the morning after the general election; amid the chaos – of the country and of her home, beset by builders – she was measured and thoughtful, eloquent in her answers.

Q. THE WHITE REVIEW — Since so much of your work deals with personal experience, and your fiction is rooted in a very recognisable reality, I'd like first to ask you about what you refer to in AFTERMATH as 'the feminist principle of autobiographical writing'.

A. RACHEL CUSK — Every time I read a review of my own work – which I don't very often – it seems to place it in a new genre of memoir writing, along with Karl Ove Knausgaard et al, which in fact isn't new – people have been doing it forever. But what Knausgaard is doing is distinct from the memoir that documents the extraordinariness of a particular life – it's the account of ordinary experience, which has arisen over the long painful process of post-modernism. It's burst out of the apparatus of fiction, which is something that's in danger of becoming more and more to do with fantasy. The contemporary novel is a reality within a reality, in that people write novels in which their ideas about character and the way things happen come from other manufactured narratives. I don't think anyone can even remember what authenticity is, now. And in the end, Knausgaard says the same thing: I'm looking in the mirror and there I am. I don't know whether that is valuable in and of itself. My point about – if not feminism then femininity, womanhood – is that it remains inherently interesting because it remains inherently radical, because women haven't finished evolving. They're still a work in progress, and there is always an inherent radicalism, a principle to a woman writing about her own life.

Q. THE WHITE REVIEW — Perhaps because women's lives are lived so much within dominant cultural scripts and preassigned roles, there's a certain form imposed on a woman's life which is outside herself.

A. RACHEL CUSK — The thing that is still alive in letters and in life is lying and misrepresentation and consensus, and saying everything's great when it's not, or saying this is what you want when you don't. That's still something that happens in lived experience: the female self, the female individual, is at odds in some way with the female group in terms of belonging, truth, ownership.

Q. THE WHITE REVIEW — Do you see Knausgaard as a feminist writer? A lot of what he writes about the mundanity of everyday life with young children reminds me of your work – the frustration of the mothers in ARLINGTON PARK, locked in a cycle of school runs and coffee mornings, for example.

A. RACHEL CUSK — I think he's a nihilist. And it's just that he's Norwegian. There's a kind of Scandiwegian thing that looking after the children if you're a bloke isn't such a big deal. That's his reality, that's pretty normal where he comes from. And it's strange for us to read a man writing like that about children because we're so gendered and Victorian.

American female literary critics have always said that men write well about domesticity. Richard Yates, John Updike – those people have written about domestic relationships more confidently than women have. Women think that families are toxic material, that it's something people shouldn't use, that to be successful you have to subscribe to male values, which are apparently anti-domestic. When I wrote A LIFE'S WORK I remember very much being deep in the grip of that assumption and thinking I couldn't possibly write about motherhood. There was one life that I lived; on the other hand, I wondered what I was going to write about.

Q. THE WHITE REVIEW — It is the problem Virginia Woolf writes about in A ROOM OF

ONE'S OWN: 'This is an important book, the critic assumes, because it deals with war. This is an insignificant book because it deals with the feelings of women in a drawing room.'

A. RACHEL CUSK — Yes. If a woman were to write about the Napoleonic Wars I'm sure she would feel absolutely secure and safe, but the terror of writing about women's experience is absolutely there. I don't think a man feels brave in writing about domesticity. He's not conditioned either way, and if that's what he wants to write about that's what he'll write about.

Q. THE WHITE REVIEW — Do you feel politicised as a feminist writer?

A. RACHEL CUSK — Yes. That's why I do what I do. That's why I don't write historical novels about the First World War.

Q. THE WHITE REVIEW — Are you engaged in feminist politics, or activism?

A. RACHEL CUSK — No. I suppose OUTLINE was true to myself: I don't want to exist as an exterior person in the world. I really like writing, and increasingly I'll become less visible. I was very young when I was first published, and I don't know why my writing career has involved so much scrutiny. I mean, I am quite self-exposing but not in a look-at-me, attention-seeking way. I just use myself as the material and, given that it hasn't sold very many books, I want no more of that exposure.

Q. THE WHITE REVIEW — The word 'authenticity' recurs in your work. Thomas in THE BRADSHAW VARIATIONS and Christine in ARLINGTON PARK both use it when they're describing the difficulty they have in understanding themselves as individuals within the context of their families. Similarly, in OUTLINE Faye says, 'I wasn't sure it was possible, in marriage, to know what you actually were, or indeed to separate what you were from what you had become through the other person.'

A. RACHEL CUSK — It has to do with how to find one's selfhood within established forms of living created by other people, particularly when enacting social roles that pre-exist. In my work, authenticity is something that happens at a structural level, a sentence level. I try to write sentences that aren't the product of sentences written by other people, or indeed cultural perceptions – I try to find a true phrase or observation. In a sense it's the same quest as trying to uncover why people feel false or unreal. They feel unreal because they are at a great distance from the last time they felt real, which very often is childhood, or youth.

Q. THE WHITE REVIEW — You've used the word 'authenticity' of Knausgaard too, when describing the way he portrays narrative's distance from reality as a pre-eminently personal, rather than artistic, crisis. 'He shows us, by the route of life, that there is no story, and in so doing he finds, at last, authenticity. For that alone, this deserves to be called perhaps the most significant literary enterprise of our times.'

A. RACHEL CUSK — I wonder whether Knausgaard's authenticity becomes inauthentic at some point across the six volumes, because he's created a formula. I'm writing a sequel to OUTLINE, and the most important thing about that sequel will be to break the form that I'm using and take it somewhere else.

Q. THE WHITE REVIEW — How would that work?

A. RACHEL CUSK — I don't know yet. I always have read a lot of Greek drama, but at the moment I'm up to my neck in it. The thing that struck me, not so much about Euripides but very much about Aeschylus, is how language in these dramas is absolutely an event, it's absolutely an object, it's as real and concrete as a table. That relationship between objects and language creates the possibility of violence. The only way that you could ever inspire change in a piece of writing is by citing that root. That's as far as I've got in my head: how would you actually break through what you're doing and permit it to become something else?

Q. THE WHITE REVIEW — You've said you suffered a 'creative death' after *AFTERMATH* – did *OUTLINE* stem from a need to find a new form for the novel?

A. RACHEL CUSK — I suppose it was finding a form that could represent the particular truth of what I had to say at that moment in time. It was amazingly difficult to think of that, because it's about the opposite of what would ever make you write a novel.

Q. THE WHITE REVIEW — What would that be?

A. RACHEL CUSK — Abundance. The desire to externalise yourself, and put yourself into space. That kind of negative equity – you see it in plenty of modern novels. Camus is the person who is at the back of all of this. There are plenty of novels that take on this economical style in order to signal very plainly that 'the people here are alienated and this is about bleakness'. That really was not what I wanted to say, I didn't want bleak. This isn't necessarily a bleak book, it's about what life becomes when you move beyond its established or recognisable forms for living, and, I suppose, what it might become.

In *OUTLINE* I only get as far as the very first thing, a new kind of reality which is only surface. That's the only thing you can read, the surface – there's no prior knowledge, there's no assumption. In the end, that might become migration into completely wild and experimental ways of being, acting in an unconditioned, unfettered way. The sequel's going to have a lot more sex in it. 'Authenticity' – you can use that word in the context of female sexuality.

Q. THE WHITE REVIEW — Is the idea of woman as 'outline', as the 'corresponding negative' to man (as embodied in Faye and Anne) associated with the traditional, hierarchical conception of sexuality, wherein women are perceived as blank slates for men's fantasies? Anne considers her husband her 'creator', and without him she finds herself without 'a native language of self'.

A. RACHEL CUSK — The question is, what reality would they enact if they were actors? How is she, Faye, going to create reality rather than just receive it? At some point, because she's going to live, the question for the next book is whether having lost your belief in reality as a quasi-narrative – we all have that belief, it's what gets us out of bed in the morning – whether you can ever believe in it again sufficiently to care. So that's book two.

Q. THE WHITE REVIEW — When she's talking about her travels, Angeliki, the successful novelist in *OUTLINE*, tells Faye, 'Being there without my husband caused me to feel, in an entirely new way, what I actually am.' Is Angeliki's finding her creativity or authenticity without her husband in any way a reflection of your feelings as a writer?

A. RACHEL CUSK — Well, no. It's an interesting moment in female development, which I must have had at some point. To become a writer basically means you're weird. You can have an extremely detailed grasp of certain aspects of living and then other things are left totally untouched. Writing is innocence, in a way.

That's something that happens to women often as adults, in their careers, that maybe they regain some innocence by having children and being out of the world and then realising that they can become important again. I think that's what Angeliki is striving for. For me that process is never quite like that, but in female life, particularly if it includes children and marriage, there are so many cycles of loss of worldliness and loss of interaction with the outside followed by cycles of regaining that and feeling powerful. So, feeling weak and feeling powerful: that's what Angeliki is saying.

Q. THE WHITE REVIEW — She says that after being away from them because of illness, she sees her husband and child with greater objectivity.
A. RACHEL CUSK — Yes, and they don't need her. Their needing her was what gave her a sense of purpose.

Q. THE WHITE REVIEW — Is that sense of objectivity related to Faye's desire for objectivity in the stories she hears?
A. RACHEL CUSK — No, she's in a far distant place, really. What she's hearing in Angeliki's and in all the others' stories, except for Paniotis who doesn't have this quality, is people who are still in the story. She is just on the other side of that, saying 'I don't believe in it any more.' Other people can be very close to that line, they can start to see that they're moving in and out of a constructed narrative, as their story of self and resistance, but she is absolutely out of it, she's gone over that line and is out of it.

Q. THE WHITE REVIEW — Do you see Angeliki as counterpoint to some of the wives in your previous novels? I'm thinking of Claudia from *The Bradshaw Variations*, the archetypal tragic female artist, who is desperate to get to her studio at the bottom of her garden but never makes it – it's implied that her children are her only creative outlet, which is something Angeliki, who is also both a mother and an artist, transcends.
A. RACHEL CUSK — She's the next evolution of the Claudia person. She is the expressive woman, whose expression nonetheless has to take very, very secure and recognisable forms, and has to be recognised.

Q. THE WHITE REVIEW — She's 'the famous feminist writer'.
A. RACHEL CUSK — This is where we're at with womanhood; there has to be a tangible success or a tangible bit of status. That reality has to be very stable. One of the things I have noticed in my many years of being a writer and hanging around a bit in the world of writers, is how a lot of male writers set great store by their public successes. That was all taken extremely seriously, whereas I totally don't ever care. It's sort of self-importance I suppose – and I'm not saying male writers are self-important, it's just that I remember noticing that those people cared more, and maybe it's that they cared more about themselves than I do. Those things meant more to them, those forms of public recognition or reality. Women have caught up with that, and that's what I'm describing in Angeliki, the person who can say, 'I'm becoming this and I can see what I am because it's reflected. If I didn't have those things I don't know who I would be.'

Q. THE WHITE REVIEW — Is that 'authentic'?
A. RACHEL CUSK — No, not at all. That's the whole point about the Angeliki story. And at the end Faye and Paniotis have a conversation in which Faye says, well I've met her before

and she didn't even remember, and Paniotis says that wasn't her, that was a different person, this Angeliki has never met you.

Q. THE WHITE REVIEW —— So her struggle is to combine her public and private selves? It's a struggle which so many of your characters embody, but the ones who get furthest in subverting it — like Tonie, and you yourself as described in *Aftermath* — feel uncomfortable, 'unsexed', like 'hermaphrodites', or the 'self-hating transvestite'. Tonie doesn't want to define herself through her husband; she wants 'her own conflict of female and male, her own synthesis'. There's this idea that women have to take on traditionally male values to succeed, but does this come at the cost of their identity as women?

A. RACHEL CUSK —— I refuse to subscribe to those values, even though my economic, practical life has been very male: I've never been financially supported by anyone, I've always paid for my own family and been the main breadwinner, so it's a very 'male' set of things that I'm doing.

Q. THE WHITE REVIEW —— But women who do 'male' things are still expected to reconcile this with some notion of traditional femininity.

A. RACHEL CUSK —— Yes. I don't think the woman writer is any different from the woman anything, in that the apparent struggle for women is to live equality in their private lives, and I'd say the vast majority fail to do that because it is so hard to do, and then what happens is that you feel trapped and dependent. If I translate that into a world of writing, I've always imagined that if I didn't have to worry about bills and a mortgage and children's shoes, strangely, I would write poetry. The novel is such a workhorse, it's so absolutely, intimately connected to how we order our life, and form. So I imagine that in that life of freedom from care I would write poetry.

Q. THE WHITE REVIEW —— In *Arlington Park* the women conform in public, as they feel they have to, and play the role of wife and mother, but in private each of them is in turmoil.

A. RACHEL CUSK —— That's what I mean about female identity being radical, that dissonance between interior life and exterior appearance. That is still interesting, although it's becoming slightly less interesting, in that sometimes I see the world of mothers at the school gate, and I think, is there any way out of this other than aspiration, other than becoming more confident and more consumerist and looking better and having nicer things at the school gate?

Q. THE WHITE REVIEW —— *Outline* could be read as an annihilation of that. We don't know what Faye looks like, what she has.

A. RACHEL CUSK —— No. Those sentences would not be written — it's a very interesting experience having thought about this form, and it really taught me how to write it. Simply, there were a lot of things that just could not be expressed in that. What is a woman without the description of those things? And I suppose for most people that makes it a very, very difficult book to read. There's none of that titillation.

Q. THE WHITE REVIEW —— Your writing is very much located in place — suburbia, the country, Athens — even houses are evoked with personality. Is this interest in where your characters live, and contextualising their lives within their surroundings, to do with ideas of authenticity and self-definition?

A. RACHEL CUSK —— My upbringing was relatively itinerant. I grew up in America, moved here and was sent to boarding school, and my parents moved house incessantly. They were also great investors in the status of houses and grandeur. We were never sure what it was that made us, us. Was it us, or was it this thing? So those issues loomed large in my life. It would be nice to not think that way.

Q. THE WHITE REVIEW — Your books often feature itinerant characters – lodgers, au pairs, people coming into the main characters' lives from outside.

A. RACHEL CUSK — It tends to triangulate. You have a ball in a game of tennis, it allows dynamism in established relationships, and that perspective is one that I'm always in quasi-identification with anyway, the person who doesn't belong in the house, or doesn't belong in the relationship. That feels like me. When I was learning how to write, I realised that if I introduced that person, that would move and things would happen and suddenly it was all OK, and it was that perspective that liberated things and made them not flat any more.

Q. THE WHITE REVIEW — In the final chapter of *Aftermath* you write about your own divorce from the perspective of your lodger.

A. RACHEL CUSK — That was a truly bleak bit of counterpoint, that was me using that method to shoot myself in the head, I guess.

Q. THE WHITE REVIEW — Greek tragedy pervades a lot of your writing: the stories of Clytemnestra and Antigone are told in *Aftermath*, for example. Where does this interest come from?

A. RACHEL CUSK — I started reading those things in my early thirties. *The Odyssey* was the first Greek thing I read, and I found this literature that was not founded in Judeo-Christian reality so amazing. I had an extremely conservative upbringing and it was very, very hard for me to find any unconventionality in myself – well, not in myself, but to relate internal chaos to anything that might actually manifest itself as some way of living. Growing up I was internally chaotic and here was this absolutely rigid outside world that I couldn't translate myself into, and fell foul of, and was judged by, and disapproved of in. The first real liberation came with reading Freud and becoming interested in psychoanalytical writing. Freud is such a great critic, and his commentaries brought me to Greek literature. And that was a whole new way of understanding living.

Q. THE WHITE REVIEW — Particularly a new way of understanding female selfhood, through Clytemnestra, Medea, Antigone?

A. RACHEL CUSK — I suppose it's the idea of those totally emotionally violent people, the scheme of personality that could be dramatised by them. That's Freud's classic concept of it.

Q. THE WHITE REVIEW — Does this heightened emotional violence have something to do with the form of Greek drama? By convention, violent action had to take place offstage, which left language as the only means of conveying horror.

A. RACHEL CUSK — It's something that the novel should take as law, that things have to happen offstage. It's been interesting writing *Medea* around that idea of telling, because the novel has gone so far down the road of showing, and the showing is so inauthentic. Very often it becomes telling and showing, which is fantasy. So the thing that I've wrestled with in *Medea* is the violence, although it isn't shown. To me, that has to exist in a world of equivalence. Because otherwise it's a play about a really, really rare person, someone who kills their children. It's a curiosity, and that can't be right.

Q. THE WHITE REVIEW — This idea of things happening offstage seems relevant to OUTLINE, where characters speak rather than act and the reader is left to piece together the narrator's own situation very gradually, and particularly to AFTERMATH, where the story of the divorce itself, which spurs the book, is never told. How do you decide how confessional to be, as an autobiographical writer?

A. RACHEL CUSK — It's a real limitation, because this is such new terrain, and there are issues about who owns reality, who owns the story, what are you allowed to say about John over there, and I still don't know the answer to that. I've been reading Emmanuel Carrère's LIMONOV and it's good, and I can't bear the idea of googling things, so I don't really know how much of what he's talking about is fact. So maybe you just have to be absolutely unrepentant, as Knausgaard is. There's a line in LIMONOV about Limonov becoming a writer, and Carrère says something like, 'there are only two ways to be a memoirist.' I can't remember what the first one was, but the other was, 'if you mention somebody, give their name and address'. I really like that idea.

Q. THE WHITE REVIEW — Perhaps it's a question of objectivity, which in some ways the form of OUTLINE is striving for. Faye edits and corrects the stories she hears, critiquing the lack of objectivity in the storytellers she meets – she doesn't believe in the character of her neighbour's second wife, for example. Is that observational role, interpreting people's lives like a novel, an accurate representation of the process of a realist writer?

A. RACHEL CUSK — Yes, well, the process of writing. That's how she understands and can tell whether things are true or not, whether they take a convincing form, and her model for that form is all to do with writing. And the students' stories, which they speak – she elicits from them things that are recognisably true.

Q. THE WHITE REVIEW — One student sees 'the tendency to fictionalise our own experiences as positively dangerous'. Another, Cassandra, complains that she's not learning to write because she's not using her imagination. The clear inference is that Faye has taught them how to tell the truth, and that's what people need from writing. Is Faye's creative writing tuition anything like the way you teach creative writing?

A. RACHEL CUSK — Probably!

Q. THE WHITE REVIEW — Do you enjoy teaching?

A. RACHEL CUSK — I have enjoyed it very much, but I'm on long leave from that, I want to do my own work now. I did eight years or so of teaching. In the end so many writers find the same thing, that they really enjoy teaching but not the institution – inevitably, the whole reason you became a writer is that you didn't want to participate in the bureaucratic style of work. Form-filling has to happen, I guess. That's the inbuilt obsolescence of teaching creative writing, which in itself is not a very creative thing to do.

Q. THE WHITE REVIEW — Going back to Freud, there are a lot of dreams in your books.

A. RACHEL CUSK — Yeah, although it's so boring when people tell you about their dreams, I assume it's boring when people write about their dreams.

Q. THE WHITE REVIEW — Melete's dream in OUTLINE is very Freudian. These women are trying to get into the opera, but their entrance is blocked by a growing pile of sanitary towels. It's the perfect image for the stunting of female creativity.

A. RACHEL CUSK — That's a good dream. And Juliet and the cockroach coming out of her head is another good one. No, I mean, I don't dream much, but I have had extremely violent dreams.

Q. THE WHITE REVIEW — Were those your own dreams?

A. RACHEL CUSK — The cockroach one definitely was. I can't remember the other one.

Q. THE WHITE REVIEW — In your book THE LUCKY ONES, Serena says: 'I'm angry about men, marriage, children, I don't know, everything.' Do you write from a position of anger? Is emotion an authentic position to write from?

A. RACHEL CUSK — My position changes, has changed an awful lot, and I suppose I see myself encroaching on a goal, and anger might have been one stage that I've passed through to try and get there. The things that I would be angry about now would be very different from those things.

Q. THE WHITE REVIEW — What would those be?

A. RACHEL CUSK — I'm not sure I can put it into words. I suppose violence done by people blindly enacting themselves. I object to untransfigured selfhood, so using one's self as your battering ram, or anything, caring, I suppose, on that basis, and pursuing your interests on that basis. I've just become very sensitive to that, and more appreciative of self-sacrifice and smallness and humility. I suppose it's having been really bullied and bashed over the head. That makes me angry.

Q. THE WHITE REVIEW — Your writing is so observational, and THE COUNTRY LIFE, in particular, so perfectly captures the nuances of social awkwardness. Do you keep a journal of things you overhear? How do you write?

A. RACHEL CUSK — Well, I think. I think for a very, very, very, very long time, and then I look around at reality and then I try and fit those two things together. I write notes. Once I've got an idea for something I'll usually write a set of notes in that moment because otherwise I'll forget, but that's not content, that's very much form. I guess the idea of amassing highlights from things I heard on the bus is something I don't go in for, because that's not what happens when you leave your house. Sometimes you sit on the bus and nobody says anything interesting and sometimes they do, so I wouldn't want to write a book in which everything's pitched that high. The content comes to me while I'm writing, I just take what's available and chuck it in.

Q. THE WHITE REVIEW — Do you go through a lot of drafts?

A. RACHEL CUSK — No. I don't change anything. Well, I can think about it, often I do think about it for two or three years. When I'm ready to write it, I've written it, I know everything about it. It's a horrible process: most of the time I'm thinking 'what am I meant to be doing?' And then for six weeks I'm writing 5,000 words a day.

Q. THE WHITE REVIEW — Have you already thought about the third volume in the OUTLINE trilogy?

A. RACHEL CUSK — It's about the discovery of peace.

FRANCESCA WADE, MAY 2015

BEETLE

BY

JOANNA KAVENNA

SKITAFLIT, DAY 49

704 *Dawn Breaks above the grey-dusted grey-fronted houses*
903 *Well the office is looking just lovely today...*
916 *Crazy Katy has stolen my pencils again*
918 *Actually she is denying all knowledge of my pencils*
920 *Still, who else would have stolen a perfectly good set of pencils? Who?*
922 *Crazy Katy writes,* I know you're writing about me. If I want to I'll go and find it. *I say, fine, go and find it, whatever*
924 *Crazy Katy says,* I won't bother, it's too pathetic. *But of course she'll look anyway*

1100 *Mother Mary and the blessed saints, that was a long meeting...meeting...meeting...*
1105 *This morning I had three meeting meeting meeting and tomorrow I have seven meeting meeting meeting meeting meeting meeting meeting*
1109 *During the rest of my working life I will have 45,000 meeting meeting meeting meeting meeting meeting*
1454 *A pause during which I was seized by a mild bout of complete and utter futility but I think it's passed at least for the time being...*
1457 *At least for now...*
1516 *If a ten tonne truck crashes into us*
1517 *To die by your side, the pleasure the privilege is mine*
1519 *I don't mean by your side, Crazy Katy, not yours – if you're looking, which I know you are*
1523 *There is a light that never goes out*
1526 *I don't know, perhaps it could be an allegory for faith or hope or something but perhaps it could just mean:*
1527 *There is a light that never goes out...*
1735 *Thank Christ. I am going home.*

CYN23, DAY 49

901 *Oh do not ask me what I am*
902 *I know what I am*
903 *I am human I am dynamite*

MANNATING, DAY 49

1335 *Gorgons awake, I have lost my charger*
1405 *If it all goes black, it really all goes black*
1430 *So I have developed a new sense of the temporal continuum*
1445 *and instead of going forwards I am now going sideways*
1446 *Crabwise.*
1501 *So in fact these progressions by minute by minute by minute*
1504 *are not happening in a linear forwards motion but are going along to the side – edging –*
1510 *and instead of us proceeding onwards to some destination*
1511 *we are in fact edging out of the frame – the frame being I suppose mortal existence*
1512 *and the frame being in this spatio-philosophical paradigm a rectangular shape*
1513 *and us moving from one side to another...*
1514 *each one of us...*
1518 *are you following?*
(view conversation)
1528 *I didn't ask you to agree, I just asked you to listen*
1530 *or not, depending on how you feel. No one should feel obliged, of course...*
1533 *Enough obligations on our time, I know, I know how you feel*
(view conversation)
1535 *Anyway, before I was rudely interrupted by some pile of work-related total garbage*
1547 *I was saying...I was saying...Oh and I was saying...*
1549 *Are you going left to right, across the frame?*
1550 *I mean, do some of us go left-right and some go right-left?*
1551 *or is it pusillanimous to assume the frame must go one way or the other?*
1554 *Left/right right/left – perhaps such concerns in this respect are fundamentally trivial?*
1556 *Perhaps the frame is spinning on a spot, ah then, ah then the frame must be 3D because we are within it?*
1602 *The frame must be a form of space, a spatial manifestation which is somehow flat and not flat at the same time?*
1612 *Perhaps I have lost myself...*
1615 *If the theorist cannot follow his own theory, then what can be done?*
1617 *Perhaps I'll become world famous?*

1619 The ellipses in my own theory, the moments at which it falls into complete and utter nonsense...
1623 ...will make my name entirely?
1624 Saved! By my own incoherence and obscurity! Saved!

1845 I don't think the world is quite ready for my theory
1854 Alright Robert, you're not ready...
(view conversation)
1902 I understand you're not ready, nor do you want to be ready
1903 nor do you regard a state of readiness for my theory as a desirable state to find yourself in at all.
1905 But you are just one person...

1930 Oh well, I'd better stay in tonight and work on my great Theory
1940 Cancel everything...cancel everyone...
1942 ...That didn't take long...

2010 I mustn't get distracted...
2014 No one distract me!
2015 No one!
(view conversation)
2016 You mean it sounded like, No one, distract me...Like a request?
2018 No one, all you no ones, distract me! Please!

2225 So, I have crawled and crept again, across another section of my frame
2230 I'm sticking with this...
2245 No, no I'm not. I'm taking a break...

0245 Ok, that was a bad idea. Vicky was drunk already, and she's never kind when she's drunk
(View conversation)
0255 Really Vicky, you know you're not.
0300 And the same to you, honey...
0310 In this section of the frame the sky is dark,
0312 the stars are out, a billion stars, but they are even they are in the frame
0314 the whole thing everything I see is in the frame
0315 beyond the frame lies – what the hell...? Who knows?
0316 That's the stuff that gets you in the dead of the night
0319 but the frame within the frame itself – well that's everything

0320 *Everything I know and everything anyone knows*
0322 *and everything they pretend to know and everything I pretend to know*
0325 *That sort of everything –*
0345 *Well, it's been a long day*
0355 *Frankly it's not every day you develop a brand new theory of human life*
0400 *To whoever, goodnight...*

I lack expertise in most things, and find many aspects of ordinary life virtually unintelligible. Yet I know a lot about the Twitter 'tell'.

At Beetle we specialise in preemptive emotional analysis. You can derive a great deal from a simple tweet, if you read it carefully. The 'tell' is the significant anomaly, the crackle on the wire, the hint that something is not quite right. If something's not quite right, then we want to help.

Reading the 'tell' is a delicate business. Tweets are an unmediated form; they come straight from the unconscious, fired from below. A tweet is not like a piece of journalism. Layers of arbitration lie between a news article and a reader. Yet a tweet is HERE, suddenly, where nothing was before –
No forethought, and very little conscious control –
Ideas flickering like flames –
Unscripted, inner lives –
Tweet by tweet –

My cases tweet as Skitaflit, Cyn23 and Mannating. Their real names are Saskia Flint, Cynthia Scott and Andy Mann.

We're like Twitter Samaritans, only people don't come to us. They don't really know about us, it's not that sort of thing. Instead, we watch them, to check they're OK. If people are OK, society is OK.

Friendly bacteria, that's what my bosses say. We purge and cleanse, we don't infect.

The Beetle data machines are insanely fast, of course, and can process data more swiftly than you or I. No one, no human, can compete with them when it comes to filing words away, slotting preferences into manufactured taxonomies. However, the Beetle machines lack any real awareness of tone. They allocate, they reapportion, yet they cannot discern when someone is uneasy, off-colour, or well-nigh crazy. The machines approach us through our superficial qualities: which car we drive, where we go on Saturdays, how many pairs of shoes we buy each year. They are incapable of assessing delicate shifts in attitude, or feeling; they can only legislate for so many variables.

Take my apartment. I work there each day, in my grimy bedroom, in a grey-drab part of Brooklyn. I spend my days staring out of the window, looking at strangers passing by. That's a curious sight, and it never gets dull. You learn how people are ritual, how they forge patterns of resistance even as they move along. You can tell if a man is sad or happy by how he moves his cheap trainers, his shiny work shoes.

You can programme a computer to observe imperceptible differences in gait, you can get it to analyse them with reference to standardised notions of happiness, walking speed in relation to psychological turmoil, and so on. Yet the computer can't empathise, it can't imagine what it's like to be a unique individual, preparing to waste another day; panicked, furious, raging at the indifferent fates.

If one of those poor freaks outside dropped to his knees, started biting the paving slabs and barking like a dog, if another started walking backwards singing 'Love Me Tender', then, programmed the right way, our Beetle computer might be able to respond: 'Man falls to knees – send alert...' 'Animal impersonations – send alert.' 'Emitting Elvis – send alert.' But what about 'Man teeters, just briefly, just as if he is staring up at the sky, forgets himself, forgets gravity, forgets that he is a mortal being, and just stares, and when he stops staring at the endless blue like a painting that never ends, he teeters again, he nearly falls, corrects himself, walks on again.' What about that? Is that a tell?

Someone who has only ever written, 'So enjoyed the Met's new staging of Don Giovanni, ethereal and profoundly moving' or 'Delightful piece by Liesl Brooke on the Morandi exhibition at the Guggenheim' will suddenly tweet, 'I'm gonna oh my mother, oh my Jesus, oh brother, I'm gonna go wild today mamma dadda I'm so sorry, Oh my Jesus oh Humbaba, things are gonna change...' The Beetle computer sifts through this babble in a split second, searching for references to global brands, finds none, then filing the tweeter into a category of Christocentric web users ('oh my Jesus'), or sending his details to the corporate denizens of self-help ('things are gonna change'), or to a few thousand party-organisers ('go wild'). It dismisses the reference to Humbaba as extraneous to data parameters, and leaves it at that. It fails to perceive that this tweet is just very slightly unusual.
Later – boom! an explosion, a shooting in a mall, a vile act of matricide –

F

So, Beetle realised that computers can't actually do the whole damn thing. We need, oh slender irony, a few jowly mortals such as myself, our own jowly mortal experiences allowing us to edge towards a fragile understanding of those around us. Though my body is falling apart, though I am the physical antithesis of a roboworker, my mind discerns, my mind imagines, and this is why I am still, just about, in my job.

7 a.m. Usually 'Skitaflit' rises.
This morning, her first communication is at 7.04 a.m.

She tweets incessantly –
Dawn breaks above the grey-dusted, grey-fronted houses...
That sort of thing...
I rise, Skitaflit adds. *I rise and stare at the filmy furtive street.*
(That makes me balk. Can the street really be 'filmy' or 'furtive'? I wonder, but I log her phrases anyway.)

Then there's a pause. She might be staring at the filmy furtive street but also I think she is showering, dressing herself with practised efficiency, eating breakfast. Sometimes she comments on the news.
Weird about what happened in Madrid...
Bad scene in the Pacific.

All around the world, millions of people are commenting on the news...
Between 8 a.m. and 9 a.m. Skitaflit is silent. Great and mighty are the edifices of modern technology and well-nigh omniscient but the subway is deep, ancient, rattling through caverns built by long-dead men who had no need of mobile phone reception.

When the trains burrow deep, deep down, even the loquacious must fall silent...

When Skitaflit gets to the office the tone of her tweets changes. She is distracted, she is killing time. Her computer whirs before her. Sallow-lit, her face. She tweets lyrics from songs, she engages in mild controversies.
All day, Skitaflit tweets on.

Cyn – is more elusive. She mainly tweets quotations from philosophers. Of course, I've skimmed through a few of her emails, but they're equally unforthcoming. It was her native secrecy, her use of multiple personae, that cast Cyn as a 'potential anomaly'. Cyber-ambivalents, we call them. They use the internet, but they try to confuse it at the same time. It's ironic that Cyn's strategies of self-concealment brought her to our attention. Still, they are good strategies, and effective. I know she works in a bar in the East Village, but I can only guess at what she does with the rest of her time. There are days I wonder if Cyn is real at all. But if she isn't real, then what is she for?

Mannating has been consistent enough, spouting his satirical philosophy ever since I've 'known' him. I enjoy reading Mannating. To be honest, I even admire him. He teeters all the time on the brink of a tell and, several times, I have come close to alerting Beetle. But then, he just carries on – as normal. By his standards, anyway.

Mannating works from home (freelance copyediting, average salary $30,000 a year, i.e. he barely earns enough to pay his rent.)

He sleeps all morning, and finally, just after lunchtime, he rolls over, I imagine, gets out of bed, fixes himself a coffee, lights a cigarette (average daily consumption of caffeine, about 5 or 6 'strong ones,' average nicotine consumption, 25 Marlboros). He opens his computer, he begins again –

This afternoon – he began –

1408 *My heart aches...*
1412 *and a drowsy numbness pains my sense*
1426 *as though of hemlock I had drunk, or emptied some dull opiate to the drains one minute past*
1427 *and Lethe-wards had sunk...*

To quote Keats doesn't automatically mean that you are about to crack.
Romantic poetry, in and of itself, does not constitute a tell.
Still, I was on my guard.

1439 *My heart aches...aches...oh the burden.*
1508 *The impossible, unstoppable burden of life...*
1511 *My heart aches, my lungs ache, my head aches, my balls ache...*
1524 *My brain aches, my soul aches...my whole fragile foolish being aches, aches...*
1535 *my mind has fluttered out of my aching head, it has fluttered all the way to the window frame –*
1543 *Oh not The Frame, my Frame theory is dead and gone...I shot it, I shot a theory*

F

in Remo, or really in my bedroom, just to watch it die...

1551 *It's not 1551 in fact it's 1531 I am going backwards, I have reinserted myself into the time-space continuum and I am going backwards...*

1552 *now, from now on...no, from now on, oh Christ*

1553 *from now on and on and on – I am stuck in a particular moment of time, a dull moment, even – horror, horror help –*

1558 1532 *I escaped, it's OK, I'm going backwards again...*

1604 but 1525 *Oh I liked 1525 better the first time...*

1609 but 1516 *The astonishing thing is that I am going backwards at a different rate from onward time*

1613 but 1502 *I mean the whole thing is weird but does it matter? Shouldn't I be going backwards at the same speed as time goes forwards?*

1614 but 1500 *But backwards?*

1615 but 1456 *But why? Why should I assume that rules would apply to improbable inversions of the space-time continuum? Why?*

1628 but 1439 *My heart aches my heart aches it aches just like it did the first time*

1634 but 1415 *I have now resmoked the cigarette that I already smoked earlier*

1635 but 1413 *I have smoked the same cigarette twice! I believe this is a first for humanity...?*

1645 but 1400 *This is when I was asleep before.*

Zzzzzzzzzzzzzzzzzzzzzzzzzzzzzzzzzzzzzzzzzzzzzzzzzzzzzzzzzzzzzzzzzzzzzzz zzzzzzzzzzzzzzzzzzzzzzzzzzzzzzzzzzzzzzzzzzzzzzzzzzzzzzzzzzzzzzzzz

1652 but 1350

Zzzzzzzzzzzzzzzzzzzzzzzzzzzzzzzzzzzzzzzzzzzzzzzzzzzzzzzzzzzzzzzzzzzzzzz zzzzzzzzzzzzzzzzzzzzzzzzzzzzzzzzzzzzzzzzzzzzzzzzzzzzzzzzzzzzzzzzz

1658 but 1345

Zzzzzzzzzzzzzzzzzzzzzzzzzzzzzzzzzzzzzzzzzzzzzzzzzzzzzzzzzzzzzzzzzzzzzzz zzzzzzzzzzzzzzzzzzzzzzzzzzzzzzzzzzzzzzzzzzzzzzzzzzzzzzzzzzzzzzzzz

1720 but 1324

Zzzzzzzzzzzzzzzzzzzzzzzzzzzzzzzzzzzzzzzzzzzzzzzzzzzzzzzzzzzzzzzzzzzzzzz zzzzzzzzzzzzzzzzzzzzzzzzzzzzzzzzzzzzzzzzzzzzzzzzzzzzzzzzzzzzzzzzz

1745 but 1300

Zzzzzzzzzzzzzzzzzzzzzzzzzzzzzzzzzzzzzzzzzzzzzzzzzzzzzzzzzzzzzzzzzzzzzzz zzzzzzzzzzzzzzzzzzzzzzzzzzzzzzzzzzzzzzzzzzzzzzzzzzzzzzzzzzzzzzzzz

1802 but 1223

Zzzzzzzzzzzzzzzzzzzzzzzzzzzzzzzzzzzzzzzzzzzzzzzzzzzzzzzzzzzzzzzzzzzzzzz zzzzzzzzzzzzzzzzzzzzzzzzzzzzzzzzzzzzzzzzzzzzzzzzzzzzzzzzzzzzzzzzz

My hands were sweating as I transcribed his words. His word.

Zzzzzzzzzzzzzzzzzzzzzzzzzzzzzzzzzzzzzzzzzzzzzzzzzzzzzzzzzzzzzzzzzzzzzzzzzzz
zzzzzzzzzzzzzzzzzzzzzzzzzzzzzzzzzzzzzzzzzzzzzzzzzzzzzzzzzzzzzzzz

At first, it could have been a joke. But Mannating kept it up for 10 hours. Sending fabricated time backwards in erratic leaps which, he explained, were not inversely synchronic with real time, he tweeted
Zzzzzzzzzzzzzzzzzzzzzzzzzzzzzzzzzzzzzzzzzzzzzzzzzzzzzzzzzzzzzzzzzzzzzzzzzzz
zzzzzzzzzzzzzzzzzzzzzzzzzzzzzzzzzzzzzzzzzzzzzzzzzzzzzzzzzzzzzzzz

At midnight my time, general time, and 5.45 a.m. Mannating's time, when he, and I, had typed out Zzzzzzzzzzzzzzzzzzzzzzzzzzzzzzzzzzzzzzzzzzzzzzzzzzzzzzzzzzzzz
zzzzzzzzzzzzzzzzzzzzzzzzzzzzzzzzzzzzzzzzzzzzzzzzzzzzzzzzzzzzzzzzzzzzzzzzzzz
zzz
so many times that it had made me nauseous, when my computer screen was filled with
Zzzzzzzzzzzzzzzzzzzzzzzzzzzzzzzzzzzzzzzzzzzzzzzzzzzzzzzzzzzzzzzzzzzzzzzzzzz
zzzzzzzzzzzzzzzzzzzzzzzzzzzzzzzzzzzzzzzzzzzzzzzzzzzzzzzzzzzzzzzz
over and over again –

I drafted my report, carefully –

'Andy Mann, 42, white male, Brooklyn New York, observed in a twitter tell. Signs of mental distress. Thinks he's travelling back in time, multiple Zs across the screen. Mother alive, father deceased. Nice guy.'

I scrubbed out the last two words. I was about to send it. I paused.

I had Mannating's bank account on my screen. He was bumping along at the bottom of his debt, as always. He wasn't due to be paid anything for two weeks. He always lived on scraps, and yet, so far, he'd struggled on. Now – he was becoming –
Disturbing, even to me –
Who had previously known him, in a sense.

I wasn't sure where he thought he was. Halfway through yesterday? Was he going all the way to the 1980s? Right back to his busted low-rent childhood?

I'd seen it all, Facebook arrayed, photo by photo, Andy with his mum, with his dad, flared collars, grown men in ball-smothering shorts, kids in paddling pools, looking pensive... Of course they had no idea this fleeting idyll would one day be merged

F

with all the other Facebook lives, smeared across one lone corner of the internet.

Andy Mann grew up in rural Connecticut, his father was a weary businessman, drank too heavily, died aged 56 (aneurysm) and Andy's mother was just one more mad-with-rage housewife, draining her life into the lives of her children, rearranging the furniture, putting flowers in vases, rearranging her children, picking at them with combs and wiping them with tea towels, smearing creams onto them, bathing their little bodies, hemming them in. It was just the agonising usual, so much of the usual year by year and then Andy Mann grew and grew, got taller, gaunt, blue-eyed, haggard from an early age. He did OK in college, acquitted himself modestly, went out into the semi-friendly world, moved to New York, snuggled down into his unhomely home, his basement, where he went on and on day by day and on, until finally –
He went back in time –

I went to the tap, drank yellow city water. Skitaflit was feeling beleaguered by her colleagues, just a little bored. Nothing else. You don't go to prison for being bored.

Mannating was still typing out the letter Z...
At 2.05 a.m. my time and whatever the hell his time Mannating was still there
Zzzzzzzzzzzzzzzzzzzzzzzzzzzzzzzzzzzzzzzzzzzzzzzzzzzzzzzzzzzzzzzzzzzzzzzzz
zzzzzzzzzzzzzzzzzzzzzzzzzzzzzzzzzzzzzzzzzzzzzzzzzzzzzzzzzzzzz

Then he stopped.

For 15 minutes, nothing. For an hour, nothing. Silence for three hours. I was confused. I wondered – was he asleep? By the terms of his inverted anti-clock, was it bedtime? Had he eaten at all? Had he left the house? Had he slumped into a stupor? Should someone help him?

Should I call an ambulance?

I re-wrote my alert, added something about how he might have gone to sleep. Christ, I thought. Just send it.

Do your job, pass it on, I thought.
Still I couldn't click the mouse.

Skitaflit woke again, started her usual.

F

Dawn breaks. The milk is off. My roommate has eaten the last of the ratatouille.
I sympathised, but I confess, I was a little distracted...
I wasn't sure where Mannating thought he was – he just wasn't there, where he should be, where he usually was – virtual, but present. Now he was elsewhere –

In the great blank beyond.
Nowhere?

I prevaricated. I got nervous. My head began to itch, as if I had lice. I was hungry but I couldn't get it together to eat. I was fixed on Mannating. And where the hell was he? And what was he doing there?
And the Z?

Well I sat it out for a few hours, I really tried. I sat through Mannating's silence and I tried to observe Skitaflit as she streamed it out. Her life.

Perhaps it was hunger – perhaps it was suspense, should I send it? Should I not? – but I found Skitaflit's wry asides only annoyed me, her jibes at Crazy Katy, I started to wonder if Crazy Katy was just fine, and as Skitaflit went on and on I curled my lip. I was trying to stay in both time zones, mine – everyone's – and Mannating's, though now Mannating had become so shy and quiet I wasn't certain where we had got to in Mannating-time and meanwhile the other time, real time, had begun to seem irrelevant.
But it was clearly a bad idea, I was compelled to add – to find the real world irrelevant!
Was I having my own tell?

Skitaflit in the real world, or thereabouts, said. *I just wish I could go home early, just for one day, just once –*
I curled my lip and thought, *Then Go!*
And Cyn finally alighted on her keyboard, finally girded herself into action and wrote:
We are discontinuous beings who perish in the midst of an incomprehensible adventure...

Now that was cheerful...

On Mannating's side: still, nothing. Complete, total nothing.
I needed to send my alert. I was going to get into trouble. I could see it – before me,

scenes in a lantern show – Mannating, out there, somewhere, becoming a problem –
Still – I hovered my cursor above that righteous 'Send' and couldn't click it.

Skitaflit was going out for lunch with a man called Doug and really, I didn't want anything to do with that. Cyn had gone back to flossing her ears, or training her cat to juggle fire, or whatever she did in all those dead hours when she was nowhere near a screen, and so, I left them both.

I did it.
I left my apartment.

I opened the door and went out onto the street. I forgot to take a coat, but it was warm enough. It was a beautiful spring day, the breeze tousling the branches of the trees, and I was anxious, clandestine, walking with my head down.

The street shadow–dappled all around me, the humans moving one by one, the warmth of the sun on my face, the stars doused for the day –
I checked on Mannating. Nothing. Cyn was steeped in habitual silence. Skitaflit was whittering on. *Just had a great Chinese for lunch, who couldn't be happy. Home again home again, jiggedy jig, not home of course, the office, jiggedy jig Not with a fat pig but still with a load of beancurd and some greens Rice too –*
Lucky? I am. That's what the fortune cookies say...

Oh, Skitaflit was squaring up to the imponderables of life, she was rifling through a few core epistemologies and I hoped she would come out OK the other side –
But I didn't have time to go with her, not now.
You're on your own Skitaflit, with your chopsticks and your extra soy sauce...All alone – No one's watching you –
Skitaflit didn't seem to care anyway...

I was still walking, and the day was still unfurling in its fluttering breezy way, I was turning the corner, I was breaking the major rule of Beetle which is you never ever approach your cases in person, never approach, I found a cab, flagged it down – sat in a stupor wondering what the hell I was doing. Why?
Why today?

The cab jolted me as if it was trying to jolt me back to reality, it shuddered along some plaintive streets until we reached a zone of Götterdämmerung, a derelict ware-

house, a factory, a cesspit masquerading as an artists' studio.
The growl of the cab, fading.
I knew Mannating lived just a block away, one more parking lot, a coil of barbed wire, a tramp breathing his last into a bottle of scotch and then –

An incongruous clapperboard house, handy for the cesspits, and the parking lots and garages, as the trains went skywards – just aloft –
The rattling and grinding in the air, train by train – rattling elsewhere –
The basement window –
I'd imagined it a hundred times, and now –

Here was Mannating's grille, separating him from the nocturnal treachery of the street, the wide-eyed drugs freaks, or the kids with their brains stewed in beer, or the lonesome desperadoes, shuffling home –
And behind, within –
Mannating lurked? I didn't know –

I knocked on the door. I had an alibi. I would say I was looking for a friend called Chrissie. This imaginary Chrissie had given me her address but doubtless the address was all wrong because Chrissie was an idiot… An imaginary idiot.
No answer, I knocked again.
The door opened.

A beefy horror-fiend in a t-shirt, chest hair sprouting from the neck, a smell of beer and Bolognese.
I recoiled.
'Are you?'
Of course he wasn't. He was too old. He was too – hairy. He was wearing shorts.
I couldn't imagine Mannating in shorts.
'I was looking for a friend. He's called Andy Mann. Does he live here?'
I had forgotten about Chrissie.
'Andy who?'
'A guy? Lives in the basement.'
'No guy lives in the basement.'
'Are you kidding?' I said.
I saw his fat hairy fist clench. I stepped back –
'I just meant,' I fumbled with a scrap of paper –
'I was sure I got the right address…'
I had the right address, there was no doubt about it.

'Nope,' he said. Shaking his hairy head at me.
'You're really certain?' I said. Trying my luck. 'No one lives in the basement? No one at all?'
That made him bridle. But he was bridling anyway. He was a bridler. The sort of guy who likes to bridle. He'd been watching the sport, splattering his crotch with spaghetti, I knew the type.

He said, 'Come down the stairs, if you want. I'll show you.'
Well, this is where I'm smacked to the floor and robbed, I wondered, but I went anyway.

I followed him along the peeling corridor and into the sweaty stairwell and down some rickety stairs –
Then he pushed open a door.
The basement.
A shell. A room with a chair, and a desk.
A smell of – musk. Rats, perhaps. Sticky floors.
'Did anyone move out recently?' I asked. This morning?
'Well...' he said. More friendly now. Hanging in the doorway, enjoying my confusion. 'Well now...There was a guy, a while back. You know, weird guy.'
'Black hair? Ponytail?'
'No, not that sort of weird guy. Sort of stubby. You know, stubby head.'
'A stubby head?' I said. *What the hell does that mean?*
'Yeah, and anti-social. Didn't hardly say hello. You know?'
'But not black-haired, no ponytail, at all?'
'I told you. He was bald, if anything.'
'If anything?'
'Yeah. Come to think of it. He didn't have any hair at all.'
'A bald stubby guy, you say?'
'Stubby, yeah.'

The conversation was not progressing. The room was bare. Some other guy – I didn't understand it. I was disturbed as I trekked back up the stairs, the hairy monster ahead of me. I thanked him on the step. He said, 'Hope you find your friend.'
'Thanks again. Sorry to bother you.'
'Nothing bothers me,' he said. Giving me a nasty look.
'Yes, thanks. Thanks again...'
I receded into the clear fine air.

F

I had it all set down, annotated. Everything about Mannating was registered to this address. His computer, his bank details, everything. He had been tweeting, from the usual place, he had continued, he had tweeted, he had started going backwards, he had reversed the space-time continuum and then he had fallen asleep like some character in a fairytale.
Then he had vanished entirely – I didn't understand it.
It was my job to observe him, but he wasn't even there. How could I help him, if he wasn't where he was supposed to be? He wasn't in the cyber-ether and he wasn't in his basement –
He was –
Nowhere?
I walked one way, then the other, I was in this wasteland, dirt and dust, I opened my phone, saw Skitaflit, still going on, still busy, speaking words –

Now Cyn was typing – twice in one day – an anomaly itself – a TELL – Jesus – *Black beetle to the white bone*

And Mannating – was –

I checked my email.

Four bits of spam. A few friends, cordial, nothing – I went through them – my hands trembling –
Beetle business, one email, another five. Ten emails, then two-dozen. Just Beetle. And then –

'Zed' –
(*What the hell?*)

I opened the email – I shivered though the day was warm – even as I read –

'Don't worry, little beetle, I'll be just fine.'
Then – 'You just scuttle away, little beetle freak... I'll come see you later.'

For a moment I stood holding the phone, blinking at the screen –
Then I started running along the street – sly-eyed people around me, walking one way, another, all of them with somewhere to go –
Perhaps they knew?
I was running so fast, I could hardly see the houses as I passed them –

I dropped my phone –
Reality was blurring at the edges –
My hands, blurred – my feet –
I was scuttling along, the houses were so tall and blank – I was getting smaller and smaller, I was getting blown by the wind, ground down, I was nothing –
I couldn't get home!

LENIN WAS A MUSHROOM

BY

THOMAS DYLAN EATON

IN THE SOVIET UNION, THE TOMB OF VLADIMIR LENIN was the symbolic centrepiece of communist power. A team of morticians preserved Lenin's body by injecting glycerin and potassium acetate into the skin beneath his three-piece suit. One of the persistent challenges faced by these modern day *necromancers* was the removal of dark spots or fungi from Lenin's face and hands. Their work shrouded in secrecy, they maintained the integrity of the revolutionary leader's corpse to the extent that the Moscow mausoleum became a secular pilgrimage site, with regular opening hours and long lines of mourners each day. A blend of Marxism and Orthodox religiosity underpinned the functioning of the Lenin cult. 'We, the communists, are people of a special make. We are made of special material,' proclaimed Stalin, the former seminarian, on the eve of Lenin's funeral. Whilst the incorruptibility of a corpse evidenced sainthood in the Orthodox tradition, Lenin's body in its mausoleum belonged exclusively to the here and now of material reality. On 17 May 1991 this macabre attraction, the most important relic in the Soviet state, was the target of an infamous television hoax, broadcast from Leningrad to a nationwide audience.

'I have absolutely irrefutable proof that the October Revolution was the work of people who'd been consuming certain mushrooms for years,' claimed Sergey Kuryokhin, a composer and provocateur from Leningrad's artistic milieu. He had been invited to present his sensational thesis by the outspoken cultural programme, THE FIFTH WHEEL.[1] What sounded like an untimely rapprochement between Bolshevik zeal and heavy intoxication unfolded rapidly, with the absurd assertion that hallucinogenic fungi had displaced the personalities and physical features of leading revolutionaries: 'I simply want to state that Lenin was a mushroom.'

This ludic argument – performed as the Soviet Union lurched towards its official disbandment – mimicked the political rhetoric calling for a return to *authentic* Marxist-Leninist ideals. Kuryokhin appropriated the medium of investigative journalism, which had emerged as part of *Glasnost* and was exemplified by programmes like THE FIFTH WHEEL, to present his findings in a seventy-minute lecture hosted by the journalist Sergey Sholokhov and backed up by a wealth of historical evidence.

On screen, Kuryokhin and Sholokhov appeared in an environment befitting members of the intelligentsia, seated behind a large desk, piled high with documents and flanked by rows of teeming bookshelves. Kuryokhin was introduced as a 'political figure and actor', recently returned from a trip to Mexico. He began his lecture in

---

1. The original 70-minute broadcast on Leningrad's Channel 5 was introduced by Sergey Sholokhov with the title 'Sensations and hypotheses' on 17 May 1991. It has since become known as *Lenin-Mushroom* (*Lenin-Grib*) after it was made available by Sholokhov as a shorter 32-minute video in 1996. The content referred to in this essay is present in both versions.

E

a tone of unbending solemnity: 'My talk today concerns the most important secret of the October Revolution of 1917. Not everything in the revolution was quite as straightforward as it might appear.'

In Mexico Kuryokhin had been studying the effects of psychoactive plants on social upheaval. Profoundly impressed by murals depicting the revolution of 1910, he recognised scenes akin to those at home, 'the same exhausted people, armed with primitive tools of labour overthrowing some rulers'. Kuryokhin suspected that 'Great October' was so spectacular, so unimaginable, that it must have sprung from a hallucinogenic vision. He drew an analogy between the ritual use of peyote in Mexico and Lenin's hypothetical consumption of *Amarita Muscaria*, the fly agaric fungus long used as an entheogen by the indigenous inhabitants of Siberia.

Step by step, Kuryokhin advanced his improbable thesis, lacing his narrative with botanical and mycological terms and willfully misinterpreted primary and secondary sources from the Soviet past. A photograph of Lenin and his comrades was said to reveal a five-pointed star 'found on all Mexican shrines'. A dome-shaped object next to the inkstand in Lenin's Kremlin office was 'highly reminiscent' of Mexican cacti with psychoactive properties. When Kuryokhin stood up to compare a bisected view of Lenin's armoured car with a drawing of the root system of a fly agaric mushroom, he remained earnest as he bent out of shape the ethos of perestroika journalism to arrive at extreme conclusions. Lenin, according to Kuryokhin, was 'not only a mushroom, but also a radio wave'. His armoured-car, the *Bronevik*, from which he addressed crowds in 1917, 'served as a spawn while Lenin was the fly agaric'.

The effect on his television audience was a state of bewilderment and panic, prompting the Regional Committee of the Communist Party to publicly contradict the broadcast with an announcement to Bolshevik veterans that the thesis was bogus, because 'a mammal cannot be a plant'.[2]

The key to Kuryokhin's comic timing was to present his incongruous image of Lenin at a moment when taboos were lifting and long-suppressed thoughts about the giant of Russian Marxism were entering public discourse. The avidity with which Lenin's personality and physiognomy were being questioned reflected popular excitement for the black holes and hidden influences behind Soviet myths. The hoax was devastating because Kuryokhin had caught his audience unaware; posing as a reformist journalist, he had given voice to the uneasy sentiment that the

---

2. Sholokhov described this potentially apocryphal event in a December 2008 interview with Dima Mishenin for the Moscow-based *KRESTYANKA MAGAZINE*. It exemplifies the many legends that surround the *Lenin-Mushroom* broadcast including alleged official denials in newspapers such as *PRAVDA*, *LENINGRADSKAYA PRAVDA* and *KOMSOMOLSKAYA PRAVDA*.

fundamental relic of the October Revolution, Lenin's carnal husk in Red Square, was an extraordinarily strange entity even before the distortions of Stalinist orthodoxy.

¶ As soon as the decision had been taken to preserve Lenin's body, the 'Commission for the Immortalisation of the Memory of V. I. Lenin' embraced immortality itself as a pillar of the scientific-materialistic future. The miracle of communism in a peasant country was superseded by the miracle of Lenin as a sleeping beauty: 'Who then is the Prince who will steal through the oaken door of Lenin's mausoleum in order to bring the sleeper back to life?' implored Konstantin Melnikov, the architect of Lenin's sarcophagus. The answer was the revolutionary Russian people, whose collectivised will would bring about the victory of human reason over nature. Lenin occupied a position as a totemic last resort in the Soviet hierarchy; his mummy personified the notion of a collective body that would never die and, by extension, the permanence of Soviet power.

In the first years of *perestroika*, the reformist leadership of Mikhail Gorbachev attempted to de-canonise Lenin in the hope of rediscovering an untarnished source of communist idealism, a move ridiculed by Kuryokhin's television hoax. The gesture was a public manifestation of artistic practices that had come to prominence in Leningrad during the dark years of the 1970s and early 1980s. In his role as conductor for the multifarious 'rock group' Popular Mechanics Orchestra, Kuryokhin was at the epicentre of a burgeoning subculture, an informal association of dissatisfied young people. One of the more extreme collectives within this milieu called themselves 'Necrorealists', a moniker that carried political undertones during an era in which social and economic decay was compounded by an ageing Communist leadership.

¶ Cast as the 'savage, ugly' part in the Popular Mechanics live show, Necrorealists were radical artists in their own right, practicing film, painting, photography and performance. They were exclusively young men who appeared to be suffering from a collective breakdown. Their public drunkenness, brawling and unchannelled energies invited chaos. Dressed in medical smocks, army issue long johns and earflap caps (the outfit of the provincial surplus store) Necrorealists differed from ordinary citizens, not in breaking the rules of socialist living, but in following those rules according to their own obtuse interpretations. Under the dismal fog of Leningrad's northern marsh, this unstable rabble of loiterers, boiler-room attendants, medical orderlies and technical students pursued a grotesque existence which led them first into idiocy and then into a kind of absurd death.

Necrorealism was never a large-scale movement, but it greatly puzzled the *Komsomol* and other institutions responsible for youth welfare. Necrorealists were dysfunctional and asocial, but they could not be accused of promoting Western lifestyles like the earlier *Bitniki* and *Stilyagi* subcultures. Nor did they seem capable of organising conspiratorial activities. Their disinterest in political matters was unwavering, and it was not easy to distinguish a 'real' Necro-performance from the general eccentricity spreading amongst the urban populus in the aftermath of Brezhnev's leadership. Even the Necro ideologue, Evgeny Yufit, admitted that he was engaged in several years of 'wild and pointless' activity before realising that it constituted a bona fide worldview.

This formative period of clown-like hooliganism took place in the courtyards and hallways of communal apartments, on suburban trains and in the fetid swamps and forests beyond Leningrad's industrial sprawl. Here, the Necrorealists would churn up the rotten soil in frenzied battle charges and mass fist fights. The participants at these events were at first barely acquainted with each other, coming together for the sole purpose of expending their pent-up energy.

To the public, these formative Necro-performances must have raised disturbing questions about the young men involved. In a 1989 television broadcast on Leningrad's THE FIFTH WHEEL, the same programme that would host the *Lenin-Mushroom* lecture two years later, a team of psychiatrists and a proletarian focus group were shown film clips of the Necrorealists in action. Their stupefied responses, recorded as part of the broadcast, laid bare the extent to which a horde of so-called drunken idiots could cultivate a socially provocative and taboo breaking aesthetics:

> From the artistic standpoint it's ordinary junk, insanity! Total absurdity! The people who made this, are they mentally all right? Horrifying! No meaning in it whatsoever. This is a dreadful pathology, consisting of sexual perversions, attraction to corpses, often including elements of sadism...[3]

Such conceptual perspicuity had arrived for the Necro mob by way of a Viennese forensic textbook. Eduard von Hofmann's ATLAS OF LEGAL MEDICINE[4] was part of a growing number of found objects purloined by the group, including sacks, shovels,

---

3. The responses are quoted from an April 1989 episode of THE FIFTH WHEEL, hosted by Sholokhov. They were compiled for the exhibition catalogue, RUSSIAN NECROREALISM: SHOCK THERAPY FOR A NEW CULTURE, Bowling Green State University, Ohio, 1993. The exhibition was organised by Ellen Berry, Jacqueline S. Nathan and Anesa Miller Pogacar and was one of the first serious assessments of Necrorealism outside the Russian Federation.

4. Eduard von Hofmann (1837–1897) was a Professor of Legal Medicine and Director of the *Medico-Legal Institute* in Vienna, Austria. His ATLAS OF LEGAL MEDICINE (ATLAS DER GERICHTLICHEN MEDIZEN) is considered a pioneering textbook of forensic pathology and was published in Russian translation in 1900.

handsaws and a life-size leather mannequin. It was to have a galvanising influence on all their subsequent activities.

In hundreds of ghastly lithographs, Hofmann detailed the bodily effects of gunshot wounds, burns from fire and chemicals, murder by stabbing, suicide by hanging and death from charcoal smoke. His accounts of violent crime were based on real cases, as interpreted by a turn-of-the-century Viennese physician. In 1980s Leningrad the ATLAS OF LEGAL MEDICINE – so blatantly at odds with Soviet ideology – inspired Yufit to coin the term Necrorealism as a travesty of Socialist Realism. Indeed, Hofmann's unusual page layout, with cadavers aligned upright like the living dead, suggested a grotesque equivalent to the ideologically intensified figure of the communist. Fallen Soviet heroes had long been represented according to the classical ideals of beauty and harmony. In iconography they appeared as if they were outside the biological life cycle, showing no sign of the deprivations suffered in their service to the party.

The lives of Necrorealists were structured by this ideology. Soviet virtues of *insouciance* and *toughness* were the pre-conditions for their year-round brawling, whether they fought in snowdrifts, in the dark slush of melting snow or in the boggy mud of a sultry summer. Yet the disposition of the group changed with the discovery of Hofmann's forensic textbook. In imitation of mutilated and decaying corpses, they started to wear make-up: holosas syrup, bandages and cotton wool. Shifting awkwardly from one foot to the other, grimacing and merging with the mist, Yufit and his shabby entourage became the living dead of late Soviet leisure time, manifesting ideological immortality in a drained-out era.

We know about the Necrorealists today because they documented their activities on film, and because their impenetrable proto-art was enthusiastically accepted in the changing cultural environment of *perestroika*. When they first became adept at film-making in the early 1980s it was merely an extension of the recreational activity that Soviet citizens considered an inalienable right. The development of the amateur arts was a phenomenon of the time, and Yufit established Mzhalala Film as the Necrorealists' very own amateur utility[5]. Their 8mm and 16mm films included such vernacular classics as WEREWOLF ORDERLIES (1984), WOODCUTTER (1985), SPRING (1987) and SUICIDE WARTHOGS (1988).[6] They were produced on the margins

---

5. The expression *Mzhalala* mixes a Russian dialect term for drowsiness (*Mzha*) with a childhood babble word (*lala*). *Mzhalala Film* was established before the 1986 law permitting the formation of amateur clubs and is often cited as the first independent film studio in the Soviet Union. During *perestroika* the *Mzhalala Film* group was closely linked to both the *Parallel Cinema* movement and the Moscow-based *Cine Fantom* club of Igor and Gleb Aleinikov.

of the amateur circuit, with assistance from a studio attached to the Leningrad Optical Mechanical Factory. According to local legend, the act of film-making began by accident, when a group of Necrorealists gathered at the Finland station. Somebody had a handsaw and somebody else had a sailor's vest, and with enough odds and ends about their person, shooting began on the first part of WEREWOLF ORDERLIES.

'It was merriment for the sake of filming and filming for the sake of merriment,' recalled Yufit, underscoring the spirit of dilettantism that pervaded the group's increasingly ambitious activities. In WEREWOLF ORDERLIES, a sailor departs a suburban train, carrying a handsaw. He strides into a nearby forest, pursued by assailants wearing ankle-length medical smocks. When he climbs a tall tree and jumps to his death, the medics catch him, wrap his body in a blanket and strike the bundle with snow shovels and pitchforks.

The constraints of amateur production certainly shaped such rudimentary narratives. Early Necrorealist cinema epitomises a genre in which directors, operators and actors had to make do with basic equipment and as little as a single afternoon to complete their work. The results were tumultuous, sporadic and roughly cut together. In SPRING, a man in an earflap cap builds a suicide contraption out of knotted ropes and a wooden plank. The shoddy machine is set in motion when he cuts a rope loose, propelling himself headfirst into a tree. In SUICIDE WARTHOGS, a pot of water is brought to the boil in a dacha's overgrown garden. One man helps another into a shaft in the ground and, after doing so, hurls the scalding water into the buried man's face.

These deadpan actions are juxtaposed with clips from state-produced films of the Stalinist era. Footage of the bloodied sailor in WEREWOLF ORDERLIES is, for instance, followed by a documentary image of a white steamship at sea. Acrobats and gymnasts of the Soviet circus, young pioneers and wartime pilots are interspersed with the Necrorealists' brand of hammy and irrational violence. A darkly comic structure emerges from the mix of pathological themes and historical propaganda. It is as if the suicidal protagonists of Yufit's films are hopelessly in thrall to an ideology that glorifies self-sacrifice. The scenes of offhand brutality parody the 'immortalisation' of Soviet heroes by the official culture.

As a marginal amateur studio, Mzhalala Film organised screenings away from the prying eyes of the state, in private apartments with an audience limited to friends and acquaintances. Yet shooting the films was another matter, as the presence of motion

---

6. The films that Yufit made with the *Mzhalala Film* logo are archived at *Eye, The Film Museum* in Amsterdam, Netherlands. The collection includes WEREWOLF ORDERLIES (SANITARI OBOROTNI) 5 min (1984), WOODCUTTER (LESORUB) 6 min (1985), SPRING (VESNA) 10 min (1987) and SUICIDE WARTHOGS (VEPRI SUICIDA) 4 min (1988). Yufit's subsequent feature length films are also viewable at Eye.

picture equipment suggested to vigilant citizens that the Necrorealists might be hostile agents of some sort, possibly even spies. On at least one occasion members of the group were arrested while filming. When interrogated at the Department of Internal Affairs, Yufit could not articulate (to the satisfaction of the authorities) what it was they were trying to do, so the camera was confiscated and sent to a processing laboratory belonging to the state security services. One week later Yufit was summoned to the notorious KGB Big House in Leningrad. Upon arrival, his interlocutors informed him that they had watched the footage from the camera. Only, they couldn't see beyond the dearth of artistry. The KGB dismissed Yufit and the Necrorealists as nonentities, without political ideas. They decided not to classify their activity as illegal because the evidence was too befuddled and inept to embody anything more dangerous than the widespread moral torpor blighting 'developed socialism'.

¶ For most of the twentieth century Soviet society had been absorbed in a gigantic project, the overwhelming characteristics of which were disequilibrium and upheaval. Distorted by Stalin in the 1930s, the course by which Socialism's 'bright future' would be built was forever changing. At one time it meant the production of the means of production, at another the collectivisation of land and people, at another still the rooting out of 'wreckers' and 'traitors', and so on, exhaustingly. Yet under the premiership of Brezhnev, the mechanism of the communist project slowed.

A chasm was laid bare between the ideals of the planned economy and its social reality. This, in turn, led to a shift in the attitudes of the population to political affairs, something like a new disenchantment. The aphorism 'We pretend to work and they pretend to pay us' entered common parlance when the technocrats of *Gosplan* were pinning the blame for industrial stagnation on absenteeism, alcoholism and idleness. That citizens were not at their workplace, and didn't see any reason to work properly when they were there, was an acute problem. It did not cause stagnation, but it did contribute to a great flowering of vernacular pursuits, the only form of relief from the politicised rituals of official public life.

The typical Necrorealist, who tended to work only up to the point that his earnings covered the bare necessities, was not alone in society. A whole stratum of society shared his preference for a job that demanded minimum time and effort and left plenty of opportunities to get on with what really mattered. What really mattered in barren 1980s Leningrad was that an *ad hoc* culture had emerged from ruined communal apartments on the Fontanka and Moyka rivers. The buildings, vacated for 'capital repairs', were soon made into makeshift studios by artists led by Timur Novikov and members of Kuryokhin's Popular Mechanics Orchestra. These groups shared the Necrorealists' ethos of self-organisation and disdain for contemporary Soviet life. They were neither approved of nor supported by state agencies such as

Gosconcert and the Leningrad Artists Union, and were forced to make art and music with whatever came to hand in an economy based on scarcity.

The cinema of the Mzhalala Film group was equally spartan, evincing a world of snow, gloomy patches of forest, dilapidated wooden shacks, and waterlogged fields. The city was conspicuously absent from these settings, in its place a landscape more akin to a quagmire. In the logo for Mzhalala Film two drowned sailors are depicted with their throats slit, half submerged in a bed of reeds. They are standing in the mire of the Neva delta, the flat expanse of wilderness on which St Petersburg was founded in 1703. Until the cataclysms of revolution and civil war, this enlightenment city was the grandiose capital of Tsarist Russia. Yet from the moment it was raised on marshland, the rectilinear streets and monumental squares of Peter the Great's 'winter city' would periodically flood, the urban landscape obscured by a green miasmal fog.

Russophied as Petrograd and Sovietised as Leningrad, the city was relegated to provincial status by the Bolsheviks when they moved the central government to Moscow in 1918. By the era of stagnation, Leningrad was the embattled survivor of civil strife, purges and a brutal siege. A vast Soviet city surrounded its dilapidated core, and the protracted construction of the Brezhnev dam embodied its struggle with the floodwaters of the delta.

In this unhealthy microclimate the Necrorealist makes his appearance as a late Soviet anti-hero: lifeless, ill-natured, with a chalk face and black eye. In his overcoat he recalls the downtrodden 'little man' of a literary underworld that goes back to Pushkin; in his toughness and insouciance earlier archetypes of rough-hewn outlaws and holy fools. The anti-hero of Pushkin's 'The Bronze Horseman' is a poverty-stricken young man called Evgeny who shakes his fist and curses the flooded city's equestrian statue of Peter the Great. The monument is brought to life, driving this 'little man' out of his mind and into his death, washed out from St Petersburg on a wooden shack.

Pushkin's poem heralded the morbid and phantasmagoric tone that predominated in Russian literature of the nineteenth century, and continued to resonate in *samizdat* publications during the latter Soviet period. As practitioners of an art that shunned Socialist Realist ideals, the Necrorealists inherited much from this literary underworld.

Their sub-cultural milieu lionised Soviet outsiders like Daniil Kharms[7] whose posthumous writings became influential *samizdat* in 1970s Leningrad. Kharms wrote 'for the desk drawer' at the height of the Stalinist Terror, and his miniature stories of slapstick violence and death anticipated the abrupt plotlines of the Mzhalala Film group. 'The Carpenter Kushakov' can be read as a harbinger of Necrorealism: Kushakov repeatedly slips on ice during a thaw, acquiring a new bandage each time he injures his head. Soon he is unrecognisable, and his neighbours refuse to let him back in to their communal apartment.

Necrorealist cinema was also, initially, created 'for the desk drawer', but the circumstances changed under *perestroika* and members including Evgeny Yufit, Vladimir Kustov, Andrei Mertvyi and Oleg Kotel'nikov were able to establish them-selves in the cannon of Russian postmodernism.[8] Yet the Mzhalala Film group is not so easily assimilated into art history. Beside the ephemeral, largely undocumented nature of Necrorealist performances, there is the disquieting revelation that the differences between the unreal world of Necrorealism and the genuine absurdities of Soviet life have been obscured. After all, did not Lenin himself emerge from his hideout on the eve of the storming of the Winter Palace, disguised in a wig, with his face bandaged?

7. Daniil Kharms (1905-1942) was an iconoclastic poet and performer who was incarcerated by the Soviet state and died during the siege of Leningrad. In his lifetime he was officially a writer of children's stories, but in the Brezhnev era dozens of his short prose pieces, plays and poems began circulating amongst non-conformists in Leningrad.
8. Yufit continues to be the undisputed figurehead of Necrorealism. After participating in the 1989 film workshop of Alexander Sokurov, he began making a series of full-length and feature-length films with plots centred on genetic experi-mentation and pseudoscience. Necrorealism in the post-Soviet world has been the subject of numerous international exhibitions and film programmes, and beginning with the collaboration of the art historian Victor Mazin a body of theoretical and academic writing has been dedicated to this radical movement.

E

XXI

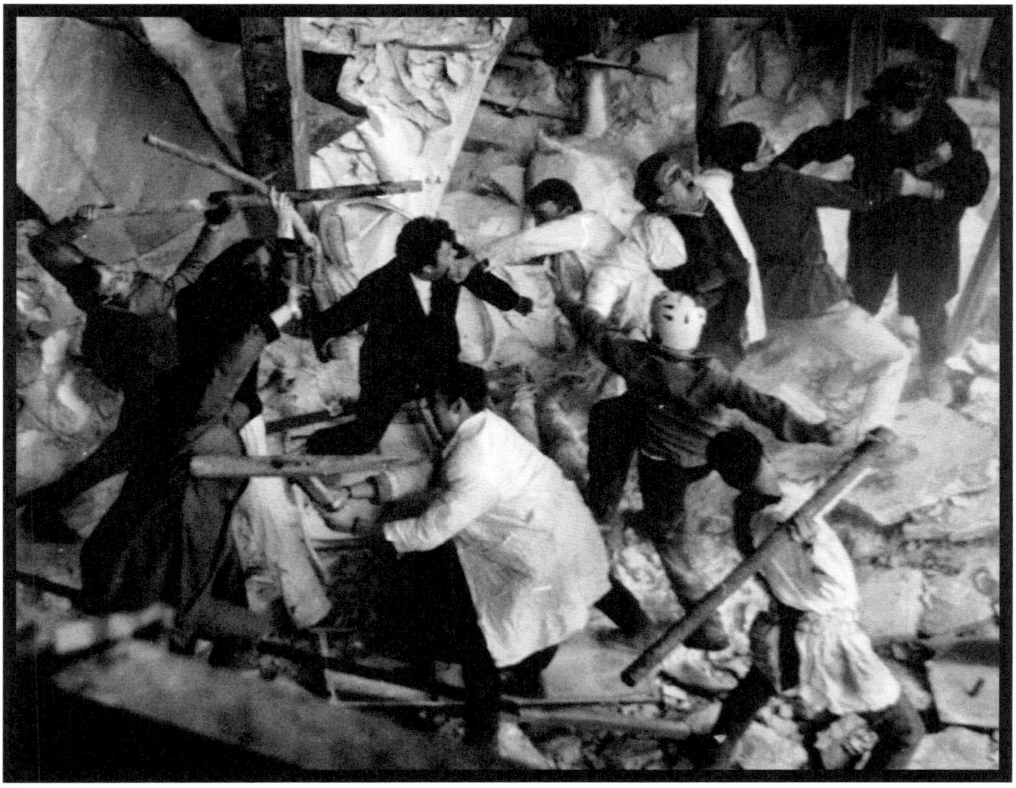

XXIII, XXIV

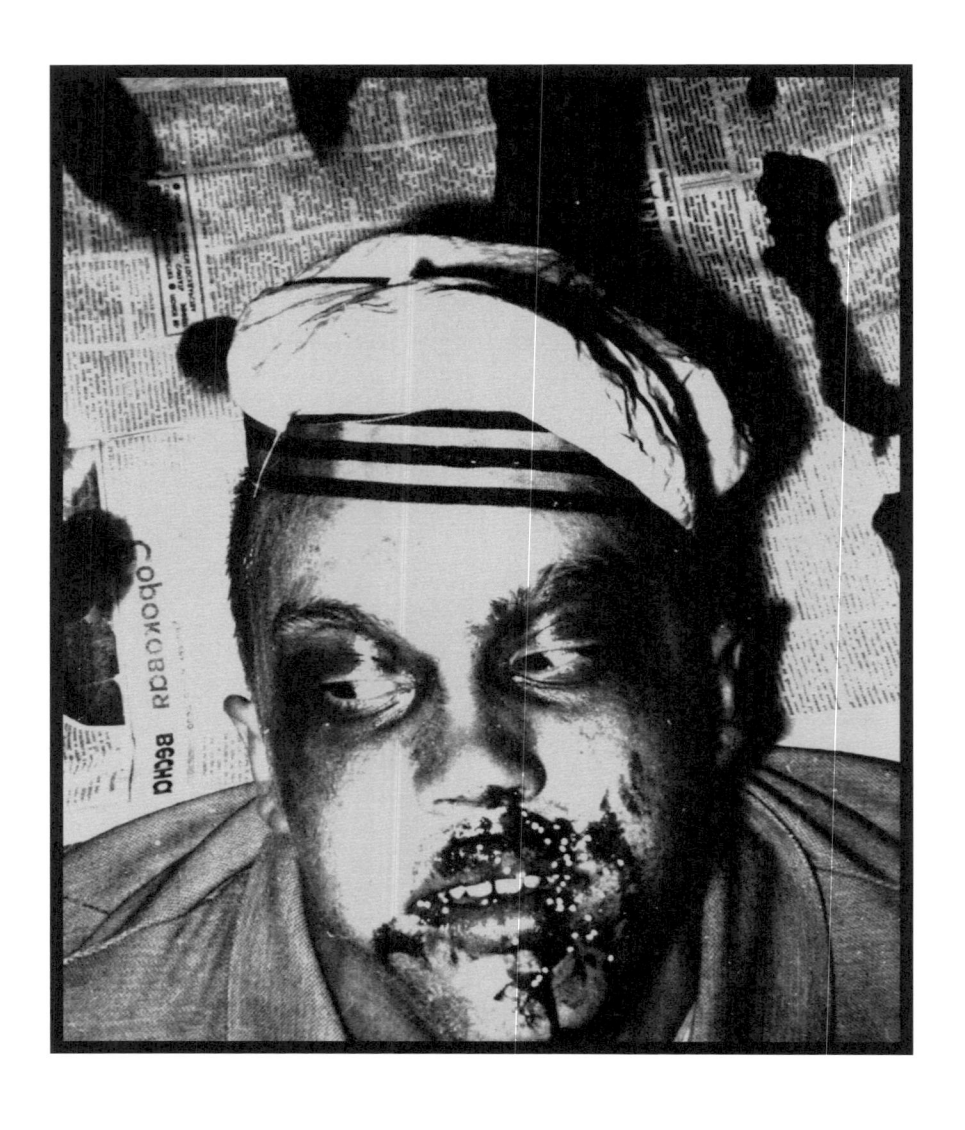

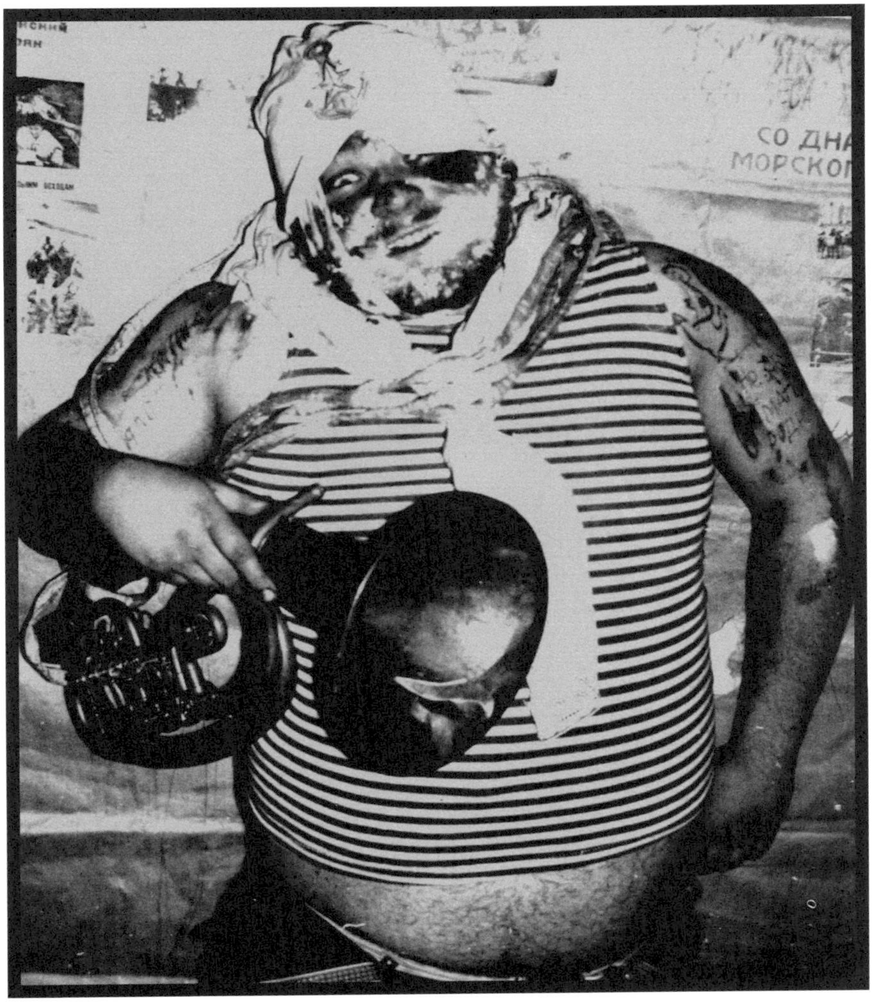

xxv

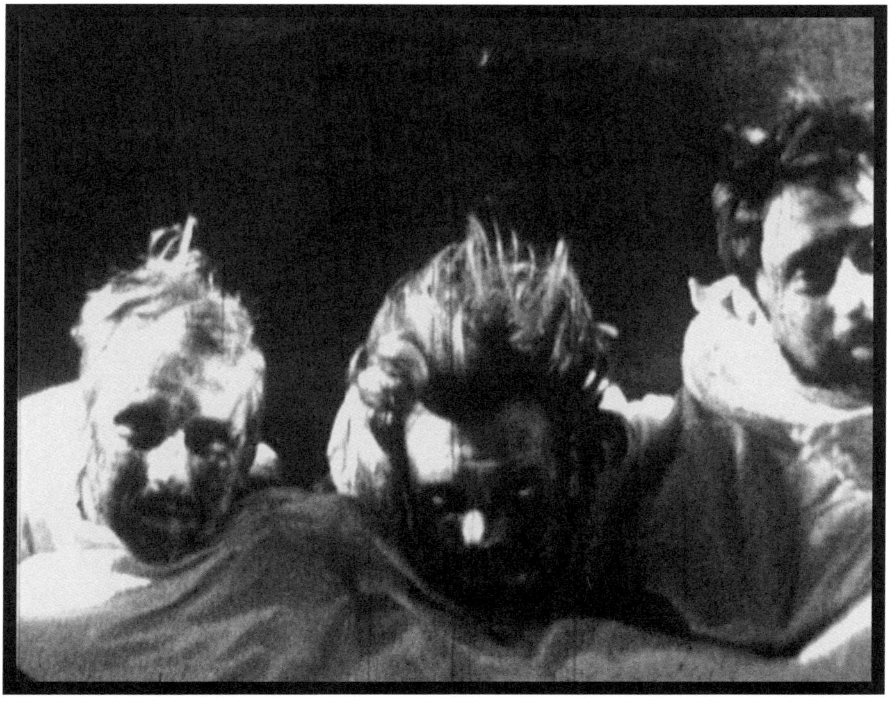

XXVI, XXVII

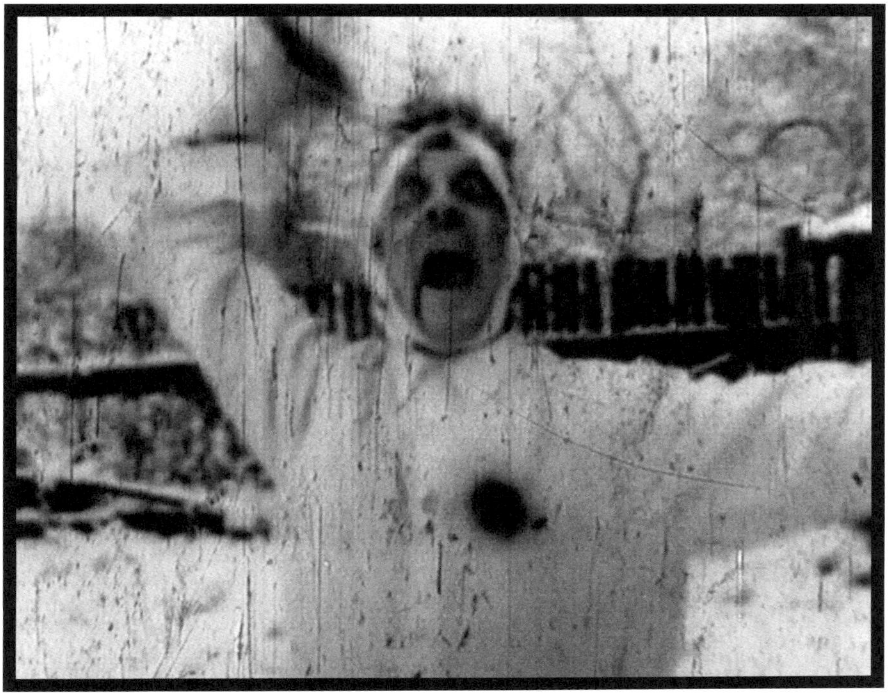

XXVIII, XXIX

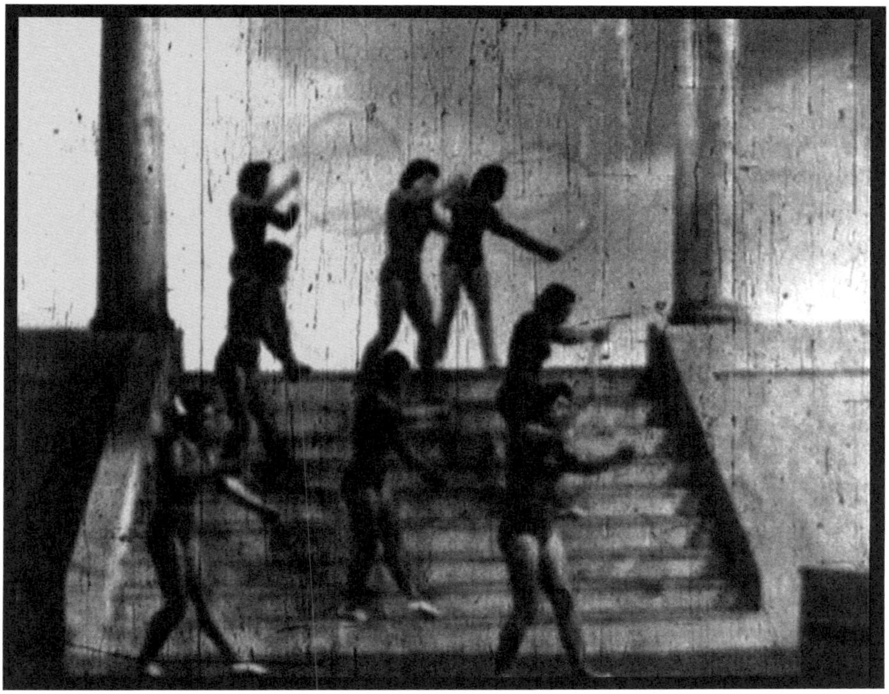

XXX, XXXI

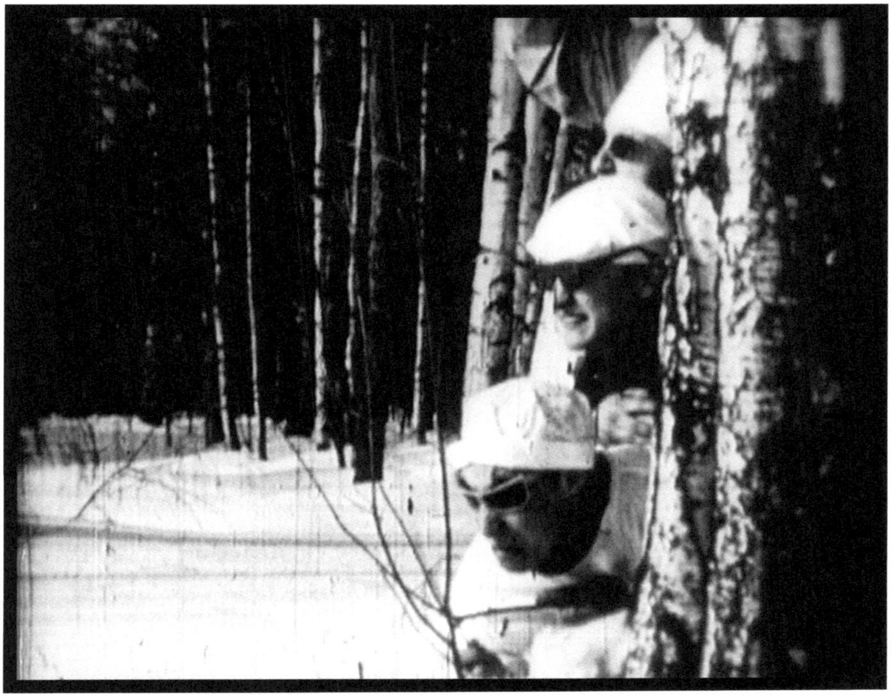

I TOLD YOU I'D BUY YOU ANYTHING YOU WANTED SO YOU ASKED FOR A SUBMARINE FLEET

by

OWEN BOOTH

I. THE TRIUMPH OF CAPITALISM

It was the end of the Cold War and capitalism had won. Everywhere people were either out of a job or making obscene amounts of money. If you didn't have a plan and a German car you were nobody.

Because I could tell you were about to leave me, I had to come up with a grand gesture.

We were sitting in the lobby of the American hotel, where the walls are painted gold and the rooms cost three times my annual salary. You were wearing your best dress and I was wearing my new suit and sunglasses because I'd spent the day going to job interviews. I'd been thrown out of the army along with everyone else.

Businessmen were prowling the edges of the room like lions. They were looking for sexy gazelles. They all noticed the way the light reflected off the gold-painted walls and lit up your face.

Spooked, I told you I'd buy you anything you wanted. So you asked for a submarine fleet. It totally served me right.

II. SERGEI THE SUBMARINE SALESMAN

I got together with a bunch of likeminded investors. We were men of vision who saw the big picture and we were going to remake the world. We hired a retired submarine captain called Yuri who drank too much and told us stories of playing cat and mouse with the Americans for forty years under the arctic sea. During a long and distinguished career he'd made more than seventy-two circuits of the globe and been married five times. Then the oligarchs had taken over and stolen everything, including his fifth wife.

We stood in the conning tower of a reconditioned Victor III class submarine fifty miles out to sea off Archangelsk, smoking brutally strong cigarettes in the grey dawn light.

The air was so cold it smelt like iron.

'She displaces seven thousand tonnes, and she'll give you fifty-five kilometres an hour at top speed,' Sergei the submarine salesman was telling us. 'Power source is two pressurised water reactors. Safe, but don't stand too close, you know?'

'What about the crew?' said Captain Yuri.

'Usual crew complement is twenty-seven officers, thirty-five warrant officers and thirty-five enlisted men; but you can probably get away with a third of that.'

'Probably?' I said.

'Underwater endurance is 90 days,' Sergei continued. 'Armament is two 650 mm torpedo tubes here and here, and four 553 mm torpedo tubes over there... somewhere.'

'Is his name really Sergei?' I whispered.

'Obviously not. No.'

'If you want something that packs a bit more punch, I know a man with a couple of discontinued Akula-class Typhoons. Can I ask if you gentlemen plan to launch any ballistic missiles?'

We all looked at each other.

I wondered: did we?

III. LEONID'S BROKEN HEART

We tracked down likely-looking crew members from Astrakhan to Vladivostok, acting on tip-offs we'd picked up in former navy bars, in towns that were now miles from dried-up inland seas. We found desperate men working in the Kazakh oilfields, in the coalmines of Siberia, riding horses on the steppes of Uzbekistan.

We weren't above the odd bit of press-ganging, when it suited our purposes.

'Lads,' Captain Yuri told our unwilling teenage recruits, as we moved silently beneath the surface of the Black Sea, 'think of this as a gap year. You'll come home with hair on your chest and thrilling tales of the ladies of the mysterious orient.'

Our First Mate Leonid came highly recommended from the academy in St Petersburg. He was still nursing a broken heart. The love of his life had gone back to Chechnya after the declaration of independence.

'She never could get the Caucasian dirt out of her hair,' he said, tearfully.

Every evening he played his guitar and sang love songs that he'd written for her. There were songs about her beautiful eyes, and the dresses she wore, and the long evenings in the mountains, and how difficult she'd found it to adapt to life in St Petersburg, and how he wanted to be a ghost and haunt the dust that rose at her footsteps.

It was depressing stuff.

Eventually we had to ask him to stop for the sake of morale.

Other than that, he was a model submariner and everyone in the crew loved him.

IV. THE SEX LIFE OF PLANTS

We took over the abandoned secret submarine base on Simushir Island, 500 miles north of Japan. The base was built inside the flooded caldera of an extinct volcano. You could have hidden half the Soviet navy in there and nobody would have known.

Fogs rolled in from the Pacific and the Sea of Okhotsk. We walked along the empty beaches and saw brown bears hunting for clams down by the waterline. Inland the streams were so thick with salmon you could walk from one bank to the other without getting your feet wet.

It rained all the time.

At night we lay in our cots in the draughty barracks, listening to the wind and the grumbling of the volcanoes up and down the Kuril archipelago. We wrote letters home and played cards and memorised the names of the fifteen different species of sea bird that nested on the island.

The Whiskered Auklet

Steller's Sea Eagle

The Short Tailed Albatross

The Black Guillemot

The Rhinoceros Auklet

The Horned Puffin

The Fork-Tailed Storm-Petrel

Etc.

One morning we were surprised by a party of Japanese eco-tourists who had anchored in the bay. We stared enviously at their beautiful and well-equipped cruise ship. They even had a helicopter.

They told us that they'd come to see the island's unique flora and fauna, having heard so much about it from their grandparents. Before the Russians had invaded at the end of the Second World War, they explained, most of these islands had belonged to Japan. Before that they'd belonged to the Ainu people.

Nobody knew who the islands had belonged to before the Ainu people.

We did our best to provide a warm welcome. In the evenings we all sat around campfires and told stories. We shared our rations, and our new guests gave us lectures and did slide shows.

'Robinson San,' Professor Ozaki the tour leader told me as we enjoyed a tin of decades-old caviar and a bottle of plum brandy, 'your undersea mission is an honourable one. I've spent most of my career investigating the sex life of plants, so I know a thing or two about grand romantic gestures. I hope your girlfriend is impressed.'

'I hope so too, Ozaki Sensei,' I said. 'I hope so too.'

I didn't tell him that you rarely answer my letters.

V. FUCHI'S PUNISHMENT

To celebrate the spirit of friendship we put together a joint scientific expedition to climb one of the volcanoes at the southern end of the Island. For three days we surveyed the scorched earth and planted insect traps among the dwarf pines. Every morning Professor Ozaki's 17-year-old daughter Chizuko got up before dawn to check the traps. She sang traditional Japanese folk songs to herself while she released the night's haul of groggy-looking spiders back into the undergrowth.

In the Ainu culture the goddess of spiders is called Yushkep. She is often called on to assist in childbirth, on account of her long, spidery fingers. The goddess of the hearth is called Fuchi. She is the guardian of the home and the judge of all domestic affairs.

Those who fail to maintain proper domestic relationships incur her punishment.

After three days we were chased off the summit of the volcano by a terrific thunderstorm. As we packed up the tents hailstones ricocheted off the rocks like AK47 rounds. Seconds before every lightning strike our hair would stand on end. We couldn't get the smell of ozone out of our clothes for weeks.

When we got back to the base we were informed that Engineer Pavel had been mauled by a bear and three of the junior officers had stolen a dinghy and struck out for Sakhalin under cover of darkness.

VI. A LAZY BEETLE IS NO BETTER THAN A COCKROACH

We needed money. We successfully pitched to run the North Atlantic cocaine route for one of the more enterprising Colombian drug cartels. Every two weeks we made the journey from the Caribbean to south-west Spain, where we unloaded our cargo a couple of miles off the Costa de la Luz. In the dawn light the barren hills above Zahara de Los Atunes gazed blankly down on us as we waited for the speedboats.

The cartel gave us two goons to make sure we didn't disappear with the merchandise. Their names were Hector and Hector. They wore beautiful shirts and looked like identical twins. They spent their days smoking everyone else's cigarettes and gambling in the mess hall.

They told us all about women.

'Women are more dangerous than cocaine,' said Hector Number One.

'Women are more dangerous than the Brazilian Wandering Spider, which is the most dangerous spider in the world.'

'One bite from a Brazilian Wandering Spider,' said Hector Number Two, 'you get a parolito that lasts for three days. You are like Superman, ey? Then your chimbo falls off. Then you die.'

Hector and Hector's proudest possessions were a pair of racing beetles, which they kept in separate matchboxes. They slept with the matchboxes under their pillows. The beetles were named Campo Elías Delgado and Griselda Blanco. Back home in Cartagena, Hector and Hector told us, these two beetles were famous. It was a point of honour that neither had ever lost a race.

Every morning the beetles were given a run-out on the long steel mess hall tables. Their feet made tiny clicking sounds as they scrabbled for grip, trying to escape the cigarette smoke that Hector Number One blew at them through a straw.

'The worst thing you can do to a racing beetle is let him get lazy,' Hector Number Two explained to us. 'A lazy beetle is no better than a cockroach.'

'And what do we do to cockroaches?' asked Hector Number One.

Hector Number Two took off one of his 2000-dollar snakeskin loafers and slammed it on the steel table tabletop.

The two little beetles jumped three inches in the air.

VII. WHAT HAPPENED TO ANTON THE COOK

Anton the cook had a heart attack and died fifty miles off the Cape Verde Islands. We held a short service on deck and buried him at sea at sunset. The surface of the water was as still and dark as glass. A huge flock of migrating seabirds flew overhead and the Hectors took turns on the anti-aircraft gun, trying to bring down as many of them as they could. Their tracer bullets lit up the evening sky like fireworks.

Captain Yuri offered me a cigarette.

'Some of the lads are getting itchy,' he said, as we watched the display.

'Itchy, how?' I said.

'Itchy you-know-how'.

'What do you recommend?'

'It just so happens I know a place in Mindelo on Sao Vincente. Very discreet. The landlady owes me a few favours.'

'How many favours?' I asked.

'She was my second wife,' he said.

A cheer went up from the men as Hector Number Two managed to hit one of the birds with a tracer. It plunged into the sea in flames.

That night we set a course for Mindelo harbour.

VIII. WHO CONTROLS THE MEANS OF PRODUCTION

'I was a nurse,' said Señora Carilda Oliver Cejas Morales, as she picked up her twelfth glass of pontche. It was four in the morning and we were sitting on the terrace watching the lights of boats down in the harbour. 'Angola. Nineteen Seventy-Six. Before that, the army, obviously. Viva Cuba.'

She downed the drink and puffed on her gigantic cigar. She was a formidable woman. At 60 she still looked like she could knock out a horse. I could see what Captain Yuri saw in her.

'Of course, it was a marriage of convenience,' she continued. 'I wanted to see Moscow.'

'It wasn't all that convenient for me,' said Captain Yuri, refilling her glass.

'Don't be so bourgeois, Yuri.'

They saluted each other with their drinks, then knocked them back.

Señora Cejas Morales ran the only collectivised brothel in the islands. It was possibly the only collectivised brothel in the world. The workers were all unionised. They all received equal wages as well as a share in any profits. They had free healthcare and free contraception. There were no pimps. Every year they elected a president, and every year it was Señora Cejas Morales.

There was a six-foot painting of her in the parlour. She was holding an AK47. 'It reminds our clients who controls the means of production,' she'd told the boys before they were led off upstairs.

Even the two Hectors behaved themselves impeccably in her presence. She had promised Hector Number One a ride on her horse, Simón Bolívar, next time we were in town.

'The concept of romantic love is just that: romantic,' she went on. 'It's narcissistic nonsense. Not to mention selfish. Love of an idea, a cause, even a people – now that makes sense.'

She pointed at me.

'But you're young,' she said. 'I don't expect you to understand.'

'He's doing all this to impress a woman,' said Captain Yuri. Señora Cejas Morales pushed the bottle towards me. 'Then the revolutionary council rests its case,' she said.

IX. THE FIRST AFRICAN WOMAN IN SPACE

The cocaine business was taking its toll on the sub. The propellers were all over the place and the Geiger counters in the missile hold were starting to make worrying noises. We needed to find a friendly port to carry out repairs.

We didn't have many options.

We made a deal with a failed African state and laid up for two weeks. The cartel gave Hector and Hector permission to advance us five million dollars to smooth things over with the local warlord. In return he invited us all to spend a weekend at his country retreat.

He was the fattest man any of us had ever met. He wore gold tracksuits and treated us to spectacular feasts at his hundred-foot long dining table and took us on safari in his swamp.

He told us that he'd lost count of the number of wives he had. It had got to the point where most of the local women claimed to be one of his wives whether they were or not. It made their lives easier. After all, no one was going to mess with the wife of a man famous for his sense of honour, his long memory and his unshakeable belief in the value of extreme violence.

'When I was fifteen,' he told us, as our horses picked their way through the flooded grassland, 'I fell in love with a girl who worked in the bowling alley in Bafatá. She was the most beautiful girl for fifty miles. Everyone knew it. But she wasn't interested in getting involved with boys. She wanted to be an astronaut. She wanted to be the first African woman in space.'

Upfront the two Hectors signalled for us all to stop. They'd spotted elephants.

'And so I came up with a plan,' our host went on. 'I was going to build her a rocket. Then there would be no way for her not to fall in love with me.'

He lit a cigar and shouted up to the Hectors. 'Bazooka, I think.' Hector Number Two unswung his bazooka and lifted it on to his shoulder.

'Obviously this was going to take investment. Space programmes don't come cheap. Especially not in this country. There's the talent shortage, for a start. Raw materials. Infrastructure. So that's when I had to start killing people for money.'

Hector Number One took another look through his binoculars and said something to Hector Number Two. Hector Number Two adjusted the sights on the bazooka.

'By the time I'd made my first million she'd been dead from malaria for ten years.'

There was a whoosh and a distant explosion and then it started raining elephant.

Under his umbrella our fat host sobbed, his great bulk shaking like it was the end of the world.

X. THE NORTHERNMOST GRAND PIANO IN THE WORLD

We were starting to get rich. We bought another submarine and leased it to the Spanish so they could take over the North Atlantic cocaine franchise. Hector and Hector surprised us all by deciding to stay on. They wanted to see the world, Hector Number One told us shyly.

'And lots of chimba, ey!' added Hector Number Two.

We headed north, following the mid-Atlantic ridge up to Iceland and then on towards Svalbard, 500 miles inside the Arctic Circle.

Heavy snow was falling on the sea as we sailed up the Isfjorden. It was late in the year, and the light was already beginning to fail. On either side of us the ancient, treeless mountains loomed. We passed the town of Longyearbyen and sailed on towards the abandoned coal mining settlement at Pyramiden.

Ice was starting to thicken the water at the edges of the dock where we came ashore. Snow was settling on the iron skeleton of the old coal works. In a couple of weeks the fjord would be locked up for the winter.

The Arctic wind rolled down from the tops of the mountains and made the fillings in our teeth ring.

We explored the deserted town. We wandered the corridors of the empty hospital and the old sports hall. The dry air had preserved every poster on the walls, every piece of paper in the filing cabinets, every role of film in the projector room of the cultural centre.

Leonid the First Mate found an old Red October grand piano in the concert hall and played us something. Even though it was yet another song about his Caucasian ex-girlfriend, something in the way the chords rolled out of that untuned piano tugged at all our memories.

Everyone had to sit down for a bit and think about what they'd lost.

Captain Yuri thought about his five wives and his son who'd died in Afghanistan in the eighties.

Hector and Hector thought about their mothers.

The boys thought about the love affairs they hadn't even had the chance to embark on yet.

I thought about you and the light on your face reflecting off the gold walls of the American hotel, roughly ten thousand years ago.

On the way back to the sub we passed a solitary walrus who had got lost on his way to the breeding grounds. He had come ashore to look for signs of his fellows or try to catch the scent of female walrus. Instead he'd found the bust of Lenin that watched over the town.

He was squaring off with the old leader of the people, hoping that if he just stuck to his usual patterns of behaviour then things would eventually start to make sense.

XI. WHAT WE THOUGHT WE WERE TRYING TO PROVE

We crossed the North Pole under twelve feet of ice and travelled through the Bering Straits and down into the Pacific again. We spent a couple of weeks in Hawaii learning how to surf before we headed into the vast emptiness of the South Pacific Ocean. We skirted the edge of the south-west basin at a depth of two hundred feet as storms roared above us. Six miles below, the Australian and Pacific tectonic plates slow-danced in the darkness of the Kermadec trench.

Whales and dolphins followed us around the coast of Australia. Off the horn of Africa we were chased by Somali pirates. In the Philippines we took up with a group of nomadic fishermen and compared notes on the seagoing life.

Along the way various crew members fell in love and had their hearts broken.

We bought two more submarines and leased them to a Jamaican outfit who were looking to diversify. It was almost getting too easy. We hooked them up with Señora Carilda Oliver Cejas Morales and our warlord friend and all of a sudden we had a full service on offer.

The tales of our enterprise had begun to spread. We were contacted by journalists and documentary film-makers. They wanted to know what we thought we were trying to prove.

I was beginning to wonder myself.

Twenty miles off Buenos Aires one night I was convinced I could hear tango music at three in the morning. I was up on deck smoking too much. We were heading south again. Phosphorescing microorganisms glowed in our wake for miles.

Why won't you return my calls?

Do you want me to wrestle an octopus for you? Would that be enough?

What am I supposed to do with the crew?

Eventually the inevitable happened and Hector and Hector fell out over an obscure South American point of honour. Nobody really understood what it was about.

The duel took place on a former prison island in the Southern Indian Ocean. It wasn't much more than a rock. It had been uninhabited for over fifty years, except for a colony of Adelie penguins that had turned up one morning after a hurricane. They eyed us all suspiciously as the Hectors paced out the duelling ground in the dawn light. Thankfully the booming surf drowned out their endless, irritated barking.

'You don't have to do this,' I shouted at Hector Number One.

He paused and cupped his ear at me.

I walked over to him. In the grey light the sand under my feet was as white as bone.

'You don't have to do this.'

'Of course I have to do this,' he said. 'You can't have a duel if only one person turns up.'

He was wearing a crisp white shirt and white trousers. Hector Number Two, who was moving the sand around with his foot twenty yards away, had the same outfit on. They looked fantastic.

When they turned and fired everyone held their breath.

XII. THE ROMANTIC BARENTS SEA

Up on the surface, 200-mile-an-hour winds have been churning up the Southern Ocean for over a week now. Waves as thick as blood roll over our heads. The sky is probably spectacular.

With nowhere much to go we drift on the Weddell Gyre, drawing up plans. Leonid has started writing songs again. We take this to be a good sign.

The maximum operating depth of this submarine is around 3,500 feet. Beyond that, the pressure would buckle our hull. So we hang here in the endless blue, between this world and the next, listening to the blip of the sonar and snatches of whale song.

Sergei the submarine salesman reckoned we could last ninety days without surfacing. We have food and supplies for twice that. We move around the ship quietly, conserving energy. Our heart rates have slowed right down.

We are in no rush.

In the spring our Baltic fleet will slip anchor and set sail. Our resolve is mighty. We will spend our summers off Novaya Zemlya, in the middle of the romantic Barents Sea. We will winter on the edge of the Challenger Deep.

And when the time comes we will surface off capital cities around the world and rain our atomic love down upon them.

And then you'll know how much you mean to me.

SPONSORS

LISTEN!

Sorry we couldn't get it together in time to send you a real ad. For now, you can just stare at this blank space or go to know-wave.com and just listen.

KNOW WAVE

THE ICE PLANT   theiceplant.cc

London Review OF BOOKS / *the* **PARIS REVIEW**

Paris, meet London

The Paris Review brings you the best in imaginative writing.

The London Review of Books brings you the best in essays and commentary.

From now until the end of August, you can **get a years' subscription to both magazines for one low price, anywhere in the world.**

You will receive:

- An annual print subscription to *The Paris Review* (4 issues)
- An annual subscription to the *London Review of Books* (24 issues)
- FREE digital access to any issue covered by your print subscription with both the **LRB App** and the **Paris Review App**
- Access to all locked *LRB* online content, including the entire **online archive**
- Our **no-risk guarantee**: cancel any time: receive a full refund on unposted issues

www.theparisreview.org/lrb

AA BRONSON
+
GENERAL IDEA
APRIL – MAY

DONALD URQUHART
JUNE – JULY

THOMAS EGGERER
JULY – AUGUST

MICHAEL KREBBER
SEPTEMBER – OCTOBER

LIAM GILLICK
OCTOBER – NOVEMBER

HANNAH STARKEY
DECEMBER – JANUARY

MAUREEN PALEY. 21 HERALD STREET, LONDON E2 6JT +44 (0)20 7729 4112 INFO@MAUREENPALEY.COM WWW.MAUREENPALEY.COM

A digital subscription to *Granta* includes access to over one hundred and thirty back issues. That means . . .

Diana Athill Margaret Atwood Iain Banks Julian Barnes Ned Beauman Fatima Bhutto Roberto Bolaño Anne Carson Eleanor Catton Noam Chomsky Bret Easton Ellis James Ellroy Louise Erdrich Jonathan Franzen Janine di Giovanni Nadine Gordimer Mark Haddon Seamus Heaney A.M. Homes Nick Hornby Kazuo Ishiguro A.L. Kennedy Stephen King Nicole Krauss Doris Lessing Nelson Mandela Hilary Mantel Ian McEwan David Mitchell Lorrie Moore Herta Müller Alice Munro David Peace Mary Ruefle Salman Rushdie Taiye Selasi Will Self Gary Shteyngart Zadie Smith Rebecca Solnit Andrea Stuart Paul Theroux John Updike Binyavanga Wainaina Joy Williams and Jeanette Winterson

. . . to name a few. Subscribe now for just £12 per year.

GRANTA.COM

THE TOM-GALLON TRUST AWARD 2016

Prize of £1,000 for a short story
And £500 for the runner-up
(published or unpublished)
Deadline: 31st October 2015

For entry forms and information
www.societyofauthors.org/tom-gallon

SoA twitter: @Soc_of_Authors

THE SOCIETY OF AUTHORS PRIZES

TLC The Literary Consultancy

Literary Values in a Digital Age

MANUSCRIPT ASSESSMENT AND EDITORIAL ADVICE SINCE 1996

Bridging the gap between writers and the publishing industry, TLC works worldwide to provide market-aware services to writers writing in English at all levels.

EDITORIAL

- Detailed critical assessments by professional editors for writing at all stages of development
- In-house matching to one of our 80+ readers across fiction, non-fiction, short stories, poetry, scripts and screenplays
- Links with publishers and agents, and advice on self-publishing
- Copy-editing, proofreading and ghostwriting

MENTORING

- Six online one-to-one sessions with a professional editor
- Includes separate manuscript assessment and industry day with an agent and publisher

EVENTS

- Masterclasses and skills workshops
- Literary Adventure writing retreat 26th September – 2nd October at Casa Ana, Spain

T 020 7324 2563
E info@literaryconsultancy.co.uk
W www.literaryconsultancy.co.uk

The Literary Consultancy
@TLCUK

Supported using public funding by
ARTS COUNCIL ENGLAND

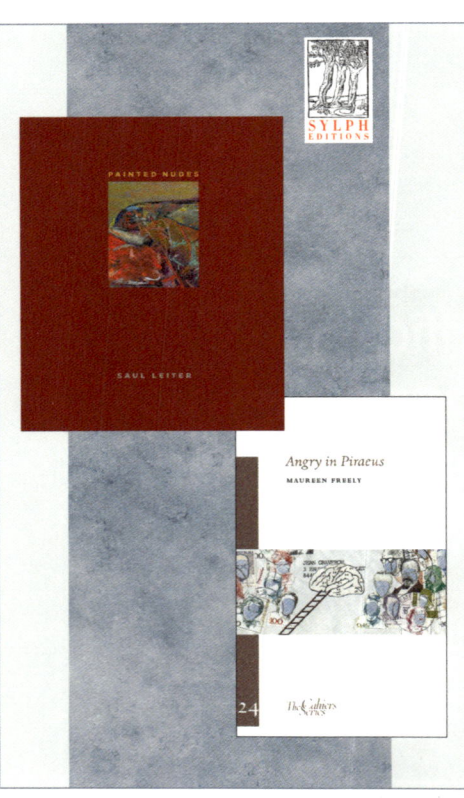

NEW FROM SYLPH EDITIONS

Painted Nudes
SAUL LEITER
With an Introduction by Mona Gainer-Salim

"Leiter's work is finally getting the recognition it deserves—and the received history of American colour photography is being revised accordingly."—*Guardian*
Cloth £38.50

Angry in Piraeus
MAUREEN FREELY
With Collages by Rie Iwatake

This is the story of the creation of a translator, as Maureen Freely explores what in her childhood led her to become a traveler across the spaces that exist between languages. The author's words are complemented by delicate collages, created by Japanese artist Rie Iwatake.
Paper £13.50

Distributed by the University of Chicago Press www.press.uchicago.edu
Trade enquiries to: UPM, 0117 9020275 Distributed by John Wiley, 01243 779777

THE WHITE REVIEW

SUBSCRIBE!

SUBSCRIBE TODAY TO SUPPORT THE WHITE REVIEW
AND SAVE 25% ON NEWSSTAND PRICES

www.thewhitereview.org

Go to
www.salvage.zone
to find out about subscriptions and submissions information, and to view web exclusives.

Get the print issues for the earliest access to all our essays, and for all the poems and artwork that will remain exclusive to our print issues.

Coming up in Issue 2 and beyond: Work by Benjamin Kunkel; Jord/ana Rosenberg; Robert Knox; Katie Fox-Hodess; an exclusive translated extract from Revolutionary Yiddishland; and more.

From our webstore:
Single Issue: £10 + postage
1 year subscription: £36 + postage
Lifetime subscription: £150
Salvage tote bags: £5

enquiries@salvage.zone

SALVAGE
A NEW QUARTERLY OF REVOLUTIONARY ARTS AND LETTERS

APPENDIX

PLATES

I. MARK LECKEY, 'Circa '87', 2013, pigment-based color print, 33 × 48.2 cm
Courtesy Mark Leckey and Haus der Kunst, Munich

II — IX. MARK LECKEY, Installation view of UNIADDDUMTHS (2014–15, showing detail of 'Felix the Cat', 2014), Kunsthalle Basel. Photo by Philipp Hänger. Courtesy Mark Leckey; Gavin Brown's enterprise, New York; Galerie Buchholz, Berlin/Cologne; Cabinet, London

MARK LECKEY, Installation view of UNIADDDUMTHS, Kunsthalle Basel, 2015. Photo by Philipp Hänger. Courtesy Mark Leckey; Gavin Brown's enterprise, New York; Galerie Buchholz, Berlin/Cologne; Cabinet, London

MARK LECKEY, Installation view of UNIADDDUMTHS (2014–15, showing "Man" section), Kunsthalle Basel, 2015. Photo by Philipp Hänger. Courtesy Mark Leckey; Gavin Brown's enterprise, New York; Galerie Buchholz, Berlin/Cologne; Cabinet, London

MARK LECKEY, Installation view of UNIADDDUMTHS (2014–15, showing "Man" section), Kunsthalle Basel, 2015. Photo by Philipp Hänger. Courtesy Mark Leckey; Gavin Brown's enterprise, New York; Galerie Buchholz, Berlin/Cologne; Cabinet, London

MARK LECKEY, Installation view of UNIADDDUMTHS (2014–15, showing detail of "Man" section), Kunsthalle Basel, 2015. Photo by Philipp Hänger. Courtesy Mark Leckey; Gavin Brown's enterprise, New York; Galerie Buchholz, Berlin/Cologne; Cabinet, London

MARK LECKEY, Installation view of UNIADDDUMTHS (2014–15, showing a copy of a 13th century silver reliquary hand, 2013; 'Documentation of The Universal Addressability of Dumb Things', 2013; a copy of Touch Bionics' 'i-Limb Ultra Prosthetic Hand', 2013), Kunsthalle Basel, 2015. Photo by Philipp Hänger. Courtesy Mark Leckey; Gavin Brown's enterprise, New York; Galerie Buchholz, Berlin/Cologne; Cabinet, London

MARK LECKEY, Installation view of UNIADDDUMTHS (2014–15, showing detail of "Monster" section), Kunsthalle Basel, 2015. Photo by Philipp Hänger. Courtesy Mark Leckey; Gavin Brown's enterprise, New York; Galerie Buchholz, Berlin/Cologne; Cabinet, London

MARK LECKEY, Installation view of UNIADDDUMTHS (2014–15, showing detail of "Machine" section), Kunsthalle Basel, 2015. Photo by Philipp Hänger. Courtesy Mark Leckey; Gavin Brown's enterprise, New York; Galerie Buchholz, Berlin/Cologne; Cabinet, London

MARK LECKEY, Installation view of UNIADDDUMTHS (2014–15, showing detail of "Machine" section), Kunsthalle Basel, 2015. Photo by Philipp Hänger. Courtesy Mark Leckey; Gavin Brown's enterprise, New York; Galerie Buchholz, Berlin/Cologne; Cabinet, London

X. Photograph of THE DICE MAN, first edition

XI — XV. HENNING BOHL, 'Great Old One - 20%', 2012, marker on paper 47.4 × 35.1 cm
Courtesy of the artist, König Galerie, Berlin and Galerie Meyer Kainer, Vienna

HENNING BOHL, 'Celtic Frost', 2012, marker on paper, newspaper 68.4 × 51.5 cm
Courtesy of the artist, König Galerie, Berlin and Galerie Meyer Kainer, Vienna

PLATES

	HENNING BOHL, 'T.A.R.T.S.', 2012, marker on paper, newspaper 68.4 × 51.5 cm Courtesy of the artist, König Galerie, Berlin and Galerie Meyer Kainer, Vienna
	HENNING BOHL, 'T.A.R.T.F.I.G.H.T.', 2012, marker on paper, newspaper 68.4 × 51.5 cm Courtesy of the artist, König Galerie, Berlin and Galerie Meyer Kainer, Vienna
	HENNING BOHL, 'Great Old One at Night', 2012, marker on paper, newspaper 47.4 × 35.1 cm. Courtesy of the artist, König Galerie, Berlin and Galerie Meyer Kainer, Vienna
XVI — XVIII.	OLIVER OSBORNE, 'Caveman (Father)', 2015, silkscreen on linen, 230 × 172.5 cm Courtesy the Artist and Gió Marconi, Milan
	OLIVER OSBORNE, 'Caveman (Red)', 2015, silkscreen on linen, 230 × 172.5 cm Courtesy the Artist and Gió Marconi, Milan
	OLIVER OSBORNE, 'Rubber Plant', 2014, oil on linen, 38 × 28 cm Courtesy the Artist and Vilma Gold, London
XIX.	OLIVER OSBORNE, 'Rubber Plant', 2015, oil on linen, 38 × 28 cm Courtesy the Artist and Gió Marconi, Milan
XX.	Portrait of Rachel Cusk by Siemon Scammel-Katz
XXI.	'New Year celebration in Leningrad' (1980). Evgeny Yufit is on the left in the front row. Courtesy Evgeny Yufit
XXII.	'A brawl in Leningrad' (1984). Courtesy Evgeny Yufit
XXIII.	'Necrorealist make-up' (1983). Courtesy Evgeny Yufit
XXIV.	'Necrorealist make-up' (1983). Courtesy Evgeny Yufit
XXV.	Film still from 'Spring' (1987). Courtesy Evgeny Yufit
XXVI.	Film still from 'Spring' (1987). Courtesy Evgeny Yufit
XXVII.	Film still from 'Spring' (1987). Courtesy Evgeny Yufit
XXVIII.	Film still from 'Spring' (1987). Courtesy Evgeny Yufit
XXIX.	Film still from 'Spring' (1987). Courtesy Evgeny Yufit
XXX.	Film still from 'Werewolf Orderlies' (1987). Courtesy Evgeny Yufit
XXXI.	Film still from 'Werewolf Orderlies' (1987). Courtesy Evgeny Yufit

CONTRIBUTORS

OWEN BOOTH writes plays, short stories and poetry. He is a regular contributor to London Liars' League storytelling events, and has been published in anthologies including Influx Press's *Connecting Nothing with Something* (2013). In 2012 his audio play *The Most Dangerous Woman in the World* was recorded by Type O Productions. He is the winner of the 2015 White Review Short Story Prize.

HENNING BOHL is an artist who lives and works in Berlin. Recent solo exhibitions include *Fatal, Fatal, Kadath Fatal* at Galerie Karin Guenther, Hamburg (2015); *Kadath Fatal* at Rob Tufnell, London (2014); *Henning Bohl: Works from the Collection at the Berlinische Galerie*, Berlin (2013); *Nameloses Grauen* at Casey Kaplan, New York (2012) and *Cornet of Horse* at Johann König, Berlin (2011).

KEVIN BREATHNACH is a writer and critic. His work has appeared in the *Dublin Review*, *The New Inquiry*, *The Irish Times*, *The Stinging Fly*, *gorse* and elsewhere. He lives in Dublin.

EMMANUEL CARRÈRE, novelist, film-maker, journalist, and biographer, is the author of *The Adversary* (a *New York Times* Notable Book), *Lives Other Than My Own*, *My Life As A Russian Novel* and *Limonov*. 'In Search of the Dice Man' originally appeared in the French magazine XXI in 2014. He lives in Paris.

THOMAS DYLAN EATON is a writer and film-maker. He has contributed essays and fiction to publications including *Artforum*, *Parkett*, *Afterall Journal and Ambit*. He lives and works in Italy.

WILL HEYWARD is a book editor in New York. He has written for *The Millions*, *Music and Literature*, *BOMB Magazine*, *Vice*, *Stonecutter*, *The Australian*, and other publications.

JOANNA KAVENNA is the author of several works of fiction and non-fiction, including *The Ice Museum*, *Inglorious*, *The Birth of Love*, *Come to the Edge*, *A Field Guide to Reality* and *Tomorrow*. Her essays and short stories have appeared in the *New Yorker*, the *London Review of Books*, the *Guardian*, *Prospect*, the *New Scientist* and the *New York Times*, among other publications. In 2008 she won the Orange Prize for New Writing and in 2013 she was listed as one of Granta's Best of Young British Writers.

CONTRIBUTORS

JOHN DOUGLAS MILLAR is a writer, critic, poet and occasional organiser of events, such as the Plastic Words series at Raven Row, London, which took place this past Christmas. He is also a PhD candidate at the Centre for Research in Modern European Philosophy, Kingston University, where he is working on the troubled relationship between literature and philosophy in the twentieth century. 'A Shadow of a Shadow of a Shadow' is an edited version of an essay that will appear in a book of literary essays to be published by Sternberg Press in 2016.

TOGARA MUZANENHAMO was born to Zimbabwean parents in Lusaka, Zambia in 1975. He was brought up in Zimbabwe, and then went on to study in The Hague and Paris. He has worked as a journalist in Harare and worked for a film script production company. Muzanenhamo's debut collection, *SPIRIT BRIDES*, was published by Carcanet in 2006 and reached the shortlist of the Jerwood Anderson First Collection Prize. He has since published two further collections, *GUMIGURU* and *TEXTURES*, (both 2014). The latter also featured verses by John Eppel.

OLIVER OSBORNE is an artist based in Berlin and London. Solo exhibitions include *THE NECK* at Giò Marconi, Milan (2015); *OLIVER OSBORNE* at Catherine Bastide, Brussels (2015); and *ANNA* at Vilma Gold, London (2015). He has participated in group exhibitions at Paul Kasmin, New York; Sprovieri, London; Saatchi Gallery, London; and OHWOW, Los Angeles. He was selected for Bloomberg New Contemporaries at the ICA, London and Liverpool Biennial in 2012.

CHRIS REITZ is Assistant Professor of Critical and Curatorial Studies and Gallery Director at the Hite Art Institute at the University of Louisville. He has written for *TEXTE ZUR KUNST*, *N+1*, and *ART-AGENDA*, and has contributed to exhibition catalogues on subjects ranging from Kosovar video art to the work of Santiago Sierra.

REBECCA TAMÁS is a London–born poet currently living in Norwich, where she is studying for a Ph.D. in Creative and Critical Writing at the University of East Anglia. Her pamphlet *THE OPHELIA LETTERS* was published by *SALT* in 2013, and she is currently at work on a series of poems which focus on witchcraft, female alterity and esoteric difference. She has most recently been published in *BEST BRITISH POETRY 2014*, and *BODY*.

CONTRIBUTORS

HARRY THORNE is Assistant Editor at *THE WHITE REVIEW*. He is a freelance art writer, editor and curator based in London.

FRANCESCA WADE is a freelance writer and Associate Editor of *THE WHITE REVIEW*. Her writing has appeared in the *LONDON REVIEW OF BOOKS*, *TIMES LITERARY SUPPLEMENT*, the *TELEGRAPH* and *LITERARY REVIEW*.

SUE WILLIAMS (b. 1954, Chicago) is a feminist painter who often combines themes of gender politics and the body into her work. She came to prominence in the early 1980s with works that echoed and argued with the dominant postmodern feminist aesthetic of the time. She was awarded a Guggenheim Fellowship in 1993. Williams has exhibited her work internationally, and is a part of numerous public collections, including at the Centre d'Art Contemporain in Geneva, The Hirshhorn Museum and Sculpture Garden, the Museum of Modern Art, the New Museum, and the Whitney Museum of American Art, amongst others.